Praise For
SONYA WALGER

"Sonya Walger brings together the quiet outer worlds of her characters and the explosive passions of their inner lives with indelible beauty, richness, and precision. *Wifehouse* reads like a storm in a soundproof room. I absolutely loved it."

—Miranda Cowley Heller, *New York Times* bestselling author of *The Paper Palace*

"A magnificent, richly textured novel. I was enthralled throughout, unable to put it down... It thrums with energy."

—Kate Kemp, author of *The Grapevine*

"A fine-grained and beautifully observed piece... *Lion* is laid out like a mosaic; disparate scenes from the long arc of the two characters' lives rub up against each other in a seamless narrative that darts back and forth across time. The story functions like memory itself; the narrator's past informs the present."

—*Los Angeles Times*

"[A] startling, breakneck, wildly insouciant debut... Walger writes with a style and verve that excites and propels; she commands the speed and tempo of her narrative with precision and grace."

—*Chicago Review of Books*

"A stirring novel... Walger's story reminds us that loss braids elegantly with reverence, and it is a demonstration of how painfully irresistible it can be to construct your life around an enticing void."

—*The Washington Post*

"The first 'must-read' of the year. Sonya Walger is a grade-A novelist... Hits every single note of a masterpiece."

—*Clarion Ledger*

"I was, frankly, stunned by the energy, the force of life in this book.... After I finished the novel, I went back and reread sections, trying to figure out how she did it.... It is [clearly] a novel only one person could write."
—John Warner, *Chicago Tribune*

"A piercing autobiographical novel about a woman's relationship with her charismatic but neglectful father... It's a revelation."
—*Publishers Weekly*

"Walger employs hypnotic prose that makes it impossible for readers to look away... The portrait Walger creates of the father is complex, despite his despicable traits, which is a testament to Walger's observation of humanity."
—*Shelf Awareness*

"A haunted story of a charismatic and deeply flawed man—and the people left in his wake."
—*Kirkus*

"A complex story of memory, lies, and parenthood."
—*Financial Times*

"Beautifully written and ultimately deeply moving... a powerful debut."
—Rumaan Alam, *New York Times* bestselling author of *Leave the World Behind*

"Everything a reader could want. It's personal and vast at once: profound and fun, deft linguistically and psychologically. Best of all, there's that sprinkling of magic you get only in the rarest novels."
—Darin Strauss, author of the National Book Critics Circle Award–winner *Half a Life*

"A breathtaking novel, dreamlike and courageous, brimming with glamour and disastrous scarcities."
—Susie Boyt, author of *Loved and Missed*

WIFEHOUSE

SONYA WALGER is an award-winning actress, best known for her role as Penny Widmore on *Lost* and Molly Cobb in the first three seasons of Apple TV+'s *For All Mankind*. Other career highlights include the original Broadway production of *Frost/Nixon, Parenthood, Tell Me You Love Me, Scandal, Flashforward,* and *In Treatment*. She studied English Literature at Christ Church, Oxford, and was the host of the literary podcast, *Bookish*. Her first book, *Lion*, a semi-autobiographical novel, was published by New York Review Books in February 2025. She lives in Los Angeles, California.

WIFEHOUSE
SONYA WALGER

MANILLA
PRESS

First published in the US in 2026 by Union Square & Co.,
An imprint of Grand Central Publishing
A division of Hachette Book Group, Inc.,
1290 Avenue of the Americas, New York, NY 10104

Published in the UK in 2026 by
MANILLA PRESS
An imprint of Bonnier Books UK
5th Floor, HYLO, 105 Bunhill Row,
London, EC1Y 8LZ

Copyright © Sonya Walger, 2026
Reading group guide copyright © Sonya Walger and Hachette Book Group, Inc.
Cover art by Wikimedia Commons (bird) and Bridgeman Images: © Estate of
Ron Bone (window) and © John Worthington (painting)

All rights reserved.
No part of this publication may be reproduced, stored or transmitted in
any form or by any means, electronic, mechanical, photocopying or otherwise,
without the prior written permission of the publisher.

The right of Sonya Walger to be identified as Author of this work
has been asserted by her in accordance with the Copyright, Designs and
Patents Act, 1988.

This is a work of fiction. Names, places, events and incidents are either the products of
the author's imagination or used fictitiously. Any resemblance to actual persons,
living or dead, or actual events is purely coincidental.

A CIP catalogue record for this book is available from the British Library.

Hardback ISBN: 978-1-78658-638-4
Trade Paperback ISBN: 978-1-78658-642-1

Also available as an ebook and an audiobook

1 3 5 7 9 10 8 6 4 2

Design and Typeset by IDSUK (Data Connection) Ltd
Printed and bound in Great Britain by CPI (UK) Ltd, Croydon CR0 4YY

The authorised representative in the EEA is Bonnier Books UK (Ireland) Limited.
Registered office address: Block B, The Crescent Building
Northwood, Santry Dublin 9, D09 C6X8 Ireland
compliance@bonnierbooks.ie
www.bonnierbooks.co.uk

# BOOK ONE
WINTER

CHAPTER 1

THE WOMAN WRAPS GIFTS THAT NOBODY WANTS. BAREFOOT, ALONE in the garage, her cold hands move scissors, paper, tape. She has left everything so late. It is so late that it is early. A strip of gray light creeps beneath the garage door. It will be morning soon. Expectations will begin. The cement floor is freezing. She should have pulled on socks, but there was no time because everything must be ready in time or else...she has no idea how to finish the rest of this thought. She tapes and snips and folds and longs for sleep.

CHAPTER 2

LAST NIGHT'S OLIVES SPECKLE AND PALE IN TINY DISHES. ROUGH-ened pits like rat droppings litter the edge of the encrusted cheese board. Wine-rimmed tumblers stack the counters. Someone has twisted the wire from a champagne cork into a tiny chair. A piece of mistletoe sags from its red velvet ribbon above the door. Empty pistachio shells sit heaped like an offering atop the mantelpiece. The house is quiet. The fireplace is ashy and cold. A tap drips in the loaded sink.

Vita picks her way across the gritty floor. She wears leggings and a baggy sweatshirt. Her thick blond hair is tied loosely at the nape of her neck. Fat headphones clasp her neck. She has been awake for an hour, lying in bed, watching the light leak across the wooden floorboards, listening to an audiobook of *The Odyssey*. It is read by a famous actress. It's pretty good, she thinks, if repetitive. They are supposed to read it over the holidays. Most of her friends will race through the graphic novel the day before school starts, but Vita disdains shortcuts. Her best friend, Zoe, thinks she is out of her mind, but Vita says fourteen-year-olds are too old for picture books.

The kitchen is disgusting. Her father usually cleans up better than this. He must have been really drunk. She glances at the chimney breast. Their stockings hang limp, flat. Her mother must have finally given up on the whole charade. Perhaps she has decided that stockings are simply decor now, and not delivery systems for unsolicited junk. Jackson will be devastated. Vita has long grown tired of her mother's secondhand offerings, but Annie snapped that she, Vita, will continue to get a stocking for as long as Jackson, who is eight, continues to believe in Santa. And since Jackson displays no signs of cynicism, she had assumed she'd be getting junky earrings and chipped vanity sets for a few more years. It is typical of her mother to change her mind and not tell anyone.

Vita gingerly sifts through the loaded sink, clearing enough space to fill the kettle from the tap. She rinses a mug, pulls the coffee canister from the freezer, shovels heaped scoops into the French press. She pulls out a bag of frozen grapes, sucks one. She rolls it from cheek to cheek, pouching it, working its sweetness into herself. She will allow herself two. Perhaps three, since today will be hard.

She waits for the kettle to boil, contemplates emptying the dishwasher. Maybe once her mother is up, so she can actually see Vita doing it. No point in invisible virtue. She should go for that run. She pops another grape and searches for her sneakers. Her mother had one of her tidying frenzies in preparation for the party, as though their friends weren't all entirely used to the stacks of magazines and teetering books and the small bonfire of footwear by the back door. Her father had protested but to no avail. He hates it when she moves stuff.

She glimpsed her parents silently bickering in the yard just before the party, her mother's skirt flapping like a dark bird in the wind as she clutched a line of string lights to her chest, her father slamming the door behind him. Vita headed upstairs and from her bedroom watched her mother doggedly hammering the lights onto the pergola or whatever she is calling it now, while Brian the handyman steadied the ladder and tried not to look up her skirt. Vita lay on her bed and texted Zoe. No reply. Her mother ran upstairs. Her father moved the trash cans behind the house. They were like inverted magnets, her parents, only able to tolerate a certain proximity before one repelled the other and skittered it into a corner.

A knock at the back door. Vita ignored it. Her mother yelled for someone to answer it. Vita sighed. She greeted a couple she vaguely recognized, took their coats and scarves, smiled and nodded at platitudes about her height, hair, familial resemblances. They all hovered, uncertain, nervous as dogs in the strangely tidy kitchen. She recalled dimly that this couple had no children, despite years of trying, and wondered if it was her awkwardness or theirs that she was feeling. She knew she must get them to the sitting room, where surely an adult now was, where she could safely deposit them and escape. She escorted them in, catching her father downing a glass of champagne, wiping his mouth as he turned to face them, flinging his arms wide in welcome. Maybe that gesture and the fire and the stupid gaudy tree and the overstuffed pink sofa full of so many cushions that there was nowhere to actually sit and the sight of the drinks tray made everyone relax a little. It offended her soul to imagine why anyone would willingly subject themselves to this kind of agonizing interaction. Her father kept his hand on her shoulder. She struggled to leave but more flushed faces arrived, kissing, inquiring, mouthing greetings. Music floated. Where was her mother, where was Candace—whose idea this had been, who lived for parties and small talk, who actually enjoyed this? Vita felt like Penelope alone in her hall thronging with suitors. She slipped upstairs and lay on her bed, looking at pictures of other people's holidays.

The doorbell rang, short and cautious. This was unforeseen. No one ever came to the front door. It meant a newcomer. It meant someone who had no idea how anything worked. She waited. The party was in full swing. The bell rang again, brief but insistent.

Vita opened the door a crack. A tall man stood in the doorway, gray beanie pulled low. Her cheeks grew hot. He pushed his hat off, crushed it in his hands.

"Hi. Am I in the right place? I'm Thierry."

Vita knew exactly who he was. This was Remy's French tutor. She had an alarm set on her phone to remind her to look up from her homework every Tuesday afternoon so that she could watch this tall man park his car, cross their yard, and knock at the door of their guesthouse, where Candace; her husband, Edouard; and their son, Remy, had been living for months now. Even though Edouard was French, Remy refused to learn the language from his father, so Candace had conjured a French tutor. Thierry came once a week, tasked with the thankless job of making Remy—an eight-year-old Vita was not convinced spoke much of any language—learn a second one. Vita had never had any interaction with the tutor, but she liked looking at the way his long legs moved across the grass and the way certain muscles emerged from the sleeves of his T-shirt.

His accent was disappointingly American. His eyes matched his beanie. He had probably chosen it for that reason. She wasn't sure if she approved of this kind of grooming. She realized she hadn't yet spoken.

"Are you looking for Remy?"

She flushed as soon as she spoke. This was entirely the wrong thing to have said. It managed to simultaneously convey that she knew exactly who he was and that he could not possibly have been invited to their Christmas party. Her cheeks burned. He smiled, appearing to have noticed nothing.

"No. Not today. Candace invited me."

Suddenly Candace was jangling in the hallway. Her green silk shirt was buttoned low and stretched tight, buckling the fabric and revealing gasps of a black lace bra. Vita was both relieved and appalled.

"Thierry! You came! *Joyeux Noël!*"

She tiptoed and kissed him on both cheeks, spilling her drink. "This is how you do it in France, Vita!"

She pulled him into the living room. He smiled at Vita as he passed.

Candace was her mother's best friend. They'd met in college or something. Candace and Edouard had come to visit them when they moved back east and had liked their house so much that they had bought one of their own nearby, but it was taking so long to renovate that they had moved into the guesthouse so that Candace could oversee construction. They were moving into their home "any day now." Vita and her father privately joked that they hadn't actually bought a house and were intending to live with them forever. Her mother protested. They were no bother and they kept to themselves. They were helpful. It was nice for Jackson to have a friend his own age around. Her father disagreed vehemently, citing the diminishing woodpile, a total loss of privacy, and the guests' relentlessly barking dog. Vita wasn't sure her brother even liked Remy.

She heard a noise above her. Jackson sat on the landing, his little white legs dangling through the banisters. He was wearing the shiny black soccer shorts he'd been expressly forbidden to wear and a crumpled blue button-down.

"No pants?"

"They itch."

"You should come downstairs."

"I want to watch a movie."

"Come down and I'll put one on for you."

"Mom said no."

"We won't tell her."

"Can it be inappropriate?"

"Yup."

He scooted down the wooden stairs, dumping his butt on every tread. She ferried him past the noisy living room where she glimpsed Candace clutching the tutor's arm, her mother fake laughing, her father talking to some woman in a tight dress. And now her mother saw her and was waving them in but it was too late and they were in the passageway.

Vita flicked on the overhead light in the garage and slid past the wall of chairs, upended sofas, bookcases, end tables, copper watering cans, rattan plant stands, baskets of throw pillows, crates of artwork, furled rugs, bulging cardboard boxes, and banks of stacked plastic totes. A mattress lay on the floor, a pale raft adrift an ocean of junk. Jackson leapt on it, squirreled himself beneath the heap of blankets. A giant old flat-screen television leaned against a bureau. She found the remote beneath a beanbag and dug out a bag of popcorn she had tucked in the bookcase two days ago.

"Don't drop it or the rats will come. And don't go nosing for presents."

He nodded, gathering beanbags around him like a fortress. She put on an old movie about a lost extraterrestrial. She would not stay to watch. She only liked the endings of films. Tension overwhelmed her; only resolution satisfied. But Jackson would enjoy this one. It would terrify him and then it would make him cry, which guaranteed that he would run upstairs to come and find her, which in turn assured her some time alone in her room followed by the opportunity to rescue him. It felt good to be needed. And it felt even better to be seen to be needed. She could already hear the adults whispering approvingly, could see herself pretending not to hear them, bending to his upturned face, taking his sweaty hand in hers and escorting him back to the garage where they could lie in a hot heap and watch the ending together. She kissed him lightly on the forehead, already anticipating the sweetness of her return, and turned off the lights.

The kettle whistles. Vita plunges the French press, pours, sips. She has learned to like its scalding bitterness. She searches for her sneakers and finds them among all the other shoes tossed into an unfamiliar giant basket outside the back door. The cold is a punch to the chest. She pulls her hood over her head, takes small steps like a boxer, light on her feet, crunching the frozen grass, the snapping leaves. Nothing moves except for the dumb brown bird that jumps over and over in front of her mother's truck, trying to see its own reflection in the fender. Her parents fight about this bird. Her father says they all do it, that jumping up and down in front of shiny objects is part of the genetic coding of this species. Her mother insists that it is unique to this one bird, that it is a lone and deranged creature exhausting itself in an attempt to glimpse its ever-elusive mate. Her parents can fight about literally anything.

She taps her watch. There is no snow this year, only a deadening freeze, stricken trees, and rigid dog shit. She watches her step. Candace's dog shits everywhere.

The dumb string lights are still blazing uselessly on the porch. Her mother is such an extremist. She decorates everything. It is all or nothing with her. The frigid air burns Vita's throat. She taps her earphones to restart the audiobook, pulls her sleeves over her fists, and begins to run. She hates running. She does it every day. *The Odyssey* drones in her ears, the wine-dark sea slips and floods her brain. Her hoodie smells of woodsmoke and sweat. Last night Remy and the tutor had appeared in the garage, a vast silhouette that suddenly flopped down beside her on the mattress. Remy wiggled between them. The man had stretched out, one arm propped behind his head, and she had smelled his musky armpit and worried she had not worn any deodorant and not dared to move again until the last credit rolled.

She runs past the beech trees and the birches, skirts the field, jogs down the driveway past her mother's truck and her father's car. Three loops should do it. It's roughly six hundred steps per loop, more if she swings her arms. The house looks so complete from here, sealed up like a wedding cake. It is pretty small, their house, but it has what her father calls "presence." He loves that word.

Vita has a stitch. She slows down, gathering breath, and heads to her father's gym—the ambitious name they gave the damp outbuilding that holds a cracked weight bench, a speckled mirror, and the secondhand treadmill that he tends to as if it were his third child. The gym is Hector's temple because Hector is an actor and an actor's body is a holy vessel. Vita has grown up knowing that what her father values is on the outside. She both hates that he is an actor and is proud of him. And then she hates herself for being proud of him. It is more complicated than she would like. Zoe's father works in real estate, which must be awesome.

Avoiding her reflection, she takes a plastic bottle of water from his stash by the mirror. Her sneakers leave marks on the floor. She pulls off her sweatshirt and uses it to wipe her footprints off the padded matting that she and her father assembled one Saturday afternoon. They sang Don McLean songs as they covered the shed floor with the soft cushioned padding. It had been nice, fun even. Her mother had come in as they were finishing, had stood in the doorway while her father sat back on his haunches, looking at her expectantly, waiting for her approval. Her mother had smiled, said something about lunch. But as she turned away from them back toward the house, Vita had caught her mother's expression in the mirror, a darkening, a collapsing. It reminded her of a video on global warming they'd watched at school where a hillside fell in silence. And then her mother was gone. Her father had already returned to his flooring, stamping it down with his heel. He had not noticed. He never did.

Vita swigs from the bottle and resumes her run. She passes the garage, where last night Thierry's elbow brushed the side of her head. Her father must have left the light on; she can see it glowing along the base of the garage door. She had been grateful for how dark it had been in there last night; it was mortifying how much stuff her mother has wedged in the garage. She claims it's all essential now that she has this staging company. Which is in itself a completely bogus concept. The idea of filling a house with a load of random furniture so that people will be seduced into thinking it is a better house than it is and so pay more for a fantasy that they're not actually getting is yet more proof of how sinister adulthood really is. A couple of times the buyers have asked to buy some of her mother's junk, probably because they realized the house they have forked out for isn't that great after all. Once her mother reversed the whole way down a street to pick up some moldy loveseat sitting out on the sidewalk. Vita shudders at the memory.

Her mother used to paint, although Vita doesn't have many memories of it. One of Annie's paintings hangs in the hallway. It is of a huge fallen tree and beside it, like a toppled moon, a bright white stump. It used to hang in Vita's bedroom in their old house in California. Vita asked her mother once when she had painted it. Annie shrugged. "Ages ago," she said, drawing herself around her like a cardigan.

Her mother hates talking about the past. Her mother really only likes talking about this afternoon, or Tuesday, or next Easter.

Vita takes a deep breath, starts her final lap.

Hector stretches his long body. The duvet is light, the air is crisp, his lungs hurt. He shouldn't have smoked that cigarette last night. Back in the day it would have been a pack, easy, but now even a single one stolen on the porch is something to be reckoned with. His head feels insolent, his eyeballs hurt. He has not slept well. He drank much more than he had intended to. He rolls over, his wife's absence unsurprising. Their bed looks like a deer bed. A ruffled emptiness of sheets long cold, the imprint of a body that he lay beside all night without knowing or touching. She was irritable last night. Picking a fight over those damn lights. He hopes she's in a better mood today. He grunts and sits up.

In the bathroom, naked, he brushes his teeth. He stares at himself, his thick hair still improbably black, his chest square. He checks himself for impurities, for overnight aberrations. He is always keeping an eye on things, as though vigilance might forestall the ambush of age. He downs some pills for the headache, swills his mouth with mouthwash, still trying to coat the fur on his tongue. He wonders if his son is up yet. He has already glimpsed his daughter, like a crow with her arms flapping as she circles the back garden, a black bird hurtling with uneven pace around the wet grass. He hopes she'll change for lunch. He knows better than to ask. He smells coffee. Thank God Annie is up. He'd done what he could last night but he knows it's a mess down there. God knows why she always put out so much food. No one ever eats anything. He'd drunk too much, getting trapped with that neighbor woman. She'd been fun to talk to, but he could not help but notice she had not asked him a single question. Amazing how few people knew how to hold a conversation these days. He can't remember her name, was surprised Annie had invited her. It was probably Candace's doing. God, were they coming over for Christmas lunch as well? Any day now he was going to come upstairs and find Candace and Edouard sitting up in his bed. Ed at least had the grace to look sheepish about the situation. But Candace was used to being at home wherever she went. The entitlement was dazzling. Mesmerizing. She walked into rooms as though they were a stage lit only for her. He must call his brother at some point; where was Alexander this year? Scaling some iceberg somewhere, he forgets where. His father will know. What time are his parents showing up? Early, just to annoy Annie. He pulls on jeans, throws a sweater over his head, runs his hands through his hair. He checks his phone; still no word from the agents, obviously not, it's Christmas Day, there will be no word till January now, God forbid anyone make a creative decision over the festive period. There are about two straight weeks in the year when anyone actually works. It's always Indigenous People's Day or Diwali or something.

Vita is hurting now. Her ankles are aching and her breath comes in short gasps. Her eyes water as she shuffle-runs. Jackson appears at the kitchen window. He is openmouthed, his face crumpled with dismay. He waves at her, as though she were a plane coming in to land. He is urgent. She ignores him. He yanks open the back door, bumping the holly wreath, runs toward her, barefoot, outraged.

"Vitaaaaa!"

She pulls off her headphones. "What?"

"What happened to Christmas?"

CHAPTER 3

EVERYONE IS WEARING PAPER HATS. THEY ARE TORN AND CRUMPLED. No one's fits quite right on their head. They look like they are in a bad play. Christmas crackers lie wrenched and scattered along the table, vegetables glisten in bowls, wax drips on an errant brussels sprout. Even from this distance Annie can tell it is undercooked. For the fourth time that day Jackson replays the fiasco of his Christmas morning. Only Remy pays attention, although Hector's mother interrupts her conversation with Candace to listen ostentatiously to her grandson with what Annie considers an excess of compassion. Remy shrugs.

"But you still got your presents, right?"

Annie could kiss her friend's son. Remy frowns.

"You don't still believe in Santa, do you?"

Now Annie hates him.

"No," says Jackson, bravely.

She feels herself floating away. She looks down the table, at the food she has hastily cooked, the tablecloth she has quickly ironed, the silver Vita has sulkily laid. She has been playing catch-up all day, ever since she woke with a start on the mattress on the garage floor and, scrambling to her feet, clutching armfuls of gifts, stumbled out of the open mouth of the garage and into the faces of her astonished family. For a moment they all froze, uncertain of how to proceed. Even now, lunch almost ended, she feels behind the plot, like an audience member who has arrived late and slipped into her seat minutes after the play has started. It is not new, this sensation. She is always behind these days, always trying to catch up with the drama. She is living in the cheap seats of her own life.

She watches Hector at the opposite end of the table, flushed, intent. His paper hat is lilac, torn almost to the hilt. He leans in, elbows propped, to talk to his father about cryptocurrency, his latest obsession. Derek, who never listens but only waits to speak, sits pushed back from the table, tilted in his chair, cashmere vest stretched wide across his spreading paunch. A tiny man rides a tiny embroidered horse stretched high on his pink cashmere chest. Annie is certain Derek has never ridden a horse in his life. His teeth are reddened with wine, his cheeks claret-flushed. Everything clashes with his sweater. On Hector's left, Edouard sits, nodding. He is a patient man, thinks Annie, to tolerate this actor expounding on finance, the very field Edouard has spent the last thirty years working in. She wonders if perhaps he doesn't understand them. Not that Edouard's vocabulary is lacking; he speaks with the accented precision of a visiting academic. No, it is more his cultural capacity to contain these Americans, their slang and familial shorthand, their laxities and conformities to a world so different than the one he grew up in that she questions. Ed's family are very proper, very old French Catholics. His mother has never forgiven him for marrying a Jewess, so Candace likes to say. But Annie suspects Candace relishes the idea of being loathed.

Candace sits beside Hector's mother. They speak intently, with faces inclined to one another, confidential, conspiratorial. Candace gleams like a candle fat with wax. She is glimmering with jewelry. Hector's mother, angular with a slashed red mouth, the liver spots on her hands that no lasers will remove, works her pearls like a rosary. They look like choir boys whispering in a stall. From across the table Vita listens to them, drawn always toward the whisper of a secret.

Hector's mother rests her own hand over Vita's, red nails stroking the stubby ripped ones, careless, possessive, trapping her. Vita loves her grandmother, always has. This is surprising to Annie, but she is grateful. Hector's mother remembers birthdays, dance recitals, names of friends. In her glacial way she is attentive, she retains information. What she lacks in warmth, she makes up for in focus.

Surreptitiously, beneath the tablecloth, Remy plays a video game on his father's phone. Jackson leans in to watch. Hector's mother's mouth twitches. Annie wonders what the women are talking about. She does not care. She has nothing to confide in Hector's mother and Hector's mother loves nothing more than to be needed, confided in, relied upon. She, Annie, has failed her for years in this regard. In most regards, she suspects.

Annie gets up to clear plates. Hector's mother, as usual, has eaten nothing. Annie is not sure she has ever seen food pass her mother-in-law's lips. She lives on sparkling water and stomach acid. Vita has merely moved her food around the plate, Jackson has slicked everything that is sliced, diced, or mashed to one side and eaten only the roast beef. The men's eyes flicker up at her appreciatively as she removes their plates; the women do not register her at all. Jackson hands her his plate.

"Is it dessert?"

"Yes, in a minute."

He squirms off the chair.

"Where did Jackson go?" asks Remy, not looking up from the game.

"To look for dessert," says Vita.

"The cake thing?"

Edouard glances over.

"La bûche de Noël."

Remy grunts.

"Can you say it?"

Remy works the phone. His father repeats himself. Candace looks over. Hector's mother frowns, hating to be ignored. Remy scowls into his game. His father reaches across, tries to take the device, but the child swerves it deeper beneath the table. His father stretches fruitlessly across his son's lap.

"Say it, and you can keep playing."

"Remy, give it to Papa."

Remy reaches his hands far beneath the tablecloth, straining to not lose sight of the game, of his working thumbs.

"*La bûche de Noël*," insists Edouard.

He pushes his chair back, the better to reach his son. Remy turns his full body away from his father now, swooping his hands deep beneath the table, but this time with a clatter and a slide of cream linen he swipes the cloth, pulling the glasses, which swerve and spill and clatter on their sides. One shatters on the floor. Red wine bleeds across the cloth, blots into abandoned tissue hats and torn crackers, splatters across plates of congealed meat.

A convulsion of movement. Hector's mother jumps back as though scalded, Candace yells at Remy, Hector gets to his feet and starts mopping at the tablecloth, righting bottles, candles, dishes. Derek holds fearfully to his own glass and pushes his chair farther back from the table, tutting. Edouard grabs Remy by the arm and marches him out of the dining room. Wine drips on the floor, a candle gutters.

Candace follows her husband out of the room but, remembering her promise to her therapist to let Ed handle his son more often, drifts into the living room. She flops on the pink tartan sofa (so lovely, she must ask Annie about this fabric), dabs ineffectually where she's splashed gravy on her blouse, and gives up. She releases one more straining pearl button, folds back the placket so she can't see the stain. She flops her head back on the sofa. God, she can't wait till their own house is ready, this has gone on long enough, this being someone else's guest. Annie is amazing how she puts up with them, although Candace suspects she actually likes having them around. It is probably a useful distraction from just how useless Hector is. She doesn't know how Annie stands it. But all men are useless. Ed, too, in a different way. At least Ed works. Hector lounges around looking decorative, lifting weights in that moldy gym, quoting dreary Russians, moping about, waiting to get cast, dragging everyone down with him, then springing back to life the minute the phone rings. She's never known anything like it. How Annie puts up with it, she has no idea. It's like living with a lovesick teenager. A half-drunk glass of wine sits on the coffee table. She drinks it. Probably been there since last night but it tastes fine. Oh God, where is Remy now? she wonders. Fucking *bûche de Noël*. She kicks off her shoes, closes her eyes.

Vita slips under the table to retrieve broken glass. On her knees she gathers the dripping shattered crystal in a napkin. It glitters, seeps. She is glad to be away from the presence of the food. She is happier under the table, like a dog. She wishes she could sit down here for the rest of the day. Her grandmother peers down at her, as though at a mouse in a trap.

"Alright, my love?"

"Just cleaning up."

"Such a help, sweetheart."

The white tablecloth drops again, the scene is over. Trust Remy to cause a scene. He's an only child, which means he gets away with murder. No way she or Jackson was allowed to have phones at the table, and definitely not at Christmas lunch, but everyone just turns a blind eye to Remy because he's their guest, even though he actually lives with them.

* * *

From the kitchen Annie hears the clatter, the shriek. She hesitates. She grabs her coat and her phone, opens the back door, and steps outside into the cold. It is almost dark again, the grayness bleeding up and outward, a watercolor of wintery light, a sky the color of bathwater. She dials her mother's number. It is early morning in Melbourne. Christmas is already over for her. Her mother will be up, feeding the chickens. She will be outside with an old yellow bucket, tossing grain to her chickens, her stubby hands dipping into the loose grains, the golden nubs, and then releasing them, a shower of tiny pebbles, over and over. And the chooks will gather at her feet, clucking and appreciative, bowing and scraping at the dirt, her tiny servants.

The phone rings and rings. Annie waits. She sees her mother crossing the yard, wiping her hands on her purple velour tracksuit, patting her hips, muttering to herself, searching for the phone.

"Hi Mum."

"I was just feeding the chooks—couldn't find the phone. Pippa's crook, I have to hand-feed her these days. But Lila's bounced right back, I told you she had the blight—had to isolate her for a week—they all lost their minds, but she's quite frisky now . . ."

"Happy Christmas."

"Oh. Yes. Does Vita like the bag?"

"Vita loves the bag."

"Good. And the jumper? For Jacko? Will it do?"

"He loves it too," Annie lies.

"Well, that's something. I wasn't sure. You never know. Your kids have so much stuff, it's hard to know what . . ."

She tails off. Annie decides not to ask her mother how she could possibly know what her children do or do not have since she has never once visited them.

"Thanks for all the gifts, Mum. You good? How was your Christmas?"

"Spent the day with Helen. She grilled us some lamb steaks, with a bit of mint on the side. Bit different. I got us a pudding from Coles. He's doing quite nice puds now, tarts and that. It was alright. She's got that schnauzer. Limerick, she calls it. Can't think why. It licks everything. Sam and her girlfriend invited me over to their Boxing Day thing, but I didn't want to go."

"Why not?"

"Bunch of lezzies talking about how much they hate men. I'll stop by later in the week. Drop them off some eggs. Lila! Leave Hetti alone! Lila! How's your Christmas? Bryony behaving herself?"

Annie struggles for a moment to think who her mother means and then remembers that Bryony is Hector's mother. She never calls her by her name. She thinks of her only as Hector's mother. As though that were her sole identity. She wonders for how many people she is simply Vita or Jackson's mother.

"She's fine. I leave her to Candace. And Vita. Vita loves her grandmother. Grandmothers."

She wonders why she corrects herself, why she bothers to protect her mother's feelings.

Annie's mother has never left Australia. She has never seen where her daughter lives. She has met Vita twice, Jackson never. She does not reproach Annie for not coming to visit her more often because she herself does not travel. Bluey refuses to fly. It is simply how things are. As a young girl she flew to Tasmania to visit cousins with her parents. It was her first time on a plane, and an extraordinary extravagance for the whole family. Half an hour from Hobart, the pilot fainted, the plane nosedived, and they crash-landed in the ocean. The passengers clung to the wreckage, to the waterlogged seats, the shattered tail, slapped by the freezing oily water. Bluey's father dragged her onto the fractured wing. She was shaking so hard, she felt her little gym shoes drop off her feet. They were rescued by lifeboats. There were, astonishingly, no fatalities; even the pilot recovered consciousness as soon as he hit the water. Bluey refused to leave solid ground ever again. Not so much as a Ferris wheel, she liked to say. Annie has heard the story so often, she can recite it like a poem. Family trips were taken in a van along the coast, on occasion to Sydney. Once they drove to Uluru, but Annie was so carsick she barely saw it.

"You still there?"

"Yes, Mum. Still here. I should go and get on with dessert. I'm in the doghouse because I slept through breakfast."

"I expect Hector managed. Did you get some nice presents?"

Annie frowns. Her mother moves through life like one of her hens, pecking briefly at one kernel, then another.

"Candace gave me French lessons."

"That was nice of her."

Annie wonders, not for the first time, if her mother is sincere.

"Now Hetty's fussing. Love to you all."

The line goes dead.

Slowly, silently snow begins to fall.

CHAPTER 4

A NNIE AND HECTOR MOVED TO CONNECTICUT FROM LOS ANGELES seven years ago. It was a decision that took them both by surprise. They drove up the California coast for their first weekend alone together since their daughter's birth, leaving a gleeful four-year-old Vita with their Guatemalan housekeeper, Marta. Marta spoke little English and bought Vita cheap plastic toys that spun around and lit up and spouted songs in high-pitched mechanical Spanish. The toys were seemingly indestructible and often burst into song in the middle of the night, waking the whole family. Vita loved them and loved Marta. They ate tamales in the backyard together, their heads touching. Marta was delighted to stay while Annie and Hector drove up to Big Sur, and Vita was giddy at the prospect of two straight days with her favorite person. Hector swept them along that generous coastline with its gentle coves and astonishing drops, pines slicing the sky while the fog crept up from the water. The mist crawled up the cliffs, and the sun, an orange lozenge, dissolved itself into the clouds. They pulled up at an old staging post inn and smiled at each other as they checked in, handing their IDs to the gray-haired lady who moved with breathtaking slowness as she scratched down their names in the handwritten ledger and handed Annie a key the length of her forearm.

"No losing that," whispered Hector.

"Watch me," she whispered back.

Their room was timbered with a neat stack of logs by the fire and a brass bed loaded with whip-stitched blankets. It smelled of pine and woodsmoke. Annie ran a tub while Hector opened wine. She felt suddenly self-conscious, unsure what they would do, what they would talk about, what couples did who went away together. She wondered who they were now, without Vita's stripling body between them. (Vita still slept in their bed, had done so for years now, and they had lost the will to protest. They had sex occasionally, furtively, while Vita watched a movie on full volume downstairs.) Hector handed her a glass.

"Room for two?"

She made space as he lowered himself into the tub.

"What do you think they are doing now?"

"Watching telenovelas."

"In Spanish."

"Definitely."

"She asked me again why we don't have another kid."

"Who, Marta or Vita?"

"Vita."

Annie sipped her wine. "Did she really?"

"No. But why don't we?"

"Oh God, are we really doing this now?"

"Sure."

"Because...because I don't want another one. You're always working. And we're happy. We're good. We got through the hard stuff and it's good now. And I don't want to raise another kid in L.A."

This surprised him. He wondered if she meant it. He frowned.

"What's L.A. got to do with it?"

Annie sank lower in the tub.

"I don't want to push a stroller around a mall again. I don't want to make friends with any more women who are paid to smile. I don't want to be at a school where people keep leaving because they're going on location. If I do it again, I want to be in the countryside, with fields. I want our friends to be farmers, not agents. I want life to be very different."

Hector looked at her with surprise.

"I didn't know you disliked it so much."

"Nor did I, really. Till we started talking about it. But I do. I really do."

She warmed to her theme.

"I hate it. I hate the flat streets full of banal little box houses, each one trying to be so hard to be different from the one next to it. I hate the way nobody stays in one place. I hate the fucking relentless sunshine and the dead hills. I miss leaves on the ground. I miss people with real jobs."

Hector watched his wife talking. It was a long time since he'd seen Annie open up like this. She looked at him.

"Do you like L.A.? I mean, really, truly?"

"I mean, I think so. I like it well enough. The weather's great and it's where the work is, so I just assume that it's where we live—it's the backdrop to our life. Which is crazy, I suppose, but since we never discussed it... I don't think I realized that it was coloring everything, your life so much."

Annie leaned forward, dripping water on the floor.

"Don't you find it makes you boring, this city? It makes me numb. I've stopped feeling anything. I mean, sure, I notice when the jasmine blooms or the sheet rain closes the canyon, but everything feels so... flat here. Featureless. There's nothing to hold on to. It all feels so impermanent; maybe it's the being built for earthquakes, but it all feels like it can be disassembled like a film set, flat-packed in a moment. And because it all feels so temporary, I think I let myself drift, not really letting myself get attached to anything or anyone. I think it must happen to everyone. No one belongs here.

But everyone wants to. And everyone wants to let you know that they are so fucking busy."

"Who are all these titans of industry you're hanging out with?"

"Oh, the wives are the worst, let me tell you."

Hector leaned back in the tub, his hands behind his head.

"So, where would we go? Where would we live?"

She hesitated. But she knew. She had gone there with a boyfriend once on a fall weekend, and she had never forgotten the trees.

"Rural Connecticut. Not the fancy part. I'm talking the wrong end. Miles from anywhere. Close enough to New York for you to be able to work there, do the plays you talk about wanting, but far enough away for us to have a different kind of life. Vita is growing up in the back of a car. I want her to have some space around her, some trees, a wilderness. I'd like to see her in the distance. She's always in the foreground. She could have a pony, we could grow apples, have a bit of land."

"A pony?"

"She loves animals. We spend a fortune on riding lessons in Griffith Park so she can ride around next to a freeway on a glue gun with legs. How much could it cost to keep a pony in a fucking field?"

Hector looked at her, eyes wide. Afterward she marveled at how quickly he took to the idea. He pulled her toward him. Water splashed on the floor. He kissed her flushed forehead, ran a thumb along her chin.

"Let's keep a pony in a fucking field."

They found an old farmhouse three hours northeast of the city, four with traffic, and there was always traffic. It sat on half an acre of land and overlooked a beechwood. It was more than they wanted to spend, farther out than they had planned, and needed more work than they had hoped for, but otherwise it was perfect. Clad in peeling clapboard, it had three bedrooms, two dormer windows, and a small converted barn.

Jackson was born there. He was a quiet baby, velvety and milk sweet. He clenched the clear blue air of the farmhouse kitchen and smiled. He liked the world he found around him. The house held him snug as a window seat. Vita turned seven that year. She was suspicious of the new house, the new brother, the backyard everyone kept telling her to go play in.

None of their Los Angeles furniture belonged in this New England home with its chilly white rooms and stripped wooden floors. Terra-cotta and peach had no place in this landscape of piney green and birch gray and blue. Annie traded in her car for a truck, and Jackson spent his first year windswept and wide-eyed in the back while his mother scoured the countryside for armchairs, sinks, bookcases. Vita hated that her mother showed up to school looking like she worked in construction, mud-spattered, hair screwed off her face, arms bare and scratched from lifting and roping. It was tough, that first year. The water froze in the pipes, the roof leaked, Jackson caught croup, and Vita missed everything. Hector worried he would never work again now that he lived in the country. Certain outlets could not be used in conjunction with others (the toaster worked, but not with the hairdryer; the microwave blew out the water heater), so negotiations were required. Annie stopped drying her hair, and Hector learned when to grind his coffee beans. They fought more than they ever had. She was tired all the time, wrangling both kids while dragging herself across the countryside to another estate sale. Hector was drained, struggling with DIY skills he'd assumed would be self-explanatory. Annie came home in the evenings, hauling red-eyed children and a steamer trunk or yet another side table.

He felt they were hemorrhaging money; she felt proud of her thrift. She stored her finds in the garage, smuggling them into the house whenever Hector left it.

And yet they were happy. The children grew ruddy. Vita learned about fractions by using slices of the neighbor's apple cake; Jackson took his first steps the day Hector rode down the driveway on his new old red tractor. They had picnics under the beechwood, sledded down their hillside, lost frisbees in the long grass. Hector learned to clean gutters, tile a backsplash, lay a stone path. Annie, never a cook, learned to make soup, pesto, bread. They were right to have moved, they told themselves. It was the best thing. They did not miss the city.

CHAPTER 5

ANNIE BACKS OUT OF THEIR SODDEN DRIVEWAY. AT THE BOTTOM OF the lane the new neighbor's trash cans huddle, bulging with holiday trash. A bright pink Christmas tree stands propped against the recycling bin, electric and improbable. Annie and the children study it. It is a real tree, sprayed with thick clumps of what looks like sticky pink shaving foam that cling to the limbs. It is as shocking as a firework at breakfast. Jackson is disgusted.

"Who does that to a tree?"

Vita shrugs. "I think it's cool."

"The garbage men won't think it's cool. Bet they won't even take it, right, Mom?" He is right. It will need to be disposed of correctly, sawed into pieces, not left like a drunk in the street. They are new, these neighbors; they moved in during the fall. A mother and her kids was all Annie knew. A *divorcée*, corrected Candace, who always knew everyone. A former model-turned-reporter-activist, whatever that was, and her two sons. She had been all over Hector at the Christmas party, slender, braless, green-eyed as a lizard, her eyes flickering over every man in the room. Annie had noticed her listening to him with a rapt expression, one hand on his wrist. She arched her back when she laughed, which was often. Annie was surprised that anyone found Hector that funny. But she felt a flash of gratitude to the woman for giving her husband the attention he craved.

Annie searched her memory for the woman's name. She had known it once, had looked her up on the Internet after dropping a welcome note in her mailbox and found, with alarming speed, photo shoots from online magazines of her new neighbor in sheer gowns, her exquisite body rippling the fabric, her buttocks round and brown as a newly risen cake. She had searched further, in spite of herself, found photographs the woman had posted of her own life, laughing at a wedding in Italy, crinkling her eyes against the Caribbean sun, holding a vast conch in Bali. There was no sign of her children, anywhere. It was like reading a novel in another language. Annie had closed the laptop and poured herself a glass of wine.

The tree is still there when they return in the afternoon. The cans are empty now. The tree lies on its side, shedding its shocking pink needles, bleeding softly into the muddied snow. It lies there for days. The children cease to notice. One morning, turning up the lane, she sees a stripper's pole leaning against the trash cans. She slows down to look more closely and realizes it is the tree. Someone has finally sawn the branches off, leaving only the skinny trunk propped against the trash cans. It looks like a skinned cat. It is both no longer a tree and finally restored to itself.

It is the first day of term. She drives the children to school. The tree has gone, leaving only a tired pink ring of water on the wasted slush. The roads are grimy, the birches shingled with old snow. In the back seat, Jackson's bright head turns to watch each passing car. Remy sits beside him, glazed and mute. Like his mother, he rarely speaks before lunch. Annie watches her son in the rearview mirror. Jackson's lips move as under his breath he names the make of each car. One holds no more value for him than the other; he just likes identifying them. He blinks rarely, his eyes moving like a radar, tracking, observing, detailing. She wonders if he will be a scientist. He is meticulous, a quality neither she nor Hector shares. Hector likes things tidy, but Jackson's need to catalogue and enumerate is unique to him. She wonders if it is just the age, but Vita was expansive at this age, sprawling, soaked in friendships, cluttered with unfinished games, puzzles, dolls. It is only now she is fourteen that she has her own secret life. In the passenger seat beside her, Vita stares out unseeing, occasionally nodding, her headphones sealing the entrance to her cave.

Annie pulls up behind a long line of steaming cars waiting for drop-off. The line snakes back to the road. A teacher gestures the bundled humans indoors. They inch forward, Jackson excitable with the arrival of every friend, Remy impervious, Vita impatient. She slams the door. Annie winces. Her daughter turns back, taps on the window.

"Don't forget, I've got dance tonight. I'll catch a ride home with Zoe."

Jackson hops from foot to foot in the cold, waiting for his sister. Remy folds into the crowd.

"Come *on*, Vita."

Annie waves, watches her children's disappearing backs. She feels the familiar and yet astonishing flood of relief at returning her children to school. The shock of pleasure at the silent car. No one tells you, she thinks, no one tells you how banal these moments are and yet how hallowed. This is what passes for happiness now. This lane that leads from the school back onto the main road is a place of profound composure for her, a place of peering up at the sky and glimpsing its vastness through the trees and feeling so grateful, so relieved, so surprised that this feeling of intact-ness is still here, waiting for her to discover it again. It is the moment where she retrieves who she is, as though through some carelessness she has misplaced herself all weekend, or all summer, and now, suddenly, among these trees, here at this curve in the road, she glimpses herself again, herself alone, as a single self, not as a purveyor of food or drink or intelligence or as the means to anything at all. She is here, in her car, just as herself. A woman driving alone. Any woman. Not a mother. Not a wife. It used to take days to stagger between these identities, whole weekends to recover her former childless self. Now they are a breath and a bend in the road apart. She reassembles herself like a broken pot every morning and shatters herself anew in time for pickup.

Annie never imagined herself as a mother. It was a hollowed-out word for her. A trunk beetled by termites. She was an artist, a woman, a wife. A child would not change these immutable facts. She was entirely unprepared for everything that was to come.

Vita arrived like a comet. Annie was alone in the canyon house, peeling an avocado. She dropped the fruit and doubled up, a freight train boring through her pelvis. She waited for it to pass but there was no end to this train. She felt she might die. There was no space, no breath between these pains. There was no time for candles or music or baths. She knew she must get to the hospital, she knew this baby was coming immediately. On all fours, braying in the back of a cab driven by a bribed cabbie, both of them sweating and cursing, she made it to the hospital in the center of town. Hector joined her from set, still wearing his costume—a pinstripe suit, jacket thrown over one arm, sweating through the fitted white shirt with tiny darts that gathered in the small of his back, and a tideline of foundation flecking his collar. He was the only person on the floor wearing makeup and the nurses swooned. The doctor appeared, tests were run, blood surged, monitors alarmed. Hector paled, she was rolled out, she was sheeted and numbed and sliced open, feeling nothing but Hector's rigid grip on her hand and herself the still-silent epicenter of anesthetized panic, the need to hold steady, to keep the vessel secure. And suddenly, there was a new human in the room, a pink creature licked in creamy vernix, who before had been only a fiction but now was flesh, they had conjured her, and here she was, arching with protest, fisting the sky, blue-eyed, yes, already, eyes open and awake and outraged and this, this violence she named Vita.

It was with astonishment that she found herself loving the stranger that was Vita so absolutely and without warning. But loving her baby was not the same as loving parenthood, a distinction she found elusive for the first few years. They had just moved to Los Angeles when Vita was born, and Hector was filming most days. He left in the dark blue denim of dawn and was often not back until dusk, when the baby was asleep again. Annie spent her days alone with the baby in the steep canyon where they lived. She pushed the expensive stroller (a gift from Hector's parents) up and down the narrow streets that had no sidewalks so she bumped the stroller over the root-cracked asphalt, pressing herself and the baby into parked cars, ignoring the yells of irate drivers. The baby screamed every time she was buckled into her car seat so Annie resolved not to drive. Anywhere. They walked the city, covering miles and miles in silence. When the baby slept, she stopped, rested, ate, and stared at the passing world. When the baby woke, she fed her on a park bench, on the side of the road, in a parking lot. Were it not for the expensive stroller, people must have thought they were homeless. Annie felt homeless, exiled from her house, her body, from everything familiar. The city felt as uncharted as motherhood itself. Their house felt alien, shadowy, fraught. The baby felt both imperiled and imperious. Vita imposed her tiny will on the world. Annie was her slave and knew not how to disobey. Only when Hector came home was sanity restored.

Some days, sitting on the kitchen floor, watching Vita play with a block or a sunbeam, Annie would marvel that she had made this astonishing flesh with her body. She would scoop her up and bury her face in her daughter's yeasty neck or feast on the folds of her cheeks. She tried sketching her daughter, tried to catch the slope of her lip and the cloud of her cheek, but it was impossible. There was no catching this body. Other days, Annie sat dully watching her child play, sensing only the mug in her hands and the ache of her eyelids and the light tang of her unwashed hair. *Where have I gone?* she wondered. *Down what canyon have I fallen?*

Candace came to meet the baby. She wore a denim jumpsuit and red wedge espadrilles, brought a life-size stuffed baby giraffe and a bottle of pink champagne. The baby slept while Annie made lunch and Candace drank the champagne. (The giraffe stood in the front hall where it would remain for years, accumulating coats, sunhats, purses, until an epic rainstorm flooded the ground floor and the giraffe got mildew and had to be thrown out. "Foot rot," Annie told the inconsolable Vita, who hated all change.)

Candace raised a glass.

"Look at you, up and dressed and making eggs like nothing happened."

Annie smiled. She did not know how to tell Candace that the ruin was internal, invisible and incremental. She had no words for the aching elasticity of time. Hector had gone back to work a week after Vita's birth, had pulled on jeans and slipped away in the dark while she had lain and watched him leave. If he had strapped on wings, it could not have been more improbable an exit. She did not know how to tell her old friend that her days were measured in naps and ounces now. She had no words for the way tedium and devotion gripped her heart in cupped hands. She was milk-stained and starving for company. But she would not admit this, no, not to herself, not to Hector, not to Candace. She would dress herself and make omelets and arrange roses in jugs. She refilled Candace's glass.

"She's an easy baby."

And Candace, who had no reason not to, took her at her word and told Annie about the charming Frenchman she'd sat next to on the plane.

Annie tried to befriend women with babies, sought them out like life rafts, like broken hulls onto which she could haul herself, that they might bob in the choppy waters comparing crises, but there was no one who would meet her eye, no one to whom she dared say, "Who did you used to be?"

She sat in playgrounds that Vita was too young for, making small talk to slender women. She joined a music class where all the babies screamed and all the mothers weakly smiled. In the hallway, retrieving sandals and strollers, she caught one mother's eye and laughed, "Dear God, what have we done?" and the woman looked at her like Annie had a knife in her mouth and swept her baby home. Annie longed for a friend with whom she could weep. But every woman she met spoke only of naps and milk and teeth. So Annie sealed herself up. She, too, spoke only of naps and milk and teeth.

Hector came home in the evenings, eyes rimmed dark with mascara, eyebrows combed, all the hairs lying flat, glistening lightly, held in place with a clear gel, white teeth flashing in the half-light of the kitchen, his body taut, precise, his arms balancing scripts, a water bottle, his mouth full of stories from his set, from his parallel world. It was as though the front door were an enchanted wardrobe that opened into winter. It was unthinkable, the distance between them. It was unutterable. They met where they could. She patched together her stories from the streets, not mentioning the nap in a supermarket parking lot, nor the screaming fit two miles from home, nor that she had jogged, half running, half crying, up the canyon, singing, weeping, begging her daughter to stop the assault, and struggled breathless into the house and that Vita finally screamed herself into oblivion, right as the stroller bumped through the front door, had fallen asleep, chin tucked, head tumbled forward, a banana slimed in her hot, fat, outstretched hand.

Hector told stories about the director who was useless and his costar who was always late to set, and that next week would be a doozy because it was a courtroom episode, which meant so many lines for him to learn and hours and hours of work because of all the coverage. Coverage, she knew, meant all the times the camera had to be moved in order to tell the story from as many points of view as possible. It meant the number of angles required to make sure we saw the jury, the judge, the lawyers, the defendant, the whole courtroom. Coverage was how you told the whole story. But how did anyone tell the whole story? Who decided the point of view that mattered most? She wondered how much coverage it would take to tell hers. She thought it would probably take a microscope rather than a camera.

One night, a year after Vita's birth, Hector invited his cast for dinner. It was the first dinner party they had given since the baby. Annie braised beef and lit candles and arranged yellow anemones in tiny glass vases. She left Vita with the cleaning lady and got a blow-dry. The house was Spanish, pretty, with unexpected curves and a wide white arched fireplace. Twilight was its best light; it disguised the pokiness of the rooms and the blankness of the canyon walls that reared up behind it. The actors descended like a family. Beautiful, improbable, buoyant as children, they spilled their shared stories. They seemed happy to be there, delighted by her home, her candles, her hair. She could not tell when they were performing. She wondered if they knew. She sat next to his silvery costar, the one who was always late, a man older than Hector, a man who earned more and did less, a man Hector told her was sleeping with the wardrobe assistant. He turned his beam on Annie, he leaned his body toward her, he asked her questions, he widened his eyes and threw his head back in laughter at her answers. He made her feel delightful. Her hair felt shiny and smooth, she knew all the hairs were lying in the same direction. Her teeth felt white. She smelled fresh. He wanted her to feel this way because in her delight he found mirrored his own meaning; she knew this, and she did not care. He was enjoying her company, and she his. Both were new sensations. Reluctantly, she excused herself to check on Vita. She heard the screams before she saw her. Found her red-faced and incoherent with outrage, sweating, rigid, apoplectically upright and clinging to the bars of her crib. The baby monitor lay unplugged, useless, unrestored by the cleaning lady who had vacuumed earlier.

Vita had been screaming for an hour, maybe more. Swamped with guilt, Annie rushed to her, swept her into her arms, her gulping, outraged child, heat radiating from her ramrod body. She stroked her daughter's back, swaying from side to side, soothing her. Vita took a long, ragged breath, burped, and sighed out a stream of hot vomit down Annie's back. Annie felt it like a snake. It soaked her silken back. Her daughter lay her head on Annie's neck and hiccupped. The room smelled evil. Annie cleaned her daughter, changed her, found fresh bedding, sang to her as she lay her down in darkness before running to her own bathroom, where she saw the streak of rancid milk down her back, her hair clumped and darkening, her ear flecked with vomit. She peeled off the ruined silk shirt and stepped in the shower, rinsing her hair, then soaping it thoroughly to get rid of the smell. She wiped the carefully applied mascara from where it now stained her cheeks, dug out an old T-shirt, and slipped it over her head.

She came back downstairs restored to her mother self. The actor smiled at her, acted as though nothing had changed, as though she were not now sitting before him with dripping hair and a wiped face in a crumpled T-shirt. As though she had not just been swapped out for someone completely different upstairs. He smiled, patted her hand, and resumed their conversation. She would always love him for this. She listened to his stories, humming lullabies under her breath.

Later Hector asked her why she had disappeared. She told him. He shook his head and laughed, congratulated her on a great evening, rested a hand on her thigh, and told her she looked sexy even in the T-shirt. She had smiled, tried to look pleased. But in bed she had lain in the darkness, wondering how to be both, the vomit-stained mother and the flirtatious host, how to marry these women on a narrow stairwell. She fell asleep and dreamed her hair was on fire.

Annie brakes at a deserted stoplight. A deer melts out of the dark tree line. It is a doe, dusky, delicate but assured. She steps in front of the stopped car, picks her way across the road. She stops at the verge and lowers her head to the speckled snow. Annie watches, barely breathing. Her phone rings. The deer raises her head, alert. Annie fumbles, answers. It is Hector, elated.

"Easter in Buenos Aires, baby."

"You got the job?"

"Can you believe they took so long?"

"That's great."

Her heart sinks. She knows what awaits her. Days and nights of managing everything alone. The freight train of responsibility coupled with the cargo of mutual resentment. The doe listens. The winter light licks her spindly back.

"Fuckers. Now it's just about points and back end, the usual."

"When do you leave?"

"Who knows? Tomorrow, knowing them. That's the other line, I must jump. Grab some champagne on your way home? We'll celebrate tonight."

Annie hangs up, watches as the doe picks her exquisite way through the trees, careful, intent, alone. She dissolves into the woods.

CHAPTER 6

HECTOR LEANS ON THE KITCHEN COUNTER, EARPIECE DANGLING, sipping his coffee. His coffee is slick with an oil that optimizes his metabolism and a meager splash of oat milk to render the whole thing palatable. He has waited all winter to hear about this role and now it is his. He closes his eyes as his agent talks. He feels the familiar vertigo of anticipation and dread that new work engenders. He had been working up to asking his father for a loan this Christmas. He is glad he refrained. It has been years since he has asked his parents for money.

He knows how much he needs work to feel himself, to feel his full self. Hector feels like a scrap, a discard when he is not working, negligible and impotent. He is good at hiding it from his family, but he knows what his inactivity costs him. He checks their bank balance daily. He is lucky that Annie is not a spendthrift, that neither of them covet luxury. But still, what she spends on furniture ("It's secondhand, Hector. Vintage! For my work!") is absurd. He is lucky, he knows this, that compared to others, he works often, or at least steadily. He has friends who have been edged off the stage, forced to take up carpentry or real estate or teaching, who have watched their careers drift slowly out of sight. He tends not to see those friends anymore. It is too awkward. No one knows what to talk about. He feels sorry for them but often comes away with the sensation that they feel sorry for him, which is confusing. But here he is on the phone with his agent, discussing restaurants in Buenos Aires. He isn't like those friends. He is a steady earner, a safe bet.

At nineteen, with two hundred dollars in his wallet and a set of hand weights rolling in the trunk, Hector drove from Boston to Los Angeles. He crossed the country in his older brother's car, a thirdhand green Volkswagen Jetta, dimpled with dents, that spat Johnny Cash and Nirvana in and out of the CD player when it overheated. He drove without stopping, pulled up in front of a low-rise apartment block in Burbank, and passed out on his best friend's brother's sofa. His best friend's brother was a sound engineer, and Hector's first job was cleaning the music studio at night. He vacuumed the deserted soundproofed rooms, emptied ashtrays and trash cans, replenished the water bottles. He rearranged the magazines in the waiting area, swept the lobby floor, and then passed out till noon on his best friend's brother's corduroy couch. He kept gas in his car and air in his tires and an adamantine belief in his own ability. He refused humiliation as though it were fattening. By day he scoured the back pages of industry magazines, searching for the open calls to auditions. Diligently he navigated his way to every one he could find, the Thomas Guide sliding off his lap, as he wound along the bleached vertebrae of Mulholland Drive or dipped down into the electric bowl of the Valley or swung into the dark heart of Hollywood. He was never late. He was word-perfect. He was polite. He was beautiful. It was just a matter of time.

But time stretched out like the desert. Everything was taking longer than he thought it would. Longer than anyone had thought it would. Back in Boston, Hector had slid into every leading role the school amateur dramatics society had to offer. The prettiest girls and their mothers had all fallen for him. He studied hard, got good grades. Everyone loved him. Except for his father. His father seemed to care only about Hector's brother, Alexander. Alexander was brilliant, won scholarships and chess championships, went rappelling on weekends. Hector chose to shine in the few places his brother's light had not reached. He took up acting because it was the one thing Alexander didn't do. His parents looked on, hopeless, fond, despairing. They had no way to help their son, no strings to pull, no words of encouragement to give because they lacked the vocabulary for trying your hardest without any guarantee of success.

Nothing in Hector's young life had prepared him for failure. Hard work he was used to, he was built for devotion. But nothing in his life had prepared him for pouring his heart and soul into something and getting nothing in return. The silences were bewildering. He had no one to tell. He thought he must be doing something wrong. For the first time in his life, Hector doubted himself. He joined an acting class. It took place in the afternoons in a dusty black box theater on the east side of town, wedged between a chicken 'n' waffles joint and a laundromat. The smell of battered food hung in the hallways and the rumble of washing machines thundered faintly through the walls. The acting coach was a ferocious Russian American with dyed red hair and a voice like a nail on glass. She made them cry. And she made them better. He watched her pick off the weak like a frigate bird descending on newly hatched turtles. Some she devoured, some she flung back onto the sand. He watched them scramble to recover, some of them grow stronger for the encounter. He loved her. He longed to be improved by her. He loved the class. He found community here, at last, young men with the same blend of despair and determination in their wide eyes, young women, all beautiful, broken, dogged. He loved them all, he loved this dark room of young people willing themselves to greatness. He loved the anonymity and the intimacy of it. He loved the proximity to success, to working actors who brought in scenes from sitcoms or series that they might shoot the very next day. He worked diligently with whatever scene or scene partner he was assigned. He never asked to swap, nor answered back when the Russian yelled. He took notes, he studied, he waited. He knew it would not take long.

As he left class one night, a middle-aged man in a suit that was too big for him stopped him in the parking lot. He introduced himself as a theatrical agent by the name of Frank Cohen. He said he liked to drop in on class from time to time to see "who was coming up" and that he thought he could "do something" for Hector. Hector tried to act cool, as though agents regularly offered to represent him, as though he weren't still waking at noon with the imprint of a corduroy couch embossed on his cheek. He sat opposite Frank in the booth of a local diner, with its low seats and tall menus, and ransacked himself for questions to ask the faded man so that he might sound discerning, but found none. He had an agent. An agent with dried egg on his lapel and a single rented room off Pico Boulevard, an agent no one else seemed to have heard of, but an agent all the same. It felt like the end of the beginning.

One night at class he watched a beautiful girl (they were all beautiful back then) working on a scene with her scene partner. She had expensive brown hair, and a mole that hovered perfectly above her top lip. Hector was transfixed. He recognized her from television. She played a cheerleader on a popular show but she could have played anything, he knew this. The Russian teacher lavished her with praise before annihilating her reedy scene partner. The girl with the mole slipped gracefully into the seat in front of Hector. He leaned forward, whispered in her ear, "Nice work."

She looked over at him, surprised.

Later they lay naked on the floor of the charming Spanish apartment that she shared with no one. As she curled into his wide tanned chest, he took in the room. Scripts, ones she had been sent to read, to audition for, to decide on, lay splayed on the floor like seagulls in flight. Frank had yet to send him out on a single audition. He got up, deliberately picked his way past them over to the bookcase. She sprawled voluptuously, watching him. It was his best performance to date, to act this casual around this much possibility, to pretend satiety in the presence of this much fallen fruit. He pulled out a slim paperback with a fish on the cover.

"God, I love this."

She shook her head, heavy-lidded, yawned.

"Never read it."

He smiled, tried not to mind.

"Read to me."

He looked down at her wide mouth, her face so pliant with success, with ease, with knowing her place in the world. He wanted a place in her world. He propped himself, folded back the front cover.

"'He was an old man who fished alone in a skiff in the Gulf Stream and he had gone eighty-four days now without taking a fish.'"

They dated for three months. In the mornings she went to work on her show, leaving him sleeping in her bedroom. He waited till he heard the grind of the garage door, the reversing car, then made himself coffee and then settled into a chair, reading every script he could find in the house. He made a list of every role he was right for, then called Frank with the list of projects. His agent blew air through his lips.

"Sonny, you're good, but they won't see you for half of these."

"Then get me in on the half that will."

He was done with waiting.

He was ready.

But Hollywood doesn't care if you are ready.

When he booked his first job, a nationwide mattress commercial, he felt a rush of joy that he knew was unseemly. It was a mixture of relief and degradation. He was meant for better than this, he knew it. Frank knew it, too, but was relieved to have procured something for his (possibly only) client. Hector felt conflicted about how to celebrate anything so palpably beneath him. He called his mother, which is what he always did when he wasn't sure how to feel. She wore her disdain like lipstick.

"Well, sweetheart, I guess it's your first job, not your last one. I'll tell your father you won't be needing the credit card anymore."

This stung Hector. He had been given the card for emergencies and only used it twice, once to take the girl with the mole out to dinner and once to buy a used pager so Frank could get hold of him. He felt both of these were career-advancing and not to be questioned. He cut the credit card in two and mailed it to his parents in an envelope with no note. He spent his first paycheck on a membership to a local gym. He told his girlfriend (he supposed that was what she was now) about his job and she acted pleased for him, but he could tell she, too, was disappointed. She wanted him to be more successful than he was. Not than she was. But she did not want to date a person who sold mattresses. It was easier to love his untapped potential than his commercial success. She dumped him two weeks later.

He booked his next job a month later (another commercial, this time for a well-known laundry detergent). Frank took him for Reubens at a diner in Beverly Hills. Hector gave his best friend's brother a set of speakers as a thank-you and then spent the rest of his earnings on a deposit on a one-bedroom studio with a minifridge and a view of a parking lot in North Hollywood. The commercials kept coming; they bought him time, steadied his self-belief. He kept going to class and kept working on his abs. He bought a secondhand laptop and began writing ideas for screenplays in coffee shops. He journaled, drove to the beach, tried surfing, met friends for ramen or egg-white omelets, and hiked the same bald brown hills. He waited. Finally, the door cracked.

He booked a sitcom with four other actors, four other unknowns, all young and determined, all acidic with ambition. He resolved to shine in their midst and he did. And people noticed. He knew the show stunk, but he refused to stink in it. It lasted only six episodes but he was on his way now. He fired his agent over a bowl of matzo ball soup. Frank slurped sadly, nodding, unsurprised.

He got a better agent, with suits as shiny as his hair. He got more auditions. He worked on his lines and his pectorals. He barely had time for class. He met more girls, but never again would he date someone more successful than he was. He kept his eyes on the horizon. He did not care about parties, about premieres. He wanted to be valued for his own worth, not for where he went or with whom. The jobs began to improve. He met friends for dinner or an uphill run up to the HOLLYWOOD sign. He liked seeing the white letters staring down at him. They felt auspicious. He knew everyone could see them but he didn't care. At twenty-four, he knew they were there only for him.

He landed a six-part series about Pearl Harbor on a prestige channel—at last, something his mother and father could rejoice in, could tell their friends. He did army bootcamp, made competitive friends with his costars. He booked the romantic lead opposite a movie star from Rajasthan. She was a Bollywood household name trying to break into America, five years his senior, who wore a tiny ruby in her nose, like a pomegranate aril. Her neck smelled of attar of roses. They fell deeply, ravishingly in love. They filmed in the studio all day and inhaled each other in her hotel room all night. He filmed as if in a dream and when they wrapped, he promised her he would visit her in India. He drove her to the airport, the car crammed with suitcases bulging with Western fashions, waved goodbye, and wiped his eyes all the way back to his apartment. A month later he was shooting another movie in Vancouver and spending a fortune on long-distance phone calls to Mumbai. She blamed him for putting his career first and not coming to see her. He blamed her for even thinking that he had a choice. He never saw her again.

    Yes, there was no doubt about it, he had worked. He had worked consistently since those early days. He was one of the lucky few. Of course, it had not been the career he had hoped for. He wondered if anyone had the career they hoped for. It became clear that despite his alarmingly good looks, he would never be a movie star. The town was full of beautiful men. He had not expected to be one of so many. He wondered if it might be easier to be a character actor, toyed with breaking his nose or dying his hair red, but was not willing to risk it. Slowly, he grew accustomed to his place in the order of things. He never lost the longing for the great role, but now, at fifty, still passing for early forties, thank God, mature but still appealing, he was resigned to taking what was offered to him and making the best of it. He was perfect for the long-suffering husband, the forbearing father. His lightly patrician air meant he was offered the white-collar roles, the positions of mild authority: the rueful editor, the exasperated bureau chief, the overworked surgeon. He was urbane and was cast as such, had always worked in big cities. Not for him the low-budget movies in the high cornfields or the flickering strip malls of Middle America. Hector had dined in towering restaurants in all the major cities of the world, restaurants with velvet booths and views of lit-up buildings, snaking rivers. He had reached across the bodies of naked women to call for room service in hotel rooms around the globe.

    But not since Annie. There has been no one else since Annie.

As he listens to his agent reel off the details of the deal, he thinks of all that must be taken care of before he leaves. The household foibles he alone knows how to manage, the paperwork he'll have to hand off to his wife. He listens to his agent and mourns the too-brief period of his life when, unencumbered by a girlfriend or a family, the arrival of a job meant only a celebratory dinner with friends. Back then he was free to take whichever job rolled his way and spin off into the world at a moment's notice. Back then he had not so much as a spider plant to worry about. He sublet his apartment, parked his car on a side street, and slipped into a new life. They were endless, back then, the possibilities of who he could be and where the world might take him. But Annie…no, that wasn't fair, it wasn't Annie, it was the children who had changed that. Annie had never cared that he traveled. She knew that was part of the deal. In the early days she came with him; later she stayed home with the kids.

These days he is offer-only. He is too old to audition. If Spielberg calls, he likes to say, then we'll talk. He doesn't call. But no more for him the waiting rooms, the long lines of eerily identical young men sprawled in chairs, studying their lines, or studiously ignoring one another, or staring glassily out of windows, into corridors, into horizons only they can see. Hector stays home and works in the garden, rereads the complete works of Chekhov, and waits for the phone to ring. And yet, sometimes, lifting barbells in his shed, Hector feels pinioned under the weight of his decaying ambition. He lives with the tang of disappointment on his tongue, faintly metallic to the taste. He is addicted to his own failure, arranging himself around the contours of who he might have been, like an actor finding his light.

The movie is a political thriller; Hector is to play the husband of an abducted ambassador. He will be in Argentina for three months, four if the movie star doesn't know her lines. The agent drones on about some polo player Hector has never heard of. Hector interrupts him.

"When do I leave?"

The agent hazards a guess, but departure is imminent.

Hector hangs up. He is restored.

He sees Edouard helping himself to firewood from the log pile. He watches him struggle, broad shoulders stooped, straining his perfectly pressed white shirt (pressed by whom? Candace surely doesn't iron), piling logs into the wheelbarrow. Usually, this sight fills him with rage. For no good reason. Candace is generous, has offered rent and been forcefully rejected, so she and Edouard have written checks for utility bills, for firewood, paid for dinners, left a hock of prosciutto on the kitchen table, a case of prosecco on the back porch. And yet it galls him to watch another man help himself to his log pile. Hector cracks open the window, calls out.

"I got the job."

Edouard looks up, startled.

They sit at the kitchen table. Edouard sips his espresso.

"When do you leave?"

"In a week or two."

"So soon? I can't believe they don't give you more notice."

Hector suppresses the thought that an offer this late in the day means the role has been offered to others, many others, before arriving in his lap. It means someone has dropped out at the last minute. This is a well-thumbed script, grubby with handling. He sees no need to share this information with Edouard.

"We will all depart *au même temps*."

"How so?"

"The floors are finally in. The contractor called Candace this morning, said we can move in next week as soon as they finish sanding."

"My God, it's actually happening."

"We'll finally be out of your hair."

Hector makes a noise with the mug near his face that he hopes suggests demurral. "Annie will miss you. We all will."

"Will she manage? With all of us gone?"

"Annie? Oh, she always manages. She's got Brian, and we can get the sitter to give her a hand with the kids. If you'd check in from time to time, see if they need firewood or shoveling out, that would be great. But no, Annie's fine."

Edouard smiles.

"Candace would not be so easy about me leaving for three months to be a movie star's husband."

Hector snorted.

"Not Annie. She's not like that."

CHAPTER 7

ANNIE SITS AT THE KITCHEN TABLE OPPOSITE THE FRENCH TUTOR. She cannot for the life of her remember his name. They texted this week to make arrangements and she forgot to save it in her phone. She wonders if she can discreetly text Candace but she has no idea where her phone is. Where had Candace even found a Frenchman out here? It was almost embarrassing how quickly her friend had uncovered a host of after-school activities and enrichment programs that Annie had never known existed. Remy, with sullen fortitude, now endured a private soccer coach, chess club, archery, and French lessons.

She should have rescheduled. She has too much to do. Patti will have been calling all morning. She has two houses for Annie to stage. Patti is the fellow parent and local Realtor with whom Annie has recently started her company. Annie mentally scans the house for where she could have left her phone. The tutor digs in his backpack, pulls out his laptop, the cover of which is decorated with a black decal of the cover art from *The Giving Tree*. In its dark branches the glowing apple logo of the computer dangles just beyond the reach of a silhouetted child and his outstretched arm. She had always disliked that book, avoided reading it to her children. She wonders why a grown man would put stickers on his laptop. She had guessed he was thirty but perhaps he is even younger. He runs his hand over his buzzed head, frowns. His eyelashes are long, dark. She gets up to search the kitchen for her phone again.

"Can I get you a drink of anything—water, tea?"

The sink is full of unwashed plates. She hopes he has not noticed. He shakes his head, concentrating.

"I don't know why this page won't load."

She must have left it upstairs. She just has to get through this one lesson and then she can forget to schedule the others. She can hear the cleaning lady clattering around in her bedroom. Thank God for Iryna, the house is a pigsty now that Hector is gone. She feels suddenly self-conscious of the mess, but also, immediately, the absurd privilege of having a cleaner and a French tutor. She wonders how to drop into conversation that Iryna only comes one afternoon a week. She wonders why on earth she cares what he thinks.

He closes the laptop with a snap.

"I don't know what's going on. Was fine earlier. *Tant pis*. We don't need it. So. Annie. Why do you want to learn French?"

"I don't. I mean, it was Candace's idea. You're my Christmas present. So to speak. Oh Christ. She thought it would be fun for me to learn French, so she gave me lessons."

He smiles.

"Why do you think she chose French?"

"Apparently, I'm impossible to buy for, but she said she wanted to give me something beautiful. My husband says I should be learning Spanish. But that's because he's working in Argentina—we're going there for Easter."

"No plans to go to France? Morocco? Quebec?"

"No plans."

He smiles.

"Not taking a job in diplomacy?"

She laughs hard at this.

"Zero diplomacy around here. No, I really don't need French lessons."

"Very good. Let's learn some useless beautiful French. My favorite kind."

"Are you French? You don't sound it. Sorry, that sounds rude."

"Born and raised in Connecticut. American dad but my mom is from Versailles. We only spoke French at home. No one thinks a French accent is cool when you're in fifth grade so I dropped that pretty fast. I've been tutoring for the last five or six years. And you're from Australia, I think?"

"Melbourne. I've lived here for years but there's no kicking these vowels. I should warn you, I'm terrible at languages. I mangle everything. The kids die when I order guacamole. So, I apologize in advance. This may well be a lost cause."

"I guarantee you I've had worse."

She smiles, astonished by the ease of this strange young man in her kitchen. She wonders if this is a gender thing. She cannot imagine walking into a house to teach a man something and being this comfortable in her skin. His body is like slack rope.

"You took French at school?"

"From Mr. Lonsdale, a bloke from Adelaide who once spent a year in Marseille. Even at thirteen we knew we'd been had."

He laughs. His teeth are astonishingly white. She keeps talking.

"Mum was scared of flying and never left Australia and my dad hated all foreigners and had an evil word for every country he'd never been to. It was not exactly a cosmopolitan upbringing."

She wonders why she is telling him this. She has put these lessons off for months, forgotten about them until Candace asked her how they were going. She had been touched by the originality of the gift, if alarmed by the imposition it implied.

Hector had snorted from his hotel room.

"Least French lessons don't take up any space."

The tutor pulls a spiral notebook from his backpack, cracks it open. It is a sketchbook, unlined, the pages creamy and thick. She is surprised. She has stacks of these exact sketchbooks stacked in plastic totes in the garage, years old, crinkled with drawings and watercolors.

"I'll ask you some questions in French. It's just a way for me to see where you're at, how much you remember, if anything at all. No pressure, don't worry if you don't understand a word, we're just getting a feel for things. Sound good?"

"It sounds terrifying. You're going to end up doing all the talking, I warn you."

"*Alors. On commence. Ça va?*"

He is immediately, undeniably French.

"Um. *Ça va.*"

"*Très bien.*"

"Are you an artist?"

She points at the sketchbook.

"No, I'm a writer. *Je suis écrivain.* I just hate lined notebooks. The blank page is less intimidating. *Que faites-vous comme travail?*"

"Uh... *Je fais maisons?*"

"*Vous êtes constructrice?*"

"Already out of my depth here... *Je suis femme maison.*"

"You are a wifehouse? Oh, a housewife. *Je suis une femme au foyer.*"

"Wow, that actually sounds worse in French. Let's go with *je suis mère.*"

"*Vous êtes une mère.* Excellent. *Et vous avez combien d'enfants?*"

"No clue."

"*Je ne comprends pas.*"

"*Je ne comprends pas.*"

"*Enfants.* Children. *Combien?*"

"*Deux?*"

"*Vous avez deux enfants. Comment-ils s'appellent?*"

"Wait, I know this one. How old are they?"

"What are their names."

"Shit. I knew that one. Sorry. I warned you. You're going to end up having a shockingly boring conversation with yourself."

"Don't worry about me. This is my job. *C'est mon travail.*"

"Okay. *Ils s'appellent Vita et Jackson.* What do you write?"

"Short stories. For now. Building up to a novel. But not yet. *Pas encore.*"

He is drenched in youth, this young man, she thinks. He is soaked in all its possibilities. He asks her something else she does not understand. The cleaning lady bursts in, clattering the vacuum behind her like a dog on a leash. She looks startled to see them seated there. Annie winces, knowing she will now have to introduce them.

"Iryna, this is my French teacher, this is . . ." She tries to mumble his name. He has already risen to his feet and stretched out his hand in greeting. The room grows darker as he stands. Iryna, eyes wide, backs away.

"Hi. I'm Thierry."

Iryna grunts, yanks the vacuum into the next room.

"Did I scare her?"

"She doesn't speak much English. Sorry."

"What for?"

"Well, having the cleaning lady here."

"*Je suis désolée.*"

"What's that?"

"It means 'I'm sorry.' You say it a lot. Might come in useful."

CHAPTER 8

"ED AND I FOUGHT ALL NIGHT."

"What happened?"

"The cryo storage place called to ask us what we want to do with our embryos. They've been there for eight years, and we have to decide whether to renew or not."

"My God, has it been eight years?"

"We went around and around in circles. Ed wants to donate them to science, but I can't, not after all I went through to get them. I can't just give them away. So, we agreed to talk about a surrogate. I think. I am so tired I don't know what we actually settled on."

"Candace, you'd go through it all again? A baby? At our age? I thought we liked having our lives back."

"Yes, but it's all over so fast. I know that now."

Annie looks at Candace as though she were a stranger. They are in a local antiques store, standing in front of a nineteenth-century Welsh dresser that Candace wants Annie to take a look at. She is as shocked as if the dresser had spoken.

"But aren't you done? With all of that?"

Candace frowns.

"I'm always a mother."

"No, obviously, I mean done with being a mother to a newborn, to a toddler. Isn't that the stuff we all just got through as best we could to get to the good part?"

"Not all of us."

Candace points at the dresser.

"Isn't it great? For the kitchen?"

"Too heavy. It will dwarf the room."

"Damn."

"You're seriously considering having a baby."

"Remy hates being an only child. He loved living with you guys."

"Remy doesn't get a say. He's not the one who will be lying awake at night for the rest of his life wondering how he fucked his kid up."

Annie feels the sting of betrayal. She is used to being in league with Candace; they have spent so much of their adult lives intertwined. She turns to inspect a farmhouse kitchen table.

"You okay?"

"I'm in shock, I think. I didn't know... I thought we were done."

"You sound like Edouard. I thought I was done too. But you don't know what you'll do until the opportunity presents itself. And they haunt you, those little cell clusters. I never forgot about them. And now that we're faced with the prospect of letting them go, I find that I can't do it that easily."

"I can't wait to hear what Léonore has to say."

Léonore is Ed's mother, a macaron of a woman, delicate, exquisite, pastel, glazed with Catholicism. Annie met her at Candace's wedding, a magnificent affair at the Plaza in New York, with old-world Parisians mingling uneasily with Upper East Side Jews and wide-armed politicians with easy smiles sealing alliances around the room. Annie had loved it, loved her place in this family, the ease of both belonging and not, of moving effortlessly between Candace's senile Floridian grandmother and her friend's exes, who had assembled to inspect the slender Frenchman who had outwitted them all. She had found herself at one point sitting beside Léonore, pale, exquisite, and knotted like a silk scarf, her huge blue eyes echoed by the antique sapphire discs on her earlobes. She nodded, digesting Annie's halting attempts in French to extol her best friend, while sizing up Annie's thrift shop slip dress, her flushed face, and her flailing efforts to keep Vita's flower girl dress actually on her body all day.

"She is lucky. To have a friend like you."

Annie could not tell if she was joking. "Oh, no. I'm the lucky one."

The new mother-in-law smiled and turned her lovely neck away.

"Oh, she'll be delighted. She thinks we're going to hell for keeping her grandchildren in a deep freeze. By the way, how did it go?"

"What?"

"The lesson. With Thierry."

"It was fun in a humiliating kind of way."

"Isn't he cute? Remy loves him."

"Where did you find him?"

"Edouard met him in the bar in town, in the old hotel. I think he works there in the evenings."

Annie examines some linen napkins.

"It must be quiet now we've all left."

"Oh, someone is still always yelling about something."

"How is Buenos Aires going?"

"You know Hector. Hates not working and then hates whatever job he's on. But he's fine, I think, all things considered."

Annie does not say that she prefers the house without him in it, that it makes both her and the children more independent, and that the autonomy is precious. She does not mind the silent erosion of his careful systems. She does not say that she does not miss him at all.

CHAPTER 9

ANNIE TOOK VITA TO THE MUSEUM THAT OVERLOOKED THE CITY and the wide ribbon of the Pacific Ocean beyond. They rode the little electric train up the hillside mountain to the white pantheon that sparkled at the top of it. Sometimes all they did was ride the train up and down the hillside. Vita loved it.

Annie stood in a gift shop, looking aimlessly at postcards. She ran her finger around the edge of a small brass sound bowl that sat on its own plump cushion. It was beautiful, complete. A sound bowl for meditation, for another life that might hold that kind of stillness and reverence and time. The ringer, a stick wadded in cloth, rested inside it. She circled it around the lip of the bowl. A soft hum rippled forth. Vita, torturing a croissant in her stroller, twisted around to see, littering the floor with papery crumbs. A young woman at the cash register sighed, brought out a broom, and began ostentatiously sweeping the floor around them. Annie apologized for the mess. The girl ignored her, sweeping aggressively around her feet. Vita leaned forward to get a better look at what she was doing and tipped the rest of the feathery pastry from her lap onto the floor. The girl rolled her eyes and began sweeping again. Vita bent down to smile at her, but the girl refused her gaze. She looked crestfallen. Annie felt volcanic. She wanted to hurt this young woman who had never been woken in the night by an implacable tyrant, had never ridden a tram up and down a hill for three hours just to kill the hours till nap. Instead, Annie pushed the little brass bowl into the mouth of the diaper bag that hung open on the back of her stroller and made for the exit. She could feel her heartbeat in her wrists, her breath short. Everything felt bright, sharp, focused. On the tram back down the hill she kept glancing around to see who was going to stop her before she got in her car. But no one did. On the drive home Vita mercifully slept. The diaper bag sat on the passenger seat, the bowl askew among the diapers, silent and useless, a mere thing. She put it on a shelf above Vita's crib but no one ever played with it.

Vita went to preschool and Annie discovered she had time again, a few precious hours to herself. She opened up the garage and pulled out her art supplies. Her watercolors had hardened into puckered discs, her brushes stiffened, her canvases buckled with the passing seasons. The garage was musty when closed, but when open she was subjected to the stares of passing hikers, the curiosity of children, the invasion of vermin. A pit bull cocked its leg and the steaming piss pooled in the doorway, trickled down to her bare feet. There was no money for a studio, nor for a nanny. She went back to the museums, the galleries, the ocean, looking for inspiration, for a seed she might pack in the earth and tend. She found nothing. She wept, often. In the night she clung to Hector.

"What shall I do? Who even am I anymore?"

And he soothed her, saying there was no rush to go back to work, that he could make enough for them both, that she could take her time to decide what to do next. And she had no words to say that what we do is who we are, that how we fill our days is how we spend our lives and this waiting, for Vita to wake up, for Hector to come home, for any feeling that would bring her back to life, hatred, envy, rage would be welcome, anything better than this inertia that was killing her by inches. Hector, worried, called his mother.

"Postpartum?"

"Vita's three, Mom."

"Then it's about time she got a job."

"She knows that. She just doesn't know what."

"Lucky girl to have the choice," said Bryony, who was late for her tennis lesson.

Annie stopped leaving the house other than to retrieve Vita from preschool. She was asleep by the time Hector came home. Candace came to visit. She drove Annie out to the desert, past the fields of white windmills churning in the pointlessly blue sky, through the mottled scrub and outrageous arms of the strange succulents, past scattered brown towns to a tiny motel with a high white wall and a gate with a code. Annie rolled out of the car. She had not spoken for the entire trip. Behind the gate there stretched a steaming azure pool that smelled of eggs. The motel wrapped itself around it in an L shape, all the rooms opening onto the sulfuric pool of water that bubbled up through millennia of igneous rock. They had the place to themselves. The owner left them the key and a coffee cake on their doorstep. They smoked weed and ate takeout in the pool and floated for hours, for days, their world framed by the lip of the pool and the quiet courtyard. This tile of blue sky was all there was, all she needed. Candace free-associated from her inflatable about her French fiancé, about wedding dresses and fundraising committees and facials, while Annie surrendered to the water and the sky and the heat. She let Candace's prattle bead off her like water. She wondered, as she had so many times before, why they were friends. And then she remembered that she was floating in this bath of amniotic warmth precisely because of this trivial, loving, and unerringly intuitive friend. There was no one better. And there was no extraordinary future awaiting her. There was only the next hour. There was only what lay in front of her.

* * *

The clouds passed. The years passed.

Vita grew tall, vocal, independent. She was ferocious, willful, imperious in her intractable need to do everything alone. Annie felt dispensable, an onlooker already in her formidable daughter's life. She watched her and waited to be needed. With her father, Vita was pliant, coquettish even. She clambered in his lap, recited her exhaustive dreams, schoolyard injustices, and victories. With Annie, she was strangely silent. She held herself aloof, playing with a dollhouse that she filled with animals because she disdained dolls. Annie invented art projects for them to do together—watercolors, making cards, printing wrapping paper—but Vita spilled the water and screwed up the paper. Once Annie asked Hector if he thought their daughter even liked her. He laughed.
"She loves you. What are you talking about?"
But Annie knew that her daughter could open and close like a water lily.
Vita began attending the elementary school a mile down the hill. Annie drove her there in the chill canyon mornings, unloaded her heavy with backpack, teetering with snacks. One day a week she volunteered in the library, and another day she helped out with art class. It began as a way to stay close to her drifting daughter, as though physical proximity might create intimacy, as though she might eavesdrop her way into her daughter's life. She winced at how quickly Vita learned to ignore her, just as she had walked past her own mother in those bleached school corridors on the other side of the world.

One evening Hector brought home an old friend who worked as a set decorator. While Hector made coffee, the set decorator laid his hand on hers and asked her if she'd like a job. She flushed as though he'd asked her on a date. She nodded, and found herself helping him find props for a play, trawling the flea markets again for the exact right slumping sofa, the perfect beaded curtain. She loved the job, had an eye for a bargain and an irremediable inability to keep receipts. Hector was relieved to watch his wife revive, if dismayed to watch his garage space disappear.

Vita turned seven. Her godmother, Candace, lay sobbing on the living room floor. Vita, startled, headed back up to her room to play with her new hamster. She liked feeding him barbecue chips when no one was looking because it was a snack she felt they both enjoyed. Her mother was holding Candace's hand, which meant she wouldn't notice what Vita was doing.

Candace wept on her friend's floor because she was deep into her third round of IVF and the best doctors were on the West Coast, everyone said so, and so Ed and she had relocated for the express purpose of getting pregnant and now she was awash with hormones and her mother-in-law kept asking Edouard where the babies were, as though they were hiding them in a closet, and he kept shrugging but Candace felt the same way, where were her babies?

"The doctor says she can only see one follicle, but I have to go through with the retrieval anyway because you never know and something might change by the morning, but I do fucking know, and I can't go through this again, I just can't."

And Annie took her hand in hers and held it hopelessly, stroking her.

"They're coming. I know they are. Your babies are coming."

But inwardly, Annie wondered. She wondered why she, who had not particularly wanted a child, who was not terribly good with them, had one, while Candace, who crawled around on all fours with Vita, who let her try on all her makeup, who sent gifts from all over the world, why she was not getting her baby.

She drove her friend to the clinic the next morning for the retrieval. Candace could barely get out of the car.

"It feels like someone strapped a fucking bowling ball to my pelvis."

Annie helped her stooping friend into the lobby. The room was full of women who could not look at each other for fear of the pity or excitement they might see there. The sofas were carefully distributed, Annie noticed, angled away from each other for maximum discretion. There were boxes of Kleenex on every mushroom-colored end table. Candace slumped in a chair. Annie handed her off to a Thai nurse with kind eyes and came back three hours later to pick up her up. Candace looked up at her with a wolfish grin.

"Five fucking eggs, baby. FIVE."

CHAPTER 10

JACKSON BURSTS INTO THE KITCHEN. LUKE'S MOTHER DROPPED HIM at the top of the lane and he ran through the woods chased by zombies and now he is exhausted by his own imagination. He flops into a chair, relieved to find Vita eating dry cereal with a spoon, reading a book propped up against the fruit bowl.

"Where's Mom?"

Vita shrugs without looking up.

"Did Dad call?"

She does not answer.

"What time is it there?"

"Two hours ahead."

"I'm gonna call him."

Jackson dumps his backpack on the floor and goes to search for the home phone. It is always somewhere unexpected, never on the cradle now that Dad is gone. He's only been gone a month and already Jackson is sensing a decline. There was no milk at breakfast and Vita's dry cereal suggests there is still none now. His mother waved it off, offered him toast instead. She is always busy, always on her way somewhere to do something else. The house feels empty. He finds the phone on the windowsill, propped between a dead plant and a dirty mug. He calls his father.

"Hi Dad."

"Hey JJ, what's up?"

"What are you doing?"

"You find me lying on my bed in my hotel room, kind of watching TV but not really, going over my lines for tomorrow. Big scene at the heliport tomorrow. How was school?"

"Maxton broke his wrist."

"Yikes. Doing what? At school?"

"I heard it snap. Playing dodgeball."

"Is he okay? Was there a teacher? They take him to hospital?"

"Yup. I guess. Where's Mom?"

"I don't know, bud. You wanna call her? Is Vee there?"

"When are you home?"

"Not for a while. But you're coming out here for spring break. That's not too far off. You'll love it, there's ice cream parlors everywhere and the hotel has a great pool and . . ."

"Yeah, you told me. I'm gonna go now."

"Call me back if you need. Tell your mom to call me."

"'Kay. Bye."

"Bye little guy. Love you."

Annie comes in, hauling grocery bags over the threshold. She calls out.

"Kids?"

Silence. Backpacks splay on the floor. The table is scattered with cornflakes, a flayed banana skin, two unfinished cans of soda, and the shavings of a sharpened pencil. The air in the kitchen is warm, still holds their breath. She yells again, heaving the bags onto the kitchen table. She slams their bowls in the sink and takes a deep breath. Iryna does not come for another five days. It's just her, alone with her outrage and her children. Her phone buzzes again, pulsing with obligations. Patti has another house. She has been outbid on a pair of sconces. A mixer at the school tomorrow night. Luke wants a playdate. Property taxes. An undeliverable package was returned to the post office. Another message from Hector.

She throws open the fridge and begins to cull, dumping forgotten leftovers into the trash can with the zeal of one bearing fresh groceries. One container misses, splattering gelatinous noodles across the floor. She sighs, swipes and mops it up with a cloth, drags the trash bags out to the cans, stuffs milk, vegetables, butter into the fridge, crams pasta, quick-cook rice, canned tomatoes on the shelves. Now she sees the dishwasher, unemptied, full of clean plates. They have sat here, her children, and eaten, played, talked, risen, and walked away from a kitchen littered with leftovers and refused to acknowledge a dishwasher of clean crockery. They have scribbled the kitchen with the scrawl of their lived lives but not paid the tiny ransom for that freedom. This is not independence. This is abuse.

She runs up the stairs, determined to catch the children in their indolence. She bursts in to Jackson's room. The bed is unmade, underwear and pajamas snarled on the floor beside half-drawn curtains. A whorl of toothpaste has been smashed into the floorboards. No sign of him. She heads to Vita's room, knock-pushes the door open. Jackson looks up, startled. He is playing a video game lying on his stomach on his sister's bed. Vita's bathroom door is closed. A toilet flushes and she comes out, headphones on, lost in her world. She startles at her mother's hectic expression.

"What's wrong?"

"What's wrong? What's wrong is that this house is disgusting! There's food everywhere, no one emptied the dishwasher, no one took out the trash. I don't see why I have to do everything in this house!"

"Mom, you don't . . ."

"I am fed up with this. I am fed up with doing everything around here and the two of you just acting as though we had servants. I will not have . . . Jackson, put that fucking game down. Vita, take off the headphones. Both of you, downstairs, now."

Jackson's eyes widen at the obscenity. Vita refuses to be pushed.

"Jesus, Mom, calm down. I'm doing my homework."

"Listening to rap music?"

"I have to write an essay on the political value of rap?"

"Jackson, get off that machine."

"But I finished my homework!"

"He did, Mom. I made him finish it first."

Annie turns around, flailing. Her daughter's room is immaculate, tucked away, folded in on itself as though she had something to hide. There is nothing to cling to in this room.

"I don't care what you're both doing. Come downstairs. I need some help."

"You can say that again."

"What did you say?"

"Nothing. Come on, JJ, let's go."

Dinner is silent. They pick at tepid food. At her insistence, the children reluctantly tell her about their days. They are all relieved when it is over and the children place their plates carefully, dutifully in the dishwasher. She watches them slink around her, furtive as cats. She hates herself for becoming her father, for ruining them with her fury. Hector would know what to do. He would play the right music, tease his sullen daughter, kick a ball with his son. He is good at that stuff.

The family has learned to live with Annie's rage. It erupts without warning like a squall at sea. The boat lists, the passengers are hurled from bow to stern, return to their seats surprised, bruised and sodden. Hector moves among them repairing, comforting, reassuring. It is over in a moment. Annie always apologizes, blames tiredness, overwork, overwhelm. The children know this about her. And Hector is always accommodating. He never asks her what is wrong. She would not know what to say if he did. It is hard to isolate the cause of her rage. She does not think of herself as an angry person. Perhaps this is the problem.

She goes upstairs with a glass of wine and runs a bath. She lowers herself into the steaming water. She feels drained, guilty, and lightly drunk. Her phone buzzes. It is the French kid. He has sent her homework. She almost laughs out loud. She must find a way to get out of this without hurting anyone's feelings. Although he is so assured, he probably would not care. She cannot remember ever being that confident.

Annie closes her eyes, mentally hangs different pictures on the wall of the master bedroom she is staging. It's a new build by a local property developer whom Patti is keen to woo. Both the house and the developer are woefully short on character. It will take more than floor lamps to disguise this vacuum. She told the French guy she was a housewife rather than attempt to explain what she does for a living. It is hard enough to articulate in English, let alone French. She wonders when in her life she stopped telling people that she was an artist. She wonders what Mrs. Riley would think of her.

Mrs. Riley was Annie's first art teacher. She joined the high school the same year as Annie, replacing a legendarily lecherous sculptor who liked to stand behind the girls and thread his arms under theirs to help them work their clay. He was eventually fired and replaced by the phlegmatic Mrs. Riley, a local artist unencumbered by any enthusiasm to impart a skill set and motivated only by access to a studio, unlimited materials, and the paid pursuit of her own agenda. She drew, painted, and sketched whatever she felt like. The kids were free to learn by watching her. Or not. Annie arrived early for her first class, eager for the one class for which she might have some aptitude. Mrs. Riley, compact, stout, iron hair cut like a helmet, stood at an easel in a spattered blue smock, painting a bowl of lemons. The rest of the class arrived, jostling with anticipation and backpacks. They chattered noisily, then subsided into restless silence. Minutes passed. Mrs. Riley dabbed her brush with cadmium, swirled it with ocher.

"I dunno what you lot are waiting for."

Annie was the first to move.

Annie loved art class, looked forward to it all week. Mrs. Riley seemed not to notice or care, as unimpressed by attentiveness as absence. Occasional remarks—"late," "no gum," "noise"—reflected concern for things that might directly affect her concentration. Otherwise, she moved through the studio as though it were empty, ignorant of anything the students did. The kids were intrigued, then bored, then pursued their own interests, reading comics, passing notes, occasionally swapping outfits to see if she would notice. She never did. Annie scrutinized the little woman's movements with total absorption, attentive to her every dab of paint. She learned by watching when to clean her brush, when to add a dab of white, when to narrow her eyes and stand back in appraisal. One afternoon, three years later, Mrs. Riley glanced over at Annie's canvas.

"That's not bad."

The class raised its head as one. No one moved. Annie's best friend, Sam, took to calling her Picasso after that.

Mrs. Riley told her to join the life drawing class on Thursdays after school. Annie loved it. The human body thrilled her. Wrinkled, laced with stretch marks, pockmarked, sunburned, dimpled. Every week a new texture, shape, line to explore. Every week she looked up from her charcoals in astonishment when the model rose from her stool, stretched, and disappeared behind a curtain to dress.

Annie sits up in the tub. She should be taking a life drawing class, not French lessons. But she has no time. She is subsumed by clutter and invented chores. It is the clutter that is making her so impatient, so short with the children, so rough with Hector, with herself, she thinks. She is corralled by stuff. It is suffocating the life out of her. She used to be an artist. She used to have a sense of humor. She will clear out the garage, she will stop ordering tablecloths, she will make space for herself. She will quit French, make waffles for breakfast, be nice to the children, pay the property taxes. She will tell Hector she misses him even if it is not true. Perhaps it will make it true. She pulls the plug and reaches for a towel.

Hector is asleep. He is too drugged to dream but in the hazy distance of wherever he is, he hears his cell phone. He struggles to the surface, reaching for it, dimly wondering if it is already time to work.

"Everything okay?"

"Were you asleep?"

"Yeah. I'm on set in... four hours."

"Oh. Sorry."

"Everything alright?"

"I think so. Hector, am I a terrible wife?"

"Could this maybe wait till tomorrow?"

"I mean it."

"There are some Ambien in the drawer on my side. Why don't you take one of those?"

"I'm a shitty mother. I'm not a very nice person."

"Oh God. What's this about? Of course you're not nice. You're much too interesting for that."

"I don't feel interesting. I feel like I've let everyone down. Myself included. And I... hang on, who's this... there's another call..."

Hector sighs, props the phone on the pillow. He pushes the eye mask back down over his eyes and closes them, waiting in the air-conditioned darkness. Outside, the hot city purrs. He dozes. He is almost asleep again when he hears his wife's voice.

"Hector?"

"Mmmm."

"Mum died."

He is awake like a switchblade. He sits up.

"What?"

"That was Sam. Helen found her. In the backyard. A heart attack, they think. The chickens were sitting on her chest. They were upset. The chickens, I mean."

Annie sounds as though she is calling from another star.

"Oh, love. Oh, Annie."

"She's dead."

"Jesus."

"I'll need to go. I have to go there."

"Yes, yes, of course. I won't be able to come, I mean, I don't think they'll let me . . ."

"No. I'll go on my own. Candace will take the kids."

"I'll ask my mother to come."

"Please don't. I should go. I . . . I need to make some calls."

"Annie, baby. I'm so sorry."

"I'll ring you later."

He holds the silent phone to his chest and stares at the white fan turning endlessly on the ceiling.

BOOK TWO
SPRING

CHAPTER 11

ANNIE HAS NO MEMORY OF GETTING TO MELBOURNE. HER BODY feels like it belongs to someone else. She wonders if this is grief or jet lag.

It is late summer in Australia. The wind is hot and damp, full of longing for rain. She has forgotten the harshness of antipodean light. She tastes salt on her lips. She has no idea when she last ate. Her eyes are dry, her nails ripped. Her cab slides through the city. Bicycles, coffee shops, a brown man yelling at a yellow dog. She has no one to rush for, she realizes, when the traffic slows. There is no one to see. The idea holds her heart in a fist. She has not been home for eight years. Jackson never met his grandmother. She had been pregnant with him, although she hadn't known it, when she last came, bringing Hector and a five-year-old Vita with her. They had stayed in a hotel.

Jackson had looked at her with dazed concern when she sat at the end of his bed in the morning and told him the news.

"Granny?" he asked. "The one on the phone?"

"Yes, darling. My mum. The one in Australia."

He leaned forward and hugged her waist.

"Oh Mom. You'll miss my soccer match. But that's okay."

Vita let fat tears roll down her cheeks.

"I told you we should have gone for Christmas."

Annie had no answer. She had not wanted to go for Christmas. For any Christmas.

She leans her head against the window of the cab. A new mall flashes by, neon and slick. They snake through the suburbs, white houses draped with bougainvillea, staked with jasmine, the cars sleek and oversized. The city has grown fat in her absence. The grammar school flashes past, the fences higher, the skirts shorter.

They are close to her home now. There is the playground. She feels panicked. She does not want to arrive yet. She taps on the glass.

"Here is fine."

She stands in the playground, her suitcase beside her. The ground is springy, buoyant beneath her feet. It is the new kind of asphalt, accident-proof. No pitted gravel here to scrape the small of your back, to scuff your elbows and shins. The merry-go-round has gone. The rec center is no longer. Now there is a climbing frame, not too high, with a rope ladder, monkey bars, swings with seats for every kind of child, infant, young, and disabled. The park is inclusive now, and utterly anonymous. It might be anywhere in the world. It is clean, silent, no broken bottles, no cigarette butts, no graffiti. Everything is welded, secure, rinsed. She sits on a swing, pushes off, arches her back to get some lift. She scans the streets, an old habit, searching for three big red dogs. There is the main road, there is the football pitch, and there, inevitably, is the ocean.

Annie's father never hit her as a child, but they all knew it was a matter of time. She grew strong as her teenage years crowded on her, pushed her body upward and outward, adding shape and dimension to her slender form. She made a few friends but never asked anyone home. Bluey worked as a secretary in the lower school and Annie took care never to run into her. Few kids knew they were even related. She was an average student, adept at not exciting attention. She cared only about art. As a child she had preferred drawing to speaking; for a year when she was five, she had communicated solely through her drawings. The doctor had shrugged and said she would grow out of it, and she had. But she continued to sketch her way through every class, illustrating her homework, essays, exam papers. At fifteen she was summoned to the headmistress for defacing school property and sent home with a letter requesting a check for one hundred twenty dollars to replace all her textbooks. Her father locked her in her bedroom for two days and forbade Bluey from bringing her food or water. He stayed home from work to make sure the terms of the punishment were upheld. Annie chewed gum to wet her mouth and refused to give him the satisfaction of saying a single word.

Through her locked door he told her he wasn't paying for her "fucking doodling" and she'd better find a job. Annie drew up flyers advertising her services as a dog walker. She took the train a few stops north, to the ritzy neighborhood. The houses were big there. They stood apart, not touching one another. She stuck flyers through the letter boxes and waited. A few days later a rich bloke who worked in advertising hired her to walk his dogs after school. Every day she clicked the three powerful, sleek Rhodesian ridgebacks onto their leashes. Their auburn brindle gleamed as they muscled the sidewalk. People turned to watch them as they rippled past. Annie liked walking them, liked the feeling of power it gave her. She went to the park near the man's house, because it was nicer than the one near hers and because she liked watching the rich boys from the private school cluster by the trees near the football field, smoking and laughing, flashing their straight teeth. Their backpacks lay scattered on the damp grass. Annie's father exploded whenever she left her bag on the floor.

"Pick that up, you fucking brat."

One day a boy looked back at her. She stood at a little distance, holding the dogs on leashes, watching the boys, unafraid.

"They yours?"

He gestured to the dogs.

"Not really."

"What's that supposed to mean?"

"Give us a ciggie."

He laughed and the other boys turned to take in the girl with the huge dogs tugging at her slender arms, hair bundled in a topknot.

His name was Ian. He lived with his mother and younger sister in the rich area a few streets down from the dog owner. His parents were divorced; his father had moved to Sydney and he spent the summers with him at the beach. Annie did not know anyone with divorced parents. It sounded luxurious. Everyone she knew was unhappily married. Except for Sam's mum, Bente, who lived alone, but she was "a big fucking hippie," as her father said, and for once, she could not argue. Ian's house was soft and quiet. The carpet in his bedroom was as thick as the quilt on her bed. He had his own TV and they would turn it on full volume and then lie on his bed and kiss until their tongues ached and their faces grew raw. Downstairs in his garage, the beautiful dogs lay panting in the darkness, drool spooling on the concrete, chins resting patiently on their paws.

One Friday after school she brought the dogs to the playground. Ian and the boys were there, jingling with loose change. Javo, a kid with white-blond hair and eyes so dark they looked black, pulled a bottle of schnapps from his backpack. It glinted like a knife in the evening sun. Two fat peaches glowed on the label.

"Where d'ya get that, mate?"

"My brother."

Javo swigged, grimaced, proffered. Annie reached for it before anyone else could. She was the only girl, protected, not just as Ian's girlfriend but because she carried herself like one of the boys. The dogs lent her an authority the other girls lacked.

She swigged hard, felt the alcoholic singe her cheeks, fought the urge to spit the medicinal peach taste across the playground. The boys laughed, jeered, drank. The roundabout, buckled and bleached, spun, or was spun. Bodies lurched, hot and yielding. Laughter spilled from mouths, belched from bellies.

Ian dragged her behind the rec center and they staggered, laughing, spinning. He pressed her up against the bins, kissed her with messy intensity. Pressed together, they slid down the rough shingle of the building. With the sun in her eyes, she felt rather than saw him tugging at his pants, then at hers. She felt too dizzy to resist.

He unzipped his pants, spat on his palm, and jabbed her till it hurt. She dug her short nails into his bumpy back to stop from crying out. So this is it, she thought. It was over before she had time to wonder how long it would take. He sat up.

"Alright?"

Annie's head spun. She rolled on her side and vomited.

"Fucking hell."

Javo appeared, his head wavering like a flag. The empty bottle glittered in his hand. He gestured with it.

"Annie spewed?"

Ian nodded, tugging at his pants, and clambered to his feet. Javo laughed. Annie sat up.

"Where are the dogs?"

She got up, adjusting her skirt, calling their names, jangling their leashes. The boys on the roundabout looked over, glazed.

"Fuck. Fuck. Fuck. Fuck."

She yelled their names. She'd left them roaming the undergrowth beneath the bottlebrush tree. She hadn't tied them up; she'd left them to find shade, knowing they were close enough for her to see. But now there was nothing but lightly flattened grass. She began calling, clapping, pleading through the scrubby corner of the park, knowing it was neither bosky nor rugged enough to conceal them. She turned back to the boys.

"You didn't see them? See anyone take them?"

They shrugged, hapless, embarrassed, drunk.

She felt panic rise like the tide. Her mouth was a beach, her stomach the ocean.

They never found the dogs. The owner stood speechless, ashen on his doorstep, one hand on his heart as though he could catch it. Annie told him his dogs must have been taken while she refilled her water bottle in the park toilets. A policeman came, took notes, asked Annie questions she struggled to answer. Suddenly her father was there. He put a hand on his daughter's shoulder, told the cop she'd told him all she could and reminded the owner that he should "take care of his own fucking pets if they mattered so much to him." He drove Annie home in silence.

The front door slammed behind them. She turned to thank him for rescuing her and took the full force of his clenched fist on her right cheek. She fell on the floor, knocking into the hallway table. Her skull felt split in two. The china shepherdess lay on the floor beside her, a chip on her flounced skirt. She could see her mother's upside-down feet motionless in the kitchen. Her father's face bent down into hers, screaming. His yellow teeth, the fillings at the back, his thick tongue moving like a flattened slug. She summoned the taste of vomitous peach from the back of her throat and spat with all her strength. The globule landed on his upper lip, flecked, foamy, a pearl. He stopped, stunned. She dragged herself upright and pulled herself up to her bedroom, hauled a sports bag from under her bed, and threw in some clothes and her sketchbooks. Grabbing her wash bag from the bathroom, Annie glimpsed herself in the mirror, her cheek blooming blue, threaded already with purple. She wiped a flannel between her legs, still sticky with Ian and blood. No one stopped her from leaving. She ran all the way to Sam's house.

CHAPTER 12

ANNIE STANDS IN THE HALLWAY OF HER PARENTS' HOME, DAMP, tired. The house is silent, waiting for her. It smells faintly of bleach overlaid with something unidentifiably sweet. She drops her keys in the dish on the hall table where the china shepherdess still cups her dimpled chin. A dead moth lies crumbled in the folds of her chipped skirt. A thin stack of mail sits propped against the mirror. Bills and circulars mostly. Annie wonders who else has a key. She wonders what she is supposed to do about that, about the bills, the house itself. There is so much to manage now. She is utterly unequipped for this moment, she realizes. Her mother dealt with everything after her father's death. It never occurred to Annie to help. She glances around at the living room where her father's armchair sits empty, hulking in the corner. Plastic crinkles dully on the chintz sofa no one ever sat on.

Her father died thirteen years ago, finally succumbing to the emphysema that had been drowning his lungs for years. He kept a sleeve of red plastic cups by that chair and slid one up to spit in, dredging phlegm like a rattling chain from his chest and gobbing it into the cup. He took the cups everywhere, because hawking into a receptacle was more dignified than flobbing in the street. He left them by the TV, the bed, the sink, once in the fridge. They were hideous, spattered with what looked like sucked-on satsuma segments. Her mother stacked them without a word and tossed them in the trash. Mother and daughter flinched but knew better than to comment. When her father grew too ill to leave the house, he sat in his brocade armchair, reading thrillers and sucking on hard candies. They were his last indulgence after the doctors told him that another cigarette would kill him. Purple-tongued, orange-lipped, he coughed up his rage and waited to die. He died at home, as he wanted, his wife in attendance, as he wanted. She had not left his side for weeks, had held his bone fingers, listening to the dredging shingle of his inhale, the shattering wash of his exhale. When finally he shuddered his final gasp, Bluey went outside for the first time in a month and looked up at the huge cloudless sky. A while later she went back in and called the doctor. Then she called Annie. Annie did not go home for his funeral. Bluey did not insist. She buried her husband with a tin of car sweets in one pocket and one of Annie's sketches folded in the other.

Annie slips off her shoes and pads into the kitchen. Her mouth is furry. She takes a glass from the drying rack, fills it at the sink. The water tastes metallic, warm, familiar. A ripe smell hovers over the compost bucket. She glances in it. Tea bags and eggshells, the remnants of an overripe banana. Her mother's last breakfast. Sam said she thought she must have died in the morning, that Helen, her mother's friend, had found her in the afternoon. For hours her mother had lain in the backyard, the chickens climbing over her body, plucking at her velveteen tracksuit, shitting on her thighs.

Annie opens the fridge. Milk, the cheap stuff. Some mushrooms, loose, trembling on the wire shelf. A six-pack of peach melba yogurts, one missing. She feels sixteen again, apprehensive, unsure. Everything is holding its breath. It has been many years since Annie was alone in this house. It feels as though her mother has nipped out to the shops, as though she might walk in with a plastic bag and a sigh at any moment. Annie stands at the window, looking out at the quiet street.

This was her mother's horizon. Bluey knew only the curve of this cul de sac, the price of butter, the weight of her keys in her pocket. There was nothing else. She never asked for more. Annie had never thought to ask her if it was enough.

She leaves her bag in the hallway. She walks slowly up the stairs. Her parents' bedroom door is closed. She feels suddenly, irrationally, afraid. She stands still as a rabbit. The sweet smell is stronger up here. A narrow table stands outside her mother's bedroom. The last time Annie was here it was lined up with orange tubes of medication, neatly labeled, serried rows of all her father's drugs. But now a white ceramic atomizer stands there, recently unwrapped, the cellophane seal curled beside it. Annie picks it up, sniffs. It is a room spray she remembers giving her mother a few years ago. She sent it hurriedly, sourced it online from a local shop, having only remembered her birthday at the last minute. It is cloyingly sweet, the clinging odor of Parma violets. Someone has sprayed the whole house with it. It is nauseating.

Annie stands before the closed bedroom door. It feels invasive, disrespectful to go in there without her. She pushes the door open. It makes a soft shushing as it grazes the nylon carpet. The air is still in here, hushed as the carpet, absorbing sound itself. For a moment, standing on the threshold, she feels entirely vacant, atmospheric, as though she were the one who had ceased to exist. The dust motes float above the perfectly made bed. The rain has stopped now and the light streaming through the lace curtain is dove gray. Annie is pure absence, obliterated, empty. There is only the room, the silent house. Her phone rings. She startles, fumbles herself into existence, finds the phone is already in her hand, by her ear.

"Hello?"

"Hi. It's Thierry. I'm outside."

"Outside where?"

"Your house."

"Oh, shit."

"You forgot. Don't worry. It happens."

"I'm in Melbourne. My mother died."

"Oh God. I'm so sorry. That's awful."

"I meant to text you, I forgot we had... it was all such a rush."

"Of course. I'm so sorry. It sounds like it was unexpected."

"It... was."

She had not ever expected her mother to die, she realizes. She had not thought her mother could be any more of an absence than she already was.

"Are you okay? Let me know if I can be of any help."

"That's kind. I'll be back next week."

"No rush, don't worry about that."

"No, I have to be back. I left the kids with Candace, there'll be a riot if I'm gone any longer."

"Then I'll see you in a week. I'm so sorry for your loss. Take care, Annie."

She hangs up, oddly touched by his formality, by his use of her name.

She sits on the bed. The faded sprigged sheets are pulled taut and smooth, folded over a mustard candlewick bedspread. A single thin pillow sits in the exact center. She reaches for it, inhales. Her mother's scent lies locked in the old cotton. Faint hairspray and the must of her scalp. A pale blue dress hangs on the door of the wardrobe. Annie does not recognize it. It is silky, with watery flowers printed all over it. Her mother has not worn dresses for years. She wonders why it is hanging there. It occurs to her, suddenly, that someone has chosen it for her mother to be buried in. She moves it aside, unhooks the bungee cord that holds the wardrobe door closed (the key was lost years ago, it has been held shut like this for as long as Annie can remember), and replaces the dress.

For all of Annie's childhood Bluey had dressed like a fifties' housewife. She wore pleated skirts and narrow blouses, did not own a pair of jeans. She liked a silky scarf tucked at her neck and was never without a white pressed handkerchief in a faux leather bag that clasped with a click. But four years after her husband's death, Bluey had met Annie at Melbourne airport wearing a bright pink tracksuit. It was lightly furred, soft to the touch as a mouse.

"Look at you, Mum."

Her mother preened.

"Helen gave it to me. Nice, isn't it? Azalea, they call it. I bought one in every color. So comfy."

They were all she wore.

Annie studies the bright stack of tracksuits folded in the wardrobe. She chooses the one that looks the newest, a daffodil yellow, and lays it on the bed. Bluey waited sixty-five years to allow herself such softness. A lifetime of clasps, buttons, fasteners, hooks and eyes, waistbands, and pin tucks in the end finally exchanged for ease, for permission. Annie will not bury her in a dress now.

She turns to her mother's dressing table. It is both ancient and girlish, with its faded frilled skirt and matching upholstered stool. She sits at it, touches the old wood, a dish with small gold earrings, an amethyst on a slender chain that Annie sent her years ago, an ugly digital watch. Faded photographs of her children are tucked in the mirror: a photo of Jackson, gap-toothed, sweaty, triumphant in a field; Vita, laughing, her head thrown back, in a gesture Annie has not seen for years.

Everything is in its place. A little jar of cold cream, a small bottle of talcum powder, a rubbery nail file, a rinsed jam jar full of rubber bands, and an old margarine tub containing three smeared lipsticks. No other makeup here, no pots of concealer or powder puffs. Annie looks at herself in the mirror, at her mother's blue eyes set in her own tired face, at her father's cheekbones high beneath her pale skin, at her dark hair beginning to thread with whispers of silver. She closes her eyes and tries to imagine her mother's face. Already it is indistinct, as though trapped behind old glass. Already her mother is static, held in place, a photograph.

CHAPTER 13

THIERRY SHOULDERS HIS BACKPACK, GETS BACK IN HIS CAR. HE IS sorry not to see Annie. She is alert, funny, down-to-earth. She makes a pleasant change from slumped adolescents. He wonders whether he can still bill her for the lesson.

She had sounded dazed on the phone. Poor woman. Talking to her from her own doorstep while she went through something enormous on the other side of the world, he had felt the strangeness of their situation. It was an unusually intimate moment to be privy to. He feels the stirrings of a short story. He jots down a few notes. He likes the setup. He drives home in a state of mild excitement. He writes until late.

Thierry doesn't mind teaching. It is steady money and leaves his mornings free to write. In the evenings he has his shifts at the bar. He is disciplined, writes every day. He toys with doing an MFA but it seems expensive, and probably unnecessary. He knows he has talent. He had a particularly encouraging refusal from a literary journal only this morning. The important thing is to keep writing.

A few days later Thierry is back at Annie's house to teach Remy, whose parents have moved in to take care of Vita and Jackson. He finds himself seated at Annie's table, while Candace makes him tea and Vita, who could be Annie's twin, prowls the kitchen, skittish and evasive. He asks Candace how Annie is doing, and from across the room the daughter shoots him a look of piercing blue, but no one seems to know how to answer his question because no one has spoken to Annie. As he climbs back into his car he snaps a photo of a little fruit tree laced in white blossoms beside the driveway and sends it to her. Because he has been in the warmth of her home and it was strange that she was not. Because he has written a story that she partly inspired. And because it seems like a nice thing to do.

Thierry is good at taking care of people. When he was eleven, he came home from school and found his father wearing a skirt. His father, an immensely tall man, was standing in front of the long mirror in the bathroom, admiring himself, smoothing his hand over his hips. It was a long gray pencil skirt, tight with a slice at the back. He could see his father's long hairless calves protruding from the slit as his hands sleeked himself in front of the mirror. He glanced sideways at his son and swiftly kicked the door closed with a click. They never spoke of it. Five years later his father left in the night with a leather suitcase, the contents of the cash register in the family-owned bistro, and all his mother's eye shadows. They had no idea where he had gone. When after two years his father wrote to him with a heartfelt apology and a phone number where he could be reached, Thierry waited for his mother to leave for work before calling. His father was tearful, abject. He asked after his wife. Thierry didn't know what to say about how his mother was, how she washed the dishes in silence, watched pirated videos of French soap operas till she fell asleep, spoke to no one other than Thierry. He did not know how to tell him that his mother was like an abandoned bird's nest, shriveled, brittle, redundant.

 He told his mother he was going on a school trip and took multiple buses up to a small town in northern Vermont. It took almost eight hours. He slept the entire way. He found the address, a narrow storefront hung with button boots and boas, old leather bags, and dusty high-necked lace blouses. His father leaned on the counter, reading a book. He wore a navy silk slip dress edged with lace. His eyes were darkened with kohl. His hair was longer, darker, a shoe-shine black, but beneath the taut sheen of the dress his chest hair was gray. He looked up at his son and spread his arms wide. Thierry wanted to turn around and leave, to get back on the bus and run to find his mother in her bistro-to-go where she slopped her vats of coq au vin into small foil containers, sealing the frilled lids with exhausted thumbs. But he let himself be drawn to his father's silken chest. He was as tall as him now.

Thierry's father invited him upstairs for dinner. He lived in a room over the store that consisted of a pullout couch, a table with two chairs, a sink, and a hot plate. He offered his son a beer, which Thierry refused. He drained pasta, grated cheese, and asked his son about school. A man with pale red hair let himself in. He wore a sweater vest and knitted tie, set down a battered attaché case, kissed Thierry's father on the lips, and reached a listless hand out to Thierry.

"I'm Rich," he said.

He did not look rich. He sat heavily on the couch and Thierry watched as his father waited on this man, handing him spaghetti, cheese, beer, just as he had watched his own mother serve his father for years. Rich told Thierry he was an accountant, that he was allergic to cats, and that he had twin daughters whom he saw every other Christmas.

Later, Thierry's father walked him back to the bus station and told his son he was sorry for the pain he'd caused, but that he was much happier now. Thierry said nothing but buried his chin in his coat. He never told his mother, or anyone, about his visit. He visited his father again a year later. His father looked unkempt this time, the apartment dustier; they ate soup from a can. Of Rich there was neither sign nor mention. As his father walked him back to the bus station, he asked Thierry in a rush if he had any money. He flushed when Thierry opened his thin wallet and pulled out a twenty. He stuffed it in his pocket without meeting his son's eye.

On the morning of his eighteenth birthday, Thierry woke to the smell of fresh croissants. His mother clattered in the kitchen. A bulky card with his name on it stood propped on the table. A bunch of newly cut keys on a red lanyard slid out of the envelope. His mother handed him a warm pastry and told him she was moving back to Paris. The car, the bistro-to-go, and the apartment were all his. Now that he was of age, she had put everything in his name. He could sell it all, pay back the loans, and have enough to live on for a few months. Her work here was done, and she wanted to live out her final years in France. She kissed him and left for work.

Three months later she was gone. Thierry put the apartment on the market, sold the bistro to a local customer, who turned it into an organic wine bar, and kept the car. After repaying the bank, he had enough for first and last months' rent on a studio at the edge of town. He never told his father that his mother had left, preferring to protect everyone's privacy. He was, essentially, alone.

He was older than his years, a good listener. This, and the odd gentleness of his height, made him popular with the girls. He was neither predatory nor effeminate. He understood the power of paying attention. He was confident without being assertive, charming without appearing to seduce. He soon realized that living alone, he could bring anyone home, at any time. He was not, to his mind, promiscuous, merely hungry for experiences. He was careful with his feelings and those of others, solicitous of all, while loving none. Girls were picked up and gently set down, quietly phased out. He preferred the company of women; they shared themselves so freely, shedding stories like outfits. Men he found illegible. Women inspired him.

Thierry's father gave him his first journal when he was nine. To begin with he wrote lists of boys he disliked and, later, his fantasy soccer teams. At thirteen he began writing short stories. He showed one he was particularly proud of to his English teacher, who told him it was "promising" but "lacked tension." Thierry was initially despondent but was too diligent a student to stay depressed for long. He reread his work and found he agreed with the assessment. He had a good ear for language, but no sense of structure. His stories were bloated with descriptive passages that led nowhere. He worked and reworked them. He won second place in a school fiction contest, had a poem published in the local paper. His mother cut it out, pinned the clipping on the café noticeboard, where over the years it grayed and curled. He kept writing, sending his stories in regularly to all the literary magazines he could find. He kept a list of his submissions and a folder of the nicest rejection letters. He wrote all day, worked nights at the local hotel bar.

Once a year his mother sent him a return ticket to Paris. He spent two weeks in her tiny high-rise in the foggy banlieues, nodding at the sulky Algerians in the elevator and occasionally sleeping with the daughter of the Senegalese family downstairs. Every year he planned to extend his trip, to take a train to Istanbul, to backpack through the Peloponnese, to hitchhike to Madrid, but every year he found himself boarding his scheduled return flight from Charles de Gaulle with relief. He liked his routines, his predictable world. He was not quite ready for adventure.

The two-bedroom above him became available. He carted his stuff up the stairwell, invited an old schoolfriend, Maya, to room with him, and started French tutoring. Maya was training to be a counselor by day, working nights in a local retirement home. They had slept together a handful of times over the years, but not so many as to be a problem. She told him when she came to look around that this would only work if they were just friends. He'd agreed with relief and shown her the apartment. They ended up having sex in his room because it seemed a waste not to and she left for her shift with a shake of her head, laughing. They understood each other, he and Maya. (Thierry was still recovering from a run-in with an attractive divorcée he'd served at the bar who had escaped from a silent meditation weekend at a nearby Buddhist retreat and had come in thirsty for tequila and conversation. They had ended up at his place and he'd assumed they'd both understood the terms, but now he found himself avoiding any calls from a number with a White Plains area code.)

Thierry listens to his pupil stumble through a French newspaper article and thinks about his new story. It still needs a twist but he doesn't know what it is yet.

CHAPTER 14

ANNIE SEARCHES HER MOTHER'S DRAWERS. SHE IS LOOKING FOR A pair of underpants, having failed to pack any. She finds rows of them, clean, tightly rolled, gray as rain. They are long, the elastic exhausted with years of washing. She wedges the phone under her chin, skims her messages as she pulls on a pair of her mother's knickers.

"Hi darling, thinking of you. Kids are missing you, but everyone's fine. Remy! Leave the damn dog alone. Sorry. Hope you're okay. We think the funeral's today? Or was it yesterday? I lose track over there. Call us soon."

"Mom! Brian broke his leg! He was taking down the string lights and the ladder slipped and he fell and his leg totally broke and he fainted. I didn't see it, but Remy told me. Edouard took him to the hospital. Vita said not to tell you while you're away, but I knew you'd want to know. Okay, love you. I miss you, bye."

"Hey, it's me. Fucking nightmare about Brian. I told you those damn lights were a liability. Can you call and see if we are covered for this? That's all we need, Brian suing us. Call me later. I know today's the day. Love you. Do you need me?"

The last sentence was addressed not to her, but to someone who had approached Hector on set. She can hear the murmur of soft voices behind him.

She skims her unread emails. Messages from online auction sites, the school, the PTA, the dance academy, the soccer coach, the airline, a hotel she and Hector once stayed in. Texts from Patti, her children, RSVP reminders, requests for a proposal, a donation, a pledge. One message catches her eye. It is a photograph of the white plum tree in their driveway in bloom, lifting its laden arms up to the sky. It is from Thierry. There is no message, just the image. She smiles, surprised.

CHAPTER 15

THE FUNERAL IS JUBILANT, LOUD, AND OPPRESSIVE. ANNIE IS SURprised at how full the church is. There must be forty people in the straight white pews. Earnest women press her hands, squeeze her arms, clasp her shoulders to communicate the depth of their loss and, presumably, hers. A few burly men give encouraging nods, elbow grasps. She does not know the last time she was touched so often. She does not know who any of them are. She notices how they reverence Helen, the only friend of her mother's she recognizes, who stands a little apart, head bowed, tears coursing unchecked. Annie greets her nervously, unsure of how to participate in this woman's grief. She feels confused by all she does not know. She had assumed her mother's churchgoing was like her mother's housekeeping, something dutiful and reflexive. She had not understood that her mother loved these people and was in turn beloved by them.

Sam blows her nose, offers Annie a tissue. Annie is dry-eyed. She is ashamed of her desiccation. A woman with gray hair and a white collar leads the service. She speaks of Bluey's warmth, her homemade cakes, her welcome of newcomers. Annie tries to imagine her mother baking for new friends but fails. The congregation rises, sings, sits. She lets Sam's motions guide her. The service ends. A murmuring and slow dispersal. Annie goes to thank the female vicar, who has kind dry hands and, surprised that Annie is not hosting a wake, offers to hook up the coffee machine, put out some biscuits, and host everyone in the hall. But Annie feels panicked at the prospect of talking to all these people. She cannot bear the responsibility of so much solicitude. Sam, at Annie's elbow, thanks the vicar, then guides her friend through the crowd, into her car, back to the house.

They sit at the kitchen table, the air-conditioning roaring, an empty bottle of wine in the trash and another one, almost empty, before them. A bag of cashews lies spilled open, scattered on the Formica tabletop. It is cold in the house but neither one adjusts the thermostat. Annie wears the mustard bedspread from her mother's bed draped across her shoulders. She drinks, licks her salty fingers. Sam nods at the kitchen.

"What will you do with it?"

"This place? Put it on the market."

"Can Helen have the chooks? She asked me to ask you."

"God yes. She okay? She seemed a mess."

"Well, she loved her."

"I know that."

Sam pops a cashew.

"Do you? I mean they really loved each other. You know they were together, right? Ever since your dad died."

"I know they were close."

"They were lovers, babe."

Annie snorts.

"Too gay for you?"

"No. Not too gay. Jesus. Too old, maybe, but not too gay. It's just Mum never... why didn't she tell me?"

"She did tell you."

"She didn't. She told me they were friends. Or she let me think they were friends. Did they... did Helen live here too?"

"Helen has her own key, if that's what you're asking. But no, she kept her own place."

Annie shakes her head.

"Maybe I just didn't want to know. Poor Mum."

"Poor Bluey. She was alright. In the end."

Annie feels irritated. Her phone buzzes and she silences it without checking. Sam nods at it.

"It hasn't stopped."

"Never does."

"How are you so busy?"

"I run a business now."

"You've always got a project."

"It's a job, not a project."

"I'm know, I'm kidding, babes."

Annie tugs the counterpane across her shoulders.

"No one teases anyone in America. It's weird."

"It's a serious business, being a Yank. I dunno how you live there."

"You can get used to anything."

"Lovey, why isn't Hector here?"

"I told you. He's on a movie, he can't just leave. He's not famous enough to just take off. I mean, maybe if his mother had died, but not mine."

"That's shite."

"It's easier without him. I can deal with everything without managing him as well. Sort out what to do with the house, wrap everything up, hang out with you."

"He wouldn't let you do that if he were here?"

"He would. Of course he would. It would just be harder."

Sam nods, drinks.

"Do you like him?"

"Do I like my husband? Ha. I hadn't thought to ask. I suppose so. Why? Do you?"

"I only met him that once. He told a lot of stories."

"That's Hector."

"I just remember thinking, 'When is she going to talk?' You were dead silent, the whole way through dinner. I couldn't believe it. I thought, 'Where the fuck has she gone?'"

Annie feels hot. She shrugs.

"He's better at telling them."

"He talks over you."

"What do you mean?"

"I asked you something about Vita, and you started talking, and then he just took over. And you let him. I kept waiting for you to tell him to fuck off."

Annie frowns, drains her wine.

"Sorry, pet. Didn't mean to hurt your feelings."

"Anything else you want to clear up for me? Mum was gay, and I married an asshole. Did I miss anything?"

Sam leans forward, her nose ring glinting under the strip light. She is glassy but loving.

"You seem miserable, babes."

"My mother just died."

"You're a fraction of yourself. You're so skinny, I can see through you. She was worried about you, too, it kept her up at night."

Annie looks at her, unsteady, through wide eyes.

"How do you know what Mum thought?"

"Because I saw her, Annie! Regularly. Nazzy and I would have her over for dinner, or I'd pop by after work and have a drink with her and Helen. She missed you. You came for the bare minimum when you visited, and you brought the bare minimum of yourself with you. I know it was rough growing up, but did you have to keep so distant?"

"Are you cross-examining me, Sam? I am not one of your witnesses."

Annie stands up, tired, unsteady. The chair screeches on the linoleum.

"Congrats on making all the right choices. Good job being the daughter I never was."

"Come on, lovey, don't get pissy, I'm telling you she cared about you, we all care . . ."

"I know. I get it. It's fine. You love me. I love you. You loved Mum. I guess I loved Mum. I'm really fucking tired. It's been a long day."

"Annie, love . . ."

"I'm passing out. I love you. Thanks for taking care of me. Of everyone. I mean it."

Annie kisses the top of Sam's head and leaves the kitchen. She trudges up the narrow staircase, the bedspread dragging behind her like a child's cape, and falls on her mother's bed, fully dressed. She hears the sound of the front door closing, and nothing else.

CHAPTER 16

ANNIE WAKES TO FIND HERSELF NAKED IN HER OLD BED. SHE HAS NO memory of coming in here or undressing. It is dark outside, the street quiet. The bed is low to the floor; she can see the faded scorch mark of a curling iron she left on the carpet when she was fourteen. Her black clothes lie in a heap by the door. Otherwise, the room is as she left it thirty-five years ago: a stack of faded teen magazines on the shelf and below it, a charcoal sketch of her mother's hands taped to the wall. On the desk, a jam jar of stubby pencils, a stack of dusty CDs, a cracked eye shadow palette of chalky pastels, a broken Rubik's cube. A faded poster of a pop star in a corset, a gift from Sam, curls on the door of the cheap pine wardrobe.

Sam showed up at school at age thirteen with a line of silver hoops along one ear lobe and a digital watch she'd pinched from one of her mum's boyfriends. She didn't have a dad and made no apology for herself or her mother, who had three kids by three different men. She did not care about fitting in. She worshipped Madonna, understood algebra, read three grades above hers, and challenged all authority without ever seeming to undermine it. Her intelligence was effortless, her integrity mesmerizing. Annie thought she was the coolest person she'd ever laid eyes on. When Sam offered Annie a ciggie at the bus stop, Annie didn't hesitate. They have been best friends ever since.

Annie stares at the ceiling, replaying her conversation with Sam. Her friend is not wrong. She does withdraw when Hector is around.

He has fallen in the habit of speaking for them both. And she has allowed it. He has mistaken her reticence for her preference for hearing him talk. He has made the mistake of taking her at face value. They both have. She had assumed she was happy with the arrangement, with all their arrangements. But now, lying in her old bed, she feels angry. She flashes on the parties she used to go to for Hector's work, the dinners and premieres where she was often the only attendee not in the film industry. In the early days she reveled in her outsider status, played up her innocence, raised eyebrows with her irreverent naivete. Hector did not mind, he liked his wife to be exotic; it demonstrated his own nonchalance, his refusal to play by Hollywood's rules. By marrying an artist, not an actress, he had set himself apart. But the performance had not aged well. She grew tired of pretending not to care or understand how movies were made. She grew passive, and then cold. What began as a refusal to be impressed by fame or talent had become a refusal to be touched by anyone or anything at all. What others took as her composure was really her refusal to participate. What was her coolness had become coldness.

She closes her eyes. Her head throbs. She stumbles to the bathroom, drinks straight from the tap. A single toothbrush rests on the basin. She wonders if it belongs to Helen. She is glad for what little pleasure her mother might, after all, have known in her life. She tries to recall when Helen first appeared in her mother's life. Annie had already left, was living in New York. They met through the church, while her father was still alive, she remembered that much. Her father had been predictably, deeply threatened by his wife's friend. But Bluey had refused to give her up.

Annie's father was seventeen when he pocketed the rent money from the brown teapot on the dresser and shuffled out into the brumal

Newcastle dawn, nursing two cracked ribs and a fractured wrist. Upstairs his father moaned in his sleep, too drunk to remember the violence he had done. Arthur Weymouth limped down to the docks, slipped onto a cargo ship to Suez, and from there onto a boat bound for Melbourne. He shared his cabin with an electrician from Bermondsey who promised him they were handing out jobs and houses to any Brit who showed up and asked for one. The reality was a little different. Arthur landed in a resettlement camp, slept in a Nissan hut with twenty other men, and spent his days digging ditches for the newly expanding sewage system. But, as he later never tired of telling his family, he had not come all that way to shovel shit. He tracked down his electrician friend, who had got a job installing neon streetlights around the compound, and offered to become his assistant, apprentice, whatever the fuck he liked, as long as he taught him the trade. Arthur applied himself, watched and learned and saved and lived on coffee and loose change, carefully wadding every note that came his way in the socks his older sister knitted and mailed him. Eventually he scrimped enough to buy a thirdhand van and stencil his own name on the side. His only extravagance was cigarettes, and he smoked each one down to the filter. He nursed his love of the queen alongside his deep conviction that England had gone to the dogs.

    He was twenty-eight when he met Bluey. He'd been called in to replace a fuse box at the local elementary school, and she was the first-grade teacher who walked him to the junction box and shyly offered him a refreshment when it was done. She blushed when he told her it was the best cup of tea he'd had since leaving England. They were married a year later, at city hall, the electrician from Bermondsey and a clerk who was on lunch break as their witnesses.

    Bluey's parents died a few months apart when she was twenty-one. She had no siblings and few friends. Whole weeks went by when the only people she talked to were the children in her classroom. She was delighted to belong to someone again. And Arthur grew despotic with her love. He made his new home a little fiefdom. No one contradicted him here. No one cuffed him about the face and told him he was a disgrace. He had no employees and no boss. He grew fat, engorged by his own opinions and Bluey's starchy puddings. He was proud of his work ethic and his immaculate van. And Bluey was grateful to find a harbor she could shelter in. Arthur loved his wife immoderately. He was a jealous man, undone if her attention faltered. He ate while keeping one hand over his wife's, removing it only to cut his food, then returning to enclose hers. Her hand lay, submissive, occasionally twitching, a pet mouse. As a child Annie would watch with fascination, later with disgust, as her mother timed her moments of liberation to cut her own steak or run to the kitchen for brown sauce.

He hit her mother often. The house thrummed with the electric imminence of violence. Arthur took effortless offense. If he came home late and Bluey wasn't there, she got hit. If he came home and she was on the phone with a friend (she knew better than to invite one over), she got hit. If she spent too long helping Annie with her homework, he backhanded her. Annie waited upstairs while it was happening because it went worse for her mother if she came down. She closed her bedroom door, turned on her Walkman, pulled out her sketchbooks, and drew her mother's hands, her mother's shoes, her mother's watery eyes. She drew over the sickening thuds. They were swift, almost silent, those beatings, only the muffled exhales, the goat bleats of her mother. Later her parents came to bed. She heard them, heavy-footed, the bedroom door clicking shut, sealing them in together.

One morning Annie woke early to find her mother in the bathroom, trying to cover her bruises. Annie watched her from the doorway. Bluey winced as she dabbed concealer on the livid blue marks along her jaw. Annie went back to her bedroom and found a paintbrush, a fine one, the one that came with her watercolor kit. She tipped her mother's face toward the window and dabbed the brush in the different little pots of peach and beige, blending and mixing until she had entirely disguised her father's marks. Bluey angled her face away from the mirror. No one spoke.

When it was done, Bluey cupped her daughter's face and looked intently in her eyes, as though she might say something. Annie waited. Bluey handed her a towel and told her to wipe down the sink.

Between rages, Arthur sulked. He refused eye contact, snarled if anything wasn't exactly where he needed it, watched the news at aggressive volumes. He liked throwing things—the newspapers, his keys, anything that came to hand. Once he hurled his dinner plate across the kitchen because Bluey glanced at the clock while he was talking. It sailed past Annie's face, exploding lasagna on the kitchen wall. He had laughed, then told Annie to clean it up. There was still the faintest orange smear above the sink, if you knew where to look, despite all Bluey's scrubbing. Like the stain, Bluey grew bleached and indistinct, fainter with each passing year, a watercolor of what was already a blurred landscape. They told no one about what happened in their house. No one ever came over.

Light begins to streak the sky. Annie gets dressed, makes the bed, then lies down on it again. She has to be at Sam's office in a few hours. She should call the children, her husband. She cannot bring herself to check her phone. She feels too tired to move. She feels trapped in the aspic of this room.

She slept on Sam's floor for three years, coming home only to pick up clothes or books when she knew her father was at work. She buried the violence inside her, dropped it like a stone in a well. Bluey left her money in an envelope tucked in her locker at school. Annie ignored her if they met in the playground. She answered to no one. She fucked the rich boy Ian, and then she fucked his friend Javo, and then she fucked Javo's brother. She slid into cars and back seats and teetered along dark steps carved into the red cliffs down to crescent slivers of beach. She had sex pressed against coarse sand, sex leaning on trees that left her hair smelling of eucalyptus, sex with a gear stick wedged in the small of her back. She learned to crumble dark hash without burning her fingertips. She scorched weed in tiny crackling joints. She learned to tolerate the burn of vodka, the berry of gin. Then she lurched back to Sam's house to pass out. She cannot imagine how Sam's mother put up with her.

Bente had lived on five of the seven continents, earning her living as a waitress, an air hostess, a magician's assistant, a preschool teacher, and a cabaret dancer. She now worked as a night nurse. She wore her thick white gold hair in a braid like a pretzel crown and smoked her ciggies with a fork so her fingers wouldn't smell. She traversed the wealthy enclaves of the dark city, rocking newborns against her chest so that women she rarely glimpsed could sleep through the night. She came home in time to make everyone breakfast, then slept all day.

Sam took care of her younger brothers, walked them to school every morning, oversaw their homework, made their dinner. In the evenings, Sam stayed home while Annie roamed. Bente asked few questions and folded Annie into their life as one more baby in need of comfort. Annie loved living there, among the loving chaos of two little brown boys wrestling on the sofa, the floor tumbled with unsorted laundry, stacks of rippled books beside the toilet. She liked drawing the boys and stuck sketches under magnets to the fridge for Bente to find when she got home. Bente sang in the bath with the door open, left soggy joints by the sink, yelled at everyone when she couldn't find her keys, spent her days off with at least one of her children wrapped around her soft white body.

Graduation loomed. Sam studied hard, readied her applications for university into crisp piles, already certain that law and its clearcut edges were what awaited her. She let Annie in when she lost her keys, then fell back to sleep while her friend undressed clumsily in the dark. Bente made Annie breakfast.

"So, pet, what's your plan?"

Annie shrugged. Bente handed her a mug of tea and asked if she'd thought about art school. It was the first time Annie had heard of such a thing. She waited for Mrs. Riley after class, who gave her the names of a couple of art schools in Sydney, and one in New York.

It was a college she'd dimly heard of that was, if the prospectus was to be believed, free for foreign students. She gathered her best sketches (a pencil study of Bente's coiled hair, a charcoal of a slumped model asleep in a chair, and a sketch of crumpled cigarette butts in a plastic ashtray), borrowed Ian's camera to take careful photographs of each one, used her mother's money to process them as slides, and slid the precious celluloids into stiff envelopes. A few months later, her mother told her there was a letter for her at home. A single bulging envelope with a US postmark stood propped against the china shepherdess. She ran to Sam's and waved the acceptance letter in her face. They danced around the kitchen table, then biked down to the ocean, shrieking all the way. They sang at the top of their lungs. The world was theirs, everything awaited them. Annie stripped off all her clothes and bound naked into the water. People stared.

It comes to her even now, lying on her old bed, the purity of that moment, the clanging sun leaping off the sand, the lacy ocean at her feet, the feeling in her hair and her hands and her heart that she was finally free. She waded naked into that sun-lipped freezing ocean, the coldness rising from her feet, swathing her ankles, her thighs, her belly, caressing the soft underswell of her breasts. She lifted her arms and strode out deeper and deeper, imagining what the people on the beach saw, a young woman with her long dark hair walking straight out into the sunlight, into the water, into the world.

CHAPTER 17

"How are your brothers?"

Sam is seated at her desk, reviewing a document. Her office is surprisingly big. Two windows overlook the city. Far below, the city rumbles silently. She answers without looking up.

"Good. Both married. Si's a social worker with two kids. Xav's getting his doctorate in Adelaide. He moved up there after Mum died."

"Bente must have been dead proud of you all."

Sam points at the document.

"Sign here and here."

Annie signs. Sam nods, scans the page.

"She was. You know Bluey used to come over and visit Mum after you left? She was too proud to admit you hadn't written to her, so she'd come round to ours in case we'd had any news. She came right up until the end. Mum told me she used to slip her cash while you were living with us."

"She paid Bente to keep me?"

"She paid her to keep you safe, you daft cow. You missed one. Sign here."

Annie signs the documents that will empower Sam to handle the sale of her parents' house and dispose of its contents. She is grateful for the surrender. She is ready to go home. In her rollaway bag she has some trinkets for her children, and one pair of her mother's underwear.

CHAPTER 18

ANNIE LEANS HER HEAD ON THE TINY OVAL WINDOW AND STARES down at the jagged bite of the city skyline beneath her. They have been circling for a while, waiting to land. It occurs to her that she is an orphan now. The word sounds lonelier than she feels. What she feels is heavy, leaden. She remembers the first time she glimpsed America. She had been unable to sleep, face pressed against the window, waiting for a glimpse of her future, armed with a single address and five hundred dollars she'd saved up that summer.

Bente had a friend in New York. She had arranged for Annie to rent a room from him. "It's just a place to land. But Ney's fussy, babes. You can't lose his key. You can't stagger in at all hours like you do here."

Ney lived in a sliver of an apartment on the fourth floor of a narrow brick building in Chelsea. He wore stained silk shirts unbuttoned to his bony waist and trailed dirty palazzo pants that gathered cat hair as he glided barefoot, always barefoot, around the apartment. He kept his cat, Mendelssohn, an aloof Persian, sprawling under his left arm the way a debutante might carry an oversize clutch. Ney had dyed blond hair and a Brazilian accent with French pretensions. Annie never once saw him leave the building. A Haitian kid whose dad ran the bodega on the corner delivered groceries. The pet store delivered a brick of kibble once a month. The apartment smelled of cat piss and patchouli. Annie's room contained a bed, a raw light bulb, and a row of hooks. The door skimmed the mattress as it opened. A rectangle of glass above the door counted as the window. Ney tutted as he showed her in, reappeared carrying a dusty velvet lampshade that he affixed to the fizzing light bulb.

"Voilà, darling. *Ambiance.*"

She loved it.

Art school was a tidal wave. The vast white building loomed over half a city block. Goths, punks, skater kids, kids in earmuffs, girls in fishnets and cowboy boots, guys in pajamas and fur coats, teachers in ripped jeans thronged in the hallways. Shaved heads, pierced noses, armfuls of bangles, of tattoos, of scars. The smell of plaster, acrylic, solvent, and panic. Berets, baseball caps, beatniks. Annie had never seen anything like this. She felt instantly, irredeemably parochial. These kids knew artists, exhibitions, references she'd never heard of. They spoke in tongues. She felt like a garish onlooker, her accent as harsh and unforgiving as the Melbourne sun. She was both deeply insecure and immensely certain of the rightness of everything. She felt emptied by the endless oceanic motion of the city, ready to be subsumed by whichever swell rolled in. She kept her mouth shut and her eyes wide open.

Back home, Annie's look had been thrift-store chic, assembled from the secondhand bins of Melbourne. She, like all the girls back home, had favored tight, bright, and short. Now, she scoured the Lower East Side for anything black. Combat boots, inky kilts, a sweatshirt slashed at the neck, laddered tights, and ripped jeans. She took herself to every museum and gallery she could get in for free. She felt marooned by the majority of what she saw, confused by what she knew was expected of her. Her bewilderment made her lonely at first.

She was unmoved by abstract expressionism, irritated by pop art, confused by performance work. She kept her opinions to herself and sought out the women painters. Finally, an Alice Neel exhibition made her blood sing. Here were bodies she recognized as her own, faces she understood. She sat cross-legged before the paintings until closing, went back again for many days after. She felt she had finally landed.

Two months after Annie's arrival, she came home from class to find Ney seated at the stained green baize card table, eating a bowl of silky canned pears. The cat looped its tail across his lap. He gestured at the ceiling with his spoon.

"Party upstairs tonight. I thought we might stop by."

The guys upstairs were twins. At least, Annie had assumed they were. In the dim light of the staircase their biceps bulged identically and their flashed smiles were interchangeable. They stood side by side in the doorway, kissed Ney on the mouth, and pointed Annie toward a bathtub stacked with ice and wine. Ney dissolved into the crowded room, hot with laughing men with bare arms. Finding no glasses, she helped herself to an open wine bottle and edged around the throng. Annie knew no one to look for but saw plenty to look at. The men barely glanced at her, preferring to soak in each other's faces. Music skittered from invisible speakers, a wheel of Brie sweated untouched on the bookcase, the kitchen sink bloomed with battered bodega roses. A woman waved at her from across the room. Annie turned around, uncertain how to respond. The woman pushed her way through the unresisting men. Her hair was curvy, bleached a brittle white; a painted-on mole hovered above her top lip. She smiled at Annie.

"Thank God you showed up."

Her full breasts almost swung free of their tiny straps as she pointed to the fire escape.

"Shall we?"

Candace was a nineteen-year-old Jewish heiress from New Haven with a dead mother, a media tycoon father she rarely saw, and a fondness for hair dye and cocaine. She worked, when she did work, for her stepmother, Miriam, who had a Broadway production company. Candace's job apparently consisted of going to the theater and getting drunk afterward.

Annie asked her once, years later, what her friend had seen in her that night. Candace, a redhead at the time, had shrugged magnificently.

"You looked interesting. And lost."

They talked for hours on that fire escape, swigging wine, sharing cigarettes. Candace poured a bump of white powder from a tiny bottle onto the back of Annie's hand, showed her how to sniff it. Annie's skull tingled. She took Candace downstairs to show her where she lived. Candace wrinkled her nose in the doorway. She grew quiet, touched her new friend on the wrist.

"Why do you live here?"

"It's cheap."

"It's awful."

A week later she showed up with a roll of trash bags and an idling cab.

"I'm rescuing you."

Candace's apartment had been furnished by her stepmother. It bulged with cream sofas and hunting scenes, a mirrored bar cart, and shelves of untouched books. Candace, unquestioning of whatever her family gave her (wealth, large breasts, a short attention span) had not thought to change a thing. Her roommate had recently moved in with her financier boyfriend and so the second bedroom with its pressed-tin ceiling became Annie's. Annie paid her way in ramen and artwork.

Slowly she unpicked Miriam's good taste, stacked the hunting scenes in the hallway closet, hung a watercolor above the fireplace, propped some sketches on the bookcase, flung a secondhand kilim over the sofa. Candace didn't care. She loved her new friend, and the flicker of dark glamour it cast on her sunlit life, to be living with an impoverished art student.

Annie assumed the role of struggling artist with absurdly privileged friends. She lived in a jewelry box on the edge of penury. They were both nervous the first time Miriam came to dinner. Annie cooked the only recipe in her repertoire, a Dutch stew that Bente had taught her; Candace poured the wine her stepmother had brought while Miriam took in the changes, one hand on her slim trousered hips, the other fingering a vast pearl earring. Annie felt self-conscious—of her art, of her non-rent-paying status, of the faint scent of mothballs rising from her thrift-store cardigan. Miriam turned back to the table, saying nothing. They spoke at dinner of the new musical Miriam was producing, of the family's summer plans on the Vineyard, the Eisenhower biography Miriam had just read. She was highly literate, political, and astute. She rarely mentioned her husband, who kept a mistress in DC whom everyone knew about but no one discussed. She asked Annie questions with the suppleness of the practiced hostess and, as she eased into her soft coat in the hallway, invited her to join them that summer.

"Bring me a sketch. As a hostess gift."

Miriam became Annie's champion. She helped herself to Annie's work, and Annie had no way to demur. She felt indebted to this family and its careless wealth. She found herself more drawn to it than she cared to admit. She split herself in two: Days, she moved between lectures and the school studio; evenings, she spent in the dark bar wiping Formica tables while students bickered about Basquiat and the bill; weekends, she drew and hid herself in the cloistered wealth of Candace's world. Dinners with Candace's family were fascinating. Senators, philanthropists, directors all leaned across Miriam's candlelit tables. Annie listened, soaked in faces and stories, and made people laugh, emboldened by her status as the unvarnished Australian. She wore her smudged eyeliner with disheveled grace. Candace yawned and tried, unsuccessfully, to get her father's attention. During one Uptown soiree in Miriam's glimmering apartment, Annie went to the bathroom and was astonished to find one of her sketches framed over the sink. Candace raised an eyebrow in the cab home.

"Clever Miriam."

"Why clever?"

"Now she owns you."

"My work, you mean?"

"Nope."

Annie never brought anyone back to the apartment. She took a lover, but only because she loved his arms. He was a third-year sculptor from Eritrea, was five years her senior, and wore cut-off T-shirts even in the dead of winter. His back was beautiful, rippled ebony. He cared only for art. He never met Candace nor even asked Annie where she lived. She lay on a futon in his tiny Chinatown apartment and sketched his deltoids; he would rise and make them a bowl of steaming lentils, and they would eat, naked, on his bed, while the rain streamed outside and brown lentils scattered on his white sheets. He spoke passionately about male artists she had never heard of. She marveled at his conviction. He did not notice whether she listened or not.

She grew tired of her fellow students, the acidic competitiveness and thinly veiled contempt that passed as critique. She grew bored of naked Polaroid collages, of drip paintings made with breast milk. Annie had only ever been interested in bodies, in the fragility of flesh. She knew she was out of step with the times. It was not the fashion to draw napes, wrists, the backs of knees, but she refused to give up her love of the human figure. She grew obsessive, frustrated by her inability to lay the curve of a cheek on paper. She drew constantly in bed, on the subway, behind the bar. Whatever talent she may have thought she had was gone, or perhaps had never been there to begin with. In frustration, she tore her sketches to shreds. They floated like blossoms at her feet. She ripped pages from her sketchbook, shredded the pages with her hands, tearing them into soft curls, small as feathers, or strips like the peeling bark of the gum trees back home. A soft mound of torn paper drifted at her feet.

One day she stretched a large canvas, painted it pale pink, and then slashed it. She glued tiny paper fragments together, piece by piece, building a branch, a budding proliferation of tiny leaves, and pushed it through the gap. The leaves tumbled through, precarious and fragile. It looked enough like female genitalia to receive the nodding approval of her classmates and enough like cherry blossoms to get bought by one of Miriam's friends. Annie tore up all her sketches and reassembled them, some on canvas, some on wood, some suspended by invisible threads like birds in flight. This was not what she had been going after. It was not what she meant at all. It felt like salvage from the wreck of her efforts. But it captured something of the frailty she had been chasing, and people liked the pieces. She felt fraudulent and always on the verge of being found out. She supposed this meant she was an artist now.

The plane kisses the tarmac, bounces lightly, then comes to a slow halt. She is home.

CHAPTER 19

JACKSON BURIES HIMSELF UNDER THE COVERS. HIS MOTHER BLOWS him a last kiss and clicks his bedroom door closed behind her. He can hear her bumping her suitcase along the landing. He is glad she is home, even if she only brought him a dumb letter opener and not a real present. He is bummed his grandmother died because he never got to meet her and Vita did; plus, his grandmother sometimes sent him LEGO sets. He wonders if he'll get an extra present on his birthday from his parents to make it up. He might suggest it. His hermit crabs scuff the sand in their cage. He turns on his side so he can see them, bathed in their purplish night-light. His dad keeps reminding him to spray them with salt water. He hasn't done it once while his mother was gone but now that she is back, he thinks he'd better get back on it. He misses his dad. He wishes he were home. He likes Candace enough but it was weird having them sleep in his parents' bedroom. Like he'd been adopted in the night. At least Candace didn't care about screen time. But it is better having Mom home. He climbs back into bed, pulls the duvet over his head again. He loves being in the dark, likes making his bed a cave he can hide in. Vita says it's no wonder he likes hermit crabs.

Vita sticks her dirty laundry in the hamper, folds her jeans for the next day, and drapes them on the back of her chair. She has photography tomorrow, places the camera she got for Christmas on her desk so she won't forget to take it to class. She can hear her mother moving about in her bedroom. She is both glad she is home and already annoyed by her. Her mother seems out of it, spacey. She supposes it's grief, but her mother is pretty checked out at the best of times. And she's not convinced her mother even really liked her grandmother. Vita at least cried when she heard the news, because Vita, unlike her mother, actually likes her relatives. She's glad her mother brought her the amethyst necklace. She touches it around her neck. She can't wait to show Zoe in the morning. She checks her phone. Zoe still hasn't responded. Although, if Vita's being honest, she doesn't really remember her grandmother. She only met her once, when she was five. She remembers a woman with white hair and being made to eat an unreasonable number of eggs. She remembers going to church and singing loudly even though she didn't know the words. She remembers being on the beach and it being too cold for the beach but her mother shushing her and telling her not to mind.

Vita brushes her teeth. She's glad Candace has left. She doesn't trust her at all. When Vita was three or maybe four, Candace, who had no kids then, had come to visit them in Los Angeles. She had brought a doll with her as a gift, a large boy doll that could stand on its own feet. He was fully clothed and came with a small baby's bottle that you could fill with water. He was designed to be fed, and then you could flick a small notch on the back of his neck, pull down his pants, and watch him pee from his small hard plastic penis. Vita had loved it. Her mother had laughed, appalled, and Candace had clapped, delighted with herself. Vita remembers the women talking and laughing behind her while she sat feeding her doll and watching it pee on the floor. Her mother spread a cloth to mop up the water, but Vita wondered what it would feel like to catch it in her mouth. She put her mouth over the little rigid penis and tasted the plasticky water in her mouth. She sucked and swallowed and sucked. Candace hooted.

"Oh my God, look at Vita!"

Her mother turned around and laughed and pulled the doll away from her daughter's mouth before Vita knew what had happened. The women laughed so hard, their eyes were wet. Candace could not stop. Her shoulders rocked and she could not speak. Vita did not like being laughed at. She felt angry. She wanted Candace to stop. She wanted her mother to make her stop. But her mother was laughing too. Vita's cheeks burned. She hated them both. She cried and so her mother gave her some sliced banana and turned on cartoons. For days afterward, Vita searched for the doll. She wanted to take it to school to show the teachers but it had vanished. Her mother said it would turn up but it never did. Her mother was good at hiding things. The sound of Candace's laughter still makes Vita flinch.

This week had been weird. It has been almost her normal life, but not really. Like being trapped in a play with all new actors, with only her and Jackson left over from the original cast. Vita dislikes theatrics. Living with her father has made her suspicious of performance. She is glad this particular show is over. She finds herself missing her father even more now that she can hear her mother unpacking next door, returning to them. Vita washes her face, weighs herself, and turns out the lights.

Annie lies in bed, awake. She has taken one of Hector's sleeping pills, but it hasn't kicked in yet. She has thanked Candace and Ed, seen them out, kissed the children, gathered the abandoned mugs that Candace orphans wherever she goes, turned out the lights, left word of her arrival for her husband. She has done all the things a returning mother is supposed to do. She is too tired to sleep. Her body does not know where she is in the world. She wonders if Candace changed the sheets. She wonders if she and Edouard had sex in her bed, if they even have sex. She wonders what Ed is like in bed. His mild manners seem inconsistent with passion, although Candace says he's a ruthless negotiator. Annie has never been sure exactly what

Ed does for a living. Something so rarefied in the financial markets that it approaches philosophy. A kind of math so abstract that it sounds vaguely spiritual. Although Ed is not spiritual. He is pragmatic, quiet, intense. Old-fashioned in his courtly manners. He faintly but reflexively raises himself from the table any time a woman leaves her seat, and again when she resumes it. Annie remembers the first time she saw him do it. They were in a famous bistro in New York; the mirrors jangled with light and money. Candace was brilliant, hectic, determined they should like each other. Annie got up to pee and, seeing Ed get to his feet, had hovered, waiting for him to join her so they could cross the room together. He had looked awkward and taken his seat again. Annie assumed he'd changed his mind. He lifted himself again when she returned. She sat down, frowning.

"Are you okay?"

Candace laughed.

"He's being polite. It's a mini bow."

"Wow."

Ed colored, his smile darkened for a moment.

"Sorry. Old habit."

"Is that a French thing?"

"I think it's an old-fashioned thing. My mother is obsessive about manners."

"Look, I've had a kid. I pee a lot. You're gonna be on your feet all night. Do you want to do like eight bobs in a row now and we can call it quits?"

Candace threw her head back and cackled.

"Old World meets New. Henry James, eat your heart out."

They had eaten and drunk and Ed had picked up the bill and they had stumbled into separate cabs. Annie had texted her approval to Candace, who had drunkenly shown it to Ed, who had smiled and kissed his girlfriend's head. And Annie had called Hector from the back of the cab and told him Candace's boyfriend was "dead posh but kinda fun." And Ed never rose from his seat for Annie again.

Annie wakes suddenly in the night. Jackson is beside her, an apparition.

"I'm wet."

"Oh, love."

She stumbles to her feet. She pulls the drenched sheets from his bed, the heavy duvet, his sodden pajamas, bundling all into the hamper. The room smells damp, acidic. She takes a towel and drapes it over the mattress, pulls fresh sheets from the cupboard. He wriggles into fresh pj's.

"My pillows."

Inexplicably, they, too, are soaked.

She feels as though she is moving through mud. She is drugged, incapable, the pillows more than she can manage. She bundles her son back to her own bed.

"Get in."

She feels his cold little back nudge against hers. She reaches back, takes his feet, and warms them on the back of her thighs.

CHAPTER 20

HECTOR WATCHES HIS COSTAR'S NOSE BEING POWDERED. IT IS AN improbable nose, perfectly straight and yet neatly rounded, nostrils symmetrical and elegantly tapered, surrendering to a long philtrum that slopes gently down into immense, pillowy lips. The nose is lightly scrunched, laughing with the makeup artist who is tending to it, a man who travels with this nose and these lips, an artist whose life is devoted to their ministry. He wears a goatee and khaki jackets with large patch pockets and glasses on his forehead. He is quiet when he is not of service, he keeps to himself on set, taps at word puzzles on his phone, and answers only to his actress. Hector finds himself riveted by this man. He is implacable, polite but withdrawn, coming to life whenever the actress is near. The features he ministers to are cartoonish in person, faintly obscene. It is the distortion of the camera and application of this artist's brush that render her so mesmerizing on celluloid. Hector is unmoved by her, probably because she is unmoved by him. He goes back to his battered edition of the complete plays of Chekhov.

When they first moved to Connecticut, Hector was so busy overseeing the new roof, repairing fences, and learning about insulation that he barely noticed the passing of time. The new house required huge outlays and continuous upkeep. He looked up from his tractor after a year and realized it was time to go back to work. He got hired on a short-lived drama about a newspaper that filmed in the city, then took a recurring arc on a long-running cop show. Nothing excited him. He read every script, threw most of them down with disgust. He complained bitterly to Annie.

"I could write better than this."

"Then why don't you?"

He started reading novels, articles, blogs in the hopes of finding a story he could adapt. He would burst into the kitchen, fresh from a new podcast or brimming with a developing news story, only to find out from his agents that it had already been optioned, was in development, or even in production. He felt like a latecomer panning for gold in an exhausted riverbed. He took to scouring secondhand bookstores to find neglected books, out-of-print mysteries, a forgotten thriller that he might adapt. He secured the rights to one dusty novel, a middle-aged romance set on a college campus, but found, after all, that he could not write it. He enrolled in an expensive online screenwriting course but never got around to completing it. He gave up trying to adapt the book himself, sent it out to a few scriptwriter friends, but there were no takers. The book sat on a shelf in his office, stacked between old scripts and new bills, where it gradually disappeared from view. He was offered the second lead in a new play off-Broadway. He loved it, even if Annie didn't. It felt thrilling to be visible again, night after night, in front of rows of people waiting in the dark to hear him speak. A young director approached him after the show, asked him if he'd be interested in playing Uncle Vanya. He struggled to hide his delight and promised to get back to him, but he knew immediately that he would do it. That was a year ago. There have been delays, venue changes, schedule shifts. Hector, privately, has been relieved. He is terrified he will not be good enough. He has rehearsed the role obsessively on his own. He knows every word of the entire play. He reads all the plays, over and over, keeping them close. He could play Ivanov, Trigorin, Nina if he had to.

A shouted laugh from the camera department. He glances over. They are adjusting a light while the makeup artist works, sharing a joke. He wishes he understood what they were saying. His Spanish is limited, and while the crew are friendly, there is an invisible line around the actors. He is both surrounded by people and utterly alone. His scenes with his costar are surreal because she is already starring in her own movie: Her very existence is a performance of a life, her costars, her assistant, her makeup artist, her driver, her bodyguard, her fortress of a trailer. He sees her only on set, where she arrives hours late every day, painted, costumed, murmuring greetings and apologies, the crew parting before her like a miracle. She has spoken maybe twelve words to him since they started filming. He is not entirely convinced she knows his name. But the world knows hers, and that is enough. The makeup artist finishes his touch-ups. She has remained sheathed in dark glasses throughout. She wears them right until the director calls action, handing them to the man with the goatee who hovers in attendance until the last possible moment. Hector, who stands opposite her now, ready for her close-up, half expects to be turned to stone by her gaze but instead sees only dark brown irises, pinprick pupils, and startlingly white eyeballs. They look bleached. She speaks so quietly, he strains to hear her. The director approaches, whispers something in her ear. The actress blinks. She repeats the scene with identical intonation. She appears to be doing nothing, feeling nothing, communicating nothing. But it will all be there in the cut. She is like a tarot card; everything can be read into that face. She replaces her sunglasses as soon as the close-up is over and shimmers back to her trailer. Like a child, she lets it be known that she is done for the day. There is more to shoot but she is tired now. The director shrugs. There is nothing to be done. Wrap is called. Hector tucks his book under his arm, walks back to his trailer. He feels a nudge at his elbow. It is the director.

"Dinner?"

The director takes him to a restaurant in the port. It is dim, with long trestle tables and benches, deliberately proletariat in design. She throws back martinis with a laugh that rumbles in her throat, lights cigarettes off the candle that drips wax onto the brown paper tablecloths. The meat arrives burnished, salty and bloody, the fries gleaming with fat, a sweaty tangle of spinach in a small dish. It is all excellent. She wears the same clothes she comes to work in, white sneakers, and very little makeup. A light sweat gleams on her collarbones. In her raspy but fluent English she tells him how much she admires his work and then lectures him on the history of Latin American cinema and the shameful lack of it in the American lexicon.

"It's Hollywood, Bollywood, or the BBC. Nothing else. I know, I went to USC, I know what they teach."

"What should I watch?"

She takes a pen from the waiter, scrawls a list on the oil-flecked, wax-freckled paper tablecloth, tears it off, and gives it to him.

"Watch them. Enough dead Russians."

He takes the list. He feels her fingers rest in his palm for a moment, strong, assertive. She looks at him hard, smiling.

"So, how do you like my country?"

He lies in bed alone, listening to a message from his wife. She is home. She sounds exhausted. He thinks about calling but decides against it. He doesn't want to wake her. And he is not ready to deal with her indifference to an evening he found complicated. He enjoyed the director, her slender ankle dangling beneath the table, the way she leaned into him, earnestly talking about movies and craft, laughing at his jokes. It was nice to be noticed.

CHAPTER 21

ANNIE WAKES TO THE SMELL OF BURNING TOAST. DOWNSTAIRS, VITA is yelling at Jackson that his breakfast is ready. Annie feels stoned, the sleeping pill unfamiliar in her body, still working its way through her system. She brushes her teeth and shudders again at the thought that her mother is dead, that she will not see her face again. It is a thought that manages to be both banal and insurmountable all at the same time. Her mind balks at it, over and over, a horse refusing a fence. She pulls jeans from the floor, a sweater, and staggers down to the kitchen. The children ignore her, chewing, pulling things in and out of their backpacks, waves of motion and noise. There is the coffee, here are the car keys. She drives the children to school without knowing how she got there, returns home to the ravaged kitchen.

Surfing crosscurrents of jet lag and caffeine, she scrapes inscrutable leftovers from the fridge into the trash. Patti calls.

"Finally! Did you get my messages? Where've you been? I've been trying to reach you all week. I have a house I need ready by the weekend. I texted you the address. Meet me at ten?"

When Jackson turned three, they enrolled him in the village preschool. At the end of his first week he bit a little girl with red hair on the swing set and was sent home. Annie yelled at the teacher, then at Jackson, then called the redhead's mother to apologize. The mother was breezy.

"God, don't sweat it. Don't we all want to bite somebody sometimes?"

That was Patti. Annie liked her immediately. She was a former fashion designer turned Realtor who had moved to Connecticut ten years earlier with her husband. They lived a few miles away in a converted barn that was all glass and air. She was the first real friend Annie had made in years. Patti was ropey with yoga muscle, dressed only in black parachute silk, and knew the value of every property within a fifty-mile radius. She drank copious cups of green tea and lingered at Annie's table for as long as her restive body would let her. Annie invited Patti and her husband to dinner. Patti seemed reluctant but eventually they came, bearing a potted camellia and a jar of olives. Her husband was a poet who rarely left the house ("saves on childcare") and looked sorrowful in high-waisted trousers and mismatched socks. He sat at the head of the table, answering questions politely but with as few words as possible, as though he had set himself a word limit for the evening. Patti was brittle, full of nervous laughter. Hector trotted out all his Hollywood stories.

Annie drank more than she had for years. Everyone felt clenched except the poet, who sipped his beer, waiting for the evening to end. It was tacitly agreed that this was not an experiment worth repeating.

But Patti and Annie remained close. When Hector left to shoot a show in the city and a huge wind ripped up their fence and tossed it into the road, Patti sent over her handyman to help Annie out. Brian repaired the fence and pointed out that they needed new gutters. Knowing Hector would protest, she asked him if he could get them done before her husband came home the following week, and the first of many collusions was pulled off. Patti stopped by one morning. Annie was in the garage, restacking a tower of chairs to accommodate an armoire she had picked up at auction. Patti whistled.

"You should open a store." Her eyes widened. "You should help me stage houses."

It was an informal arrangement; she took on what she could, although Patti always pushed for more. Brian and his nephew helped with the loading in and out. She liked the work well enough. She liked earning her own money, liked making things again, even if they were just temporary rooms. Staging houses reminded her of the dollhouse she had loved as a child, of the imagined happy family for whom she had carefully laid out beds.

She meets Patti at the cottage. It is low, white, timbered with a stone chimney, built two hundred years ago. A spreading oak tree dominates the front lawn. Patti kisses her, does not ask where she has been, for which Annie is grateful. She does not yet know how to think about her mother's death, far less talk about it.

Inside, it smells of wet dogs. Patti chatters, leads her through the house.

"Owner is eighty, doesn't want to sell, but the kids are determined to get her into a home. There's not much stuff, they got rid of most of it. See what you think."

She snatches her ringing phone and disappears into the kitchen.

The living room ceilings are low and a large cracked flatscreen television stands directly in front of a bow window. A flattened dog bed sits beside a sagging brown recliner. The stairwell is hung with a gallery of family photos, school portraits, picnics, birthdays, weddings. Every one of the frames is askew. In the master bedroom the faded rug holds a dark rectangle that the bed once occupied. The oak tree is huge at the window, it paints shifting light on the floor. The children's bedrooms are empty. A glow-in-the-dark dinosaur sticker peels off one of the scuffed doors. The house feels desolate, estranged from itself. She takes photos on her phone. Patti calls up the stairwell.

"Can you do anything with it? I've got an all-cash couple who want to see it Saturday."

Annie sits at her kitchen table, on her laptop, making lists and comparing photos of the empty rooms with photos of her inventory. Mentally she rearranges sofas, rugs, plants. Cereal bowls from the morning crust around beside her, jam congeals, cold toast puckers. Dimly she remembers the children who will need fetching, dinner that will need cooking, but not yet. A knock at the door jolts her back to her own kitchen. Through the paned glass she sees Thierry.

"Fuck."

She opens the door. He sees her expression.

"I should have texted first."

"No, it's fine, I'm just so out of it. I have no idea what day it is."

He shifts his backpack.

"Next week?"

"No, no, you're here now, come in. I'll make some tea."

She turns back to the kitchen, heads over to the kettle.

She fumbles with the lid.

"When did you get back?"

"Last night. I think. Tea?"

"Water. Thank you."

She realizes she is lightheaded, that she does not remember the last time she ate. She can see her hands moving across the sink, but they seem to have no connection to her body. Behind her, Thierry is asking her how her flight was. She hears him but it is hard to answer. She holds a glass under the tap, water is flowing, it is overflowing over her hand and wrist, cold, wet. There seems to be no way to stop it. She drops the glass into the sink and it shatters on the cold porcelain. He is at her back. He leans past her, retrieving shards from the sink.

"Sit."

She sits in a chair as still as a child, letting him move back and forth, searching for the trash, finding it, bearing broken glass in his hands. She feels suddenly cold, returned to her body, but there is no welcome there. She watches him find his way around her kitchen, making tea. It is like watching a bear paw at a cabin. His hands are huge.

He hands her the tea and pulls his chair not across from her but next to her, their knees almost touching. She is about to sip but he puts out a hand to stop her. He reaches into her mug with his forefinger and thumb and pinches the tea bag that is floating on the surface. He does not flinch. He pulls it out and drops it on the edge of Jackson's cereal bowl. It is a curiously intimate gesture. He looks at her. It feels like she has not been looked at in a long time. It sucks the air out of her. It feels like they are in the bottom of a well. Through his left eyebrow he has the trace of a pale scar so faint that it might be a trick of the sunlight.

"How are you doing?"

It is the first time anyone has asked her. She tries to answer honestly.

"I keep waiting to feel something other than tired."

"I bet. You've been through a lot. Drink your tea."

She sips. It is scalding and sweet. She keeps her eyes on the rim of her mug. He is quiet. She can feel him watching her. It is oddly peaceful to be quiet with someone in her own house. She wonders if she is supposed to say more but she cannot think what to say. She tries to remember how conversation is supposed to go but everything has deserted her.

He glances at the table, the sketches, the laptop.

"Qu'est-ce que c'est?"

"A house I'm working on."

"*Vous êtes architecte?*"

"Am I an architect? No, I stage houses that are on the market. I style them with furniture to make them more attractive to buyers."

"Cool."

She shrugs.

"If you like fake homes."

He laughs.

The lesson is over before she knows it. She remembers nothing when he leaves. She is not sure what she is learning, but it is not French.

BOOK THREE
SUMMER

CHAPTER 22

THE TRUCK SHUDDERS AS ANNIE GRINDS THROUGH THE GEARS. Thierry sits beside her, hunched slightly in the passenger seat. His knees keep banging the dashboard but he does not complain. He keeps one hand on the backpack wedged between his legs, the other elbow wedged in the window. Empty water bottles roll around his feet and a dried tangerine skin dangles from the ashtray. She wishes she'd cleaned the truck out. He leans forward, plugs his phone into the swaying cable. He wears a faded gray T-shirt. It is tight across his back. It is the same color as his eyes.

"Mind if I play some music?"

She is amazed at how freely he shares himself. Music to her is so private. She feels self-conscious with this young man in her truck, irritated that Brian's broken leg has forced her into accepting his offer of help. But she does not know many able-bodied young men who can help her move furniture at short notice. She cannot afford to be picky. French lounge music drifts from the speaker.

"What's this?"

He names a French singer she has never heard of. She relaxes a little. In the back of the truck sways a pale pink sofa. It is lashed to a pair of cream armchairs, a wooden bench, a white tulip table and four chairs, several end tables, a trembling ficus in a woven basket, a vintage trunk full of sheets, pillows, rugs, and throws. Thierry glances over his shoulder.

"Where do you get all the stuff?"

"Flea markets, estate sales, the Internet. I've always liked collecting things."

"You're a hoarder."

"So my husband says."

He glances at her and laughs. She keeps her eyes on the road. He turns the volume up a little, beats time on his thigh.

She pulls up in front of the cottage. It is mild today; the air smells of warm wild fennel. He gets out, stretches his back.

They work all morning, first carrying the remaining furniture out of the cottage into the barn, then hauling Annie's furniture off the back of the truck. Thierry swings it all easily over the side. They speak only to exchange information, directions. She points to groups of items that belong upstairs. Thierry waits, lifts, places, obedient to her requests. She is focused, intent. They return to the living room where an island of furniture awaits dispersal. Thierry sinks in a chair.

"I need to eat."

"Oh, yes, sorry, I should have . . ."

"There's a café back in town. I'll go pick us something up."

"I can go."

He shakes his head, hauls himself to his feet.

"I got you."

Through the bow window she watches him reverse her truck as though he owned it. He disappears down the driveway. She turns back to the room and unrolls a rug. She drags another over, begins layering them in a bright patchwork on the stained wooden floor.

He is gone so long that she is startled by his return. He carries a bulging brown bag that he sets down on the kitchen counter, then lays out bread, ham, cheese, tomatoes, an avocado, apples. He pulls out a beer.

"Are we allowed to drink on the job?"

She laughs.

"Sure."

She washes her hands in the tiny downstairs bathroom. Her face is streaked with dirt. Her hair is kinked with dried sweat, speckled with dust. She tries to smooth it down, runs her hands through it, then gives up, gathers it into a dark knot at her neck.

He waves her away as he peels apart the ham, the cheese, assembles sandwiches, and hands her one. He fishes a penknife from his pocket, cracks the beer. She drinks.

"This is a better lunch than I'm used to. I usually just eat whatever Jackson's left on the back seat. Are you a cook?"

"My mom ran a bistro. I grew up helping out in the kitchen. We made *cassoulet, coq au vin, blanquette de veau, croque monsieur*, the basics."

"I think we may have different definitions of *basic*."

"You don't cook?"

"I apply heat to food. On a good day we call it cooking."

"Does your husband?"

"Hector? No. I think he is frightened of food."

"What does that mean?"

"He's an actor. Actors are always aware of how they look. Their bodies become kind of a battleground. I mean, don't get me wrong, he eats. He eats egg whites and chicken and salads and stuff . . ."

She drifts off. She is aware of how pitiful she is making him sound. She does not know how to rearrange the facts in a more flattering light. Thierry does not appear to have noticed. He eats his sandwich, tells her about a documentary about organic farming he watched the night before. He is so easy in himself, in his body. Crumbs scatter on his T-shirt; he lifts it up and shakes them off. There is a glimmer of his torso, tanned, flat like a table. She changes the subject.

"So, do you like teaching, or is it just a money thing?"

"Both. I'd rather be writing, but it doesn't pay. Yet. Teaching gives me structure, and the bar keeps me solvent. And it's a great place to overhear stories."

"Is it hard, teaching kids? I wouldn't have the patience."

"All parents think that. But you're putting up with them all day long. You've lost track of how patient you already are. I'm only with them for an hour, and then I get in my car and drive away. You can do anything for an hour. It can even be fun, if you can believe it. Apple?"

"Sure. The driving-away part sounds fun. Do you teach many adults?"

"Just you."

"Oh."

"You sound disappointed."

"Embarrassed, I think."

"Why? I hope I'm still open to new stuff when . . ."

". . . when you're as old as I am?"

He shakes his head, frowns, a concertina of peel dangling from his knife.

"It seems like it might be really easy to just get stuck with what you know, with what's familiar, when you have all the . . . accoutrements."

She nods, surprised.

"What do you write?"

"I'm working on a story collection. I have eight that I like. Maybe eight and a half."

"You sound like Jackson."

"I'm working on a new one."

"What's it about?"

He hands her a slice of apple on the tip of his knife.

"It's about a beautiful woman who drives a filthy truck."

She puts a hand to her neck and laughs.

She spends the rest of the afternoon furnishing the ground floor. She works in silence, moving around the room, viewing it from every angle. She can see exactly how the room should look. She wishes they had time to paint it, to rip out the cheap bookcases, the track lighting, the flickering fluorescent bulbs beneath the kitchen cabinetry. This is how it always is. There is only so much she can do. But it feels good to focus. Thierry comes in and out, watching her, sees her nod to a chair or bench, and shifts it for her.

"It already looks like a different house. You're good at this."

She barely smiles. She is concentrating. His phone buzzes. She frowns. He takes the call, steps outside to answer it. She watches him walk around on the lawn outside. He is smiling, gesticulating. He hangs up and comes back into the house. She busies herself with some cushions.

"My mom. Sorry."

She is surprised by her own relief.

"Are you close?"

"She lives in Paris, but we speak pretty often. She likes to check in."

He watches her moving the cushions, adjusting the rug.

"Were you close? To your mom?"

She hesitates.

"Not really."

She is surprised by how hard this is to say.

"I mean, we weren't estranged or anything—we spoke, sent photos and stuff—but I didn't share anything real with her."

She checks her watch.

"I should go. I can drop you off, then I have to pick up the kids."

"What about upstairs?"

"That's tomorrow's work."

"I can't do tomorrow; I teach and have a shift. I can help this weekend?"

She feels a tug of disappointment.

"Patti needs it for Saturday. I'll figure it out, don't worry."

They drive back to her house, listening to the radio. He drums his thumb on the door. She pulls up in her driveway; Thierry's car sits parked outside the house. He tries to open the truck door but it won't budge. She leans over to help him.

"Sorry, it's so old, it sticks."

Her breast grazes his chest as she wrenches the handle.

"Thank you. For helping. I mean, it wasn't a favor, I'll pay you, of course, but thank you for doing it."

He looks at her for a moment. Then he leans over and kisses her on the mouth. It takes a full second. He rests his lips for a moment on hers, as though inhaling her. She does not move. He slides out of the truck and, without turning around, raises a hand in farewell as he walks to his car. She puts the truck in gear and crunches back down her driveway, watching him diminish in her rearview mirror until she turns onto the main road. She can feel blood singing in a vein in her neck. She is untethered, a horse in a new field.

CHAPTER 23

SHE WAKES AGAIN IN THE NIGHT. SHE DOES NOT KNOW WHERE SHE is. She remembers that her mother is dead. Like a moth, the thought circles the flame of her brain. The bed feels vast, empty. She feels hollow, a rattling seed pod. She thinks of Thierry and wonders for a second if he is thinking of her. She shakes the thought away. She goes to the bathroom and puts her lips to the cold tap to drink. She slips into Jackson's room. He is asleep, nuzzled deep beneath his duvet, only the faintest wisps of blond visible. She crawls in beside him.

"Mom?"

"Shhhh."

He disappears again into sleep. She lies beside him and listens to the house.

Brian sends his nephew, Ricky, to help her finish the cottage. Ricky is twenty, speaks in grunts and tics, and when he is not checking his phone, he picks the zits on his face with grimy fingernails. He eats highly spiced tortilla chips and leaves a trail of red powder wherever he wipes his hands. Annie can hardly bear to look at him and sends him home after the heavy lifting is done. She listens to French lounge music and works alone until it is time for pickup.

The week passes. The children go to school and return. The dishwasher fills and empties. The beds are tumbled, unmade, and made again. The fridge fills and empties. The laundry mounds and disperses. The trash fills and empties. The homework sprawls and disappears. Soccer, ballet, art class, all are attended. The tide pool of the house fills and empties, empties and fills.

When the day of her French lesson approaches, it is a relief. She has been aware of it all week. She is up early, washes her hair, softens her face with cream, applies it to her arms, her legs, her soft belly. She barely feels her body as she touches it. She is elsewhere, her mind flickering along possibilities. She shaves her legs, shapes her hair, chooses her jeans. She paints her face, holding her eyes still, making her mouth full. She looks ready for a party. She stares back at her painted self. Vita glances over at her at breakfast and asks her where she's going. By the afternoon Annie has wiped her face clean and texted him twice telling him not to come, then deleted both messages before sending. She makes sure she is upstairs at four o'clock, not loitering in the kitchen.

The knock comes a little after four. She comes downstairs, forcefully relaxed. He ducks a little as he comes in the front door. He busies himself with his laptop, asks how it went with the house and the prospective buyers. She answers him without making eye contact, clears a space at the kitchen table.

He notices the dark clumps in her long eyelashes, the sweet clean smell of her hair, the way her T-shirt clings to her breasts, tugs slightly over the mound of her belly. He thought about her during the week. He wondered at himself for kissing her. He billed her for the hours he worked for her, hesitating over whether to include the receipt for the lunch. In the end he only billed her for half of it. She paid so promptly, he wondered if he could have gotten away with the full amount.

He is friendly but businesslike. He has prepared the lesson, photocopied pages for her to study. She is nervously jokey, then diligent, applied. He drags his chair a little closer to point to a phrase. She pretends not to notice. She is both too old for this and too giddy.

She wonders why she does not clutch his wrist and ask him what he meant by kissing her. Instead, she recites French verbs, aware of every hair on her forearm, and he corrects her pronunciation, looking only at her mouth.

Suddenly he is kissing her.

Her mouth is open, soft, an apricot. This time she takes his face in her hands and holds it steady and kisses him back. A fly buzzes on the lip of the fruit bowl. His tongue is in her mouth as though it were her own. It is astonishing and utterly normal. He lifts her as easily as a cat into his lap. They are fumbling, breathing, intent. There is both no time to speak and nothing to say.

Thierry stands in the refrigerated aisle of the supermarket, wondering if he had meant to have sex with Annie.

He could not have imagined her upturned face transformed like that, her eyes teasing, unrecognizably relaxed. She laughed as he rolled off her, and again when he searched for his socks under the kitchen table; she was laughing as she saw him out the door. As though she were delighted. As though she did this all the time. As though Wednesday afternoons were the time she had set aside to let strange men make love to her on her kitchen floor. And yet, she assured him, he was the first.

He had wanted to get dressed again immediately, but she had lain, unselfconscious, bare breasted, open, her legs tangled in one leg of her jeans, one arm flung wide, not moving. She had turned her head and looked at him with those laughing eyes.

"Well, that was fun."

He snorts in front of the frozen dinners. A woman startles, pushes her cart a little farther away from him. He can still smell Annie on him. He chooses frozen cannelloni, joins the line to pay. That was fun, he thinks as he swipes his debit card. She is sexy. Not weird or desperate. Or, worse, grateful, like the woman from the bar. This had felt mutual, the attraction. Not transactional. He had, if anything, been surprised by his own fervor, not hers.

The microwave pings as he hears Maya letting herself into their apartment. He calls out.

"You're home early."

She stands in the doorway, in yellow scrubs, a parka draped over her shoulders. She looks tired, dark moons beneath her eyes. She dumps her keys, shrugs.

"Yeah. You expecting someone?"

Maya knows when her shampoo has been used, her deodorant moved, but has long decided to say nothing. It is none of her business, Thierry's love life, and as long as she doesn't have to make small talk with anyone at breakfast, she is happy to make no mention of her roommate's activities.

"No. What happened?"

She sighs.

"Mr. Leonard died."

"Banjo man?"

She nods, opening the kitchen cupboard, looking for a drink. She pours herself a tumbler of wine.

"Everyone loved him. I mean, he drove us all insane with that fucking ukulele, but I actually looked forward to seeing him every day. He was a light, you know?"

She pushes tears away with the flat of her hand.

"Fuck death."

"Fuck death."

She sits down beside him, rests her head on his shoulder. She speaks in a flat voice.

"I need a shower."

She does not move. He strokes her hair. She leans into him. Everyone is grieving something, thinks Thierry.

"How was your day?"

For a moment he thinks about telling Maya about his afternoon, but he is not ready to share his experience yet. It does not fit into any narrative he knows. And he has no sense if it is a short story or an opening chapter.

"Same old."

Maya sniffs, searches her pockets for a Kleenex. He wonders if Annie will cancel her classes altogether. There had been no mention of the next lesson when he left, no reference to seeing each other again. He figures it is up to Annie; she is the one with more to lose, he will follow her lead. He is happy to go back to teaching her French, if that is what she wants. It will be strange, sure, but nothing insurmountable. Maya is talking about Mr. Leonard again. He nods sympathetically. He has no idea what she said. He wonders if his cannelloni are still hot and how long he must sit here before he can take them into his bedroom and eat in peace. He is suddenly tired of taking care of women.

CHAPTER 24

ANNIE DOES NOT CALL. ALL WEEK SHE REACHES FOR HER PHONE over and over to tell him not to come, or to tell him that he must come immediately. She flails between shame and defiance. On Wednesday morning she makes eggs for the children, remembering again his strange hands on her body. She flips bacon, listens to Jackson describe his new favorite imaginary weapon, and remembers the weight of her French teacher on her hips. Vita searches for her sneakers in the corner where his jeans lay crumpled a week ago. She is distracted, impatient with time and her children. They dawdle and linger and prattle and still it is only eight in the morning and her phone lies silent as a brick in her hand.

When he left that afternoon, she closed the kitchen door and went straight to the bathroom to look at herself in the mirror. She searched her face but saw only her flushed skin, bruised lips, glittering eyes. She went back to the kitchen and, not knowing quite what to do next, harnessed herself to domesticity, did a load of laundry, pulled the dry clean clothes from the dryer, and pushed a hot iron through all of it—ironing T-shirts, underwear, towels, anything that could be smoothed into submission with mindless repetitive action and leave her mind free to tingle with remembered sensations.

On the kitchen floor the afternoon light scattered and regathered itself, while outside the poplars shuddered and stilled. The kids had giggled that evening, disbelieving their pressed pajamas. She had laughed with them, made pizza from scratch and a cocktail for herself. It had been a good day.

But now the week has inched by. She has sourced a coffee table for Candace, taken grapes to Brian, returned a set of chairs, paid bills, volunteered for lunch duty at the kids' school, anything to pass the days. At night, sleepless, she has found herself in the kitchen, drawing for the first time in years. One night she finds herself in the garage, rummaging through boxes. She knows what she is looking for without knowing why she needs it. She pulls out her old box of art supplies and spreads inks and paints across the kitchen table. She fills saucers with cerulean, magenta, ocher, midnight. She works feverishly, the tip of her tongue between her teeth. Here she is at last, here she is again, on the page. Everything she needs is here on the page. She has missed this.

Moonlight pools on the kitchen floor. There is nowhere else to be. She paints like a girl in a story. In the mornings it as though she has dreamt it, the only evidence the damp paper towels in the trash can, faint with paint.

She wonders, over and over, if he will call. She has rehearsed every variant of every conversation, sometimes out loud in the car. Wednesday aches its way into the afternoon. She manages to secure Steph, the local girl who babysits for so many of the school families that she is never, ever available but miraculously is free, to fetch the kids from school and take them for ice cream. Annie hovers in the kitchen, then goes upstairs, not wanting to look like she is waiting for him. She lies on her bed, trying to focus on furniture websites, craning for the knock at the kitchen door. She checks the time. It is two minutes past four. He is never late. He is reliable. She likes this about him. Her chest caves. He is not coming. He is not coming. She sits up, overwhelmed by the realization. Her brain, unbidden, floods with images of herself last week, her pale stomach pillowy in the unforgiving afternoon light, her arms winged with flesh as she reached for him, the silvering around her temples, the soft gravity of her thighs. She hates herself for hating herself but for a cold minute she sees herself as he must have and is horrified. Of course she is not what he wants. She feels the sinkhole of shame, of self-abandon. She is grotesque, she sees that now. He reached for her out of pity, or boredom, and now he is ashamed or, worse, indifferent.

She tears off the dress she spent an hour choosing, pulls on sweatpants and a T-shirt of Hector's, cancels Steph, thereby guaranteeing she will not work for them again for months, and goes to fetch the kids from school herself. She hurtles down the country roads, taking angry turns. She is furious with herself. She is humiliated not by him but by the outrageousness of her own expectations. The improbability of another encounter seems obvious now, her disappointment adolescent. She is incredulous at how readily she has deceived herself.

And yet.

It had been astonishing to be wanted. It had been astonishing to watch her own body respond in ways she had forgotten. It had been enlivening to be on edge all week, like living with a light fever. She had looked forward to seeing him. There it was. That was the crux of it. To have a horizon, to be courted by the possibility of an imminent if vanishing pleasure, had quickened her deadened senses, had awoken her impatient for each day, eager for what it might bring. Now she was left with nothing but the damp chill of disappointment, the bricking up of a window. Not for years had she felt like this.

One night in her third year of art school, Miriam asked her and Candace to join her for dinner. Annie arrived late from her shift to an Uptown low-ceilinged restaurant, where, ushered past leather booths and cut-glass cocktails and ignoring Candace's scowl, she slipped in at the end of the table as a towering *fruits de mer* was set down. The man to her right paid her no attention. He was missing a pinkie, she noticed as he reached for the shellfish. He caught her staring and winked at her as he slid an oyster down his throat.

Mark was a war correspondent. He flew in and out of war zones with a duffel bag, intermittent cell service, and inscrutable alibis. He called her from Beirut and asked her to dinner the following week. He took her back to his apartment, an open loft in Tribeca, all windows and books. The walls were hung with moody black-and-white landscape photographs taken by his ex-wife. They played chess in the bath, drinking tumblers of vintage Bordeaux. His dark chest hair grew matted in the steam, candle wax dripped in the tub. She was in love before he moved his rook.

They were together for the next five years.

Candace marveled at the glamour.

"He's old enough to be your father."

Miriam, who was friends with his ex-wife, kept her counsel. Annie didn't care. In the early years she took his unreliability for spontaneity; his absences gave her space to paint; his age was a welcome reprieve from the puerile yearnings of the students around her. He never spoke about where he had been. She had to read about it like everyone else. She was proud of what he did, of his unavailability even. They became a badge of honor, his missions and her resilience. He told her to use his place while he was gone.

"Don't waste this light."

The windows ran floor to ceiling and the view of Downtown Manhattan held her spellbound. She marveled at the amount of space he had. She moved in, sprawled her canvases on his wide-planked floors. At night she drew, painted, and cut. She graduated art school. It felt like a formality; she had long outgrown the place.

Mornings, she worked in a reputable Midtown gallery that she despised; afternoons, she assisted a well-known artist whom she worshipfully hated; evenings, she toured the openings, dreading the invitations almost as much as she feared not getting them. She scorned the art world, but it was the only one she knew.

Her life was scissored. Mark called, said he'd be back on Friday, for Labor Day, for Christmas. He was always, always late. She grew accustomed to the tang of disappointment. Her friends learned not to count on him for dinner. She learned not to dress for him on Friday nights, not to bunch tulips in vases around the loft, not to spend money she did not have on grass-fed steaks bleeding through butcher paper in the fridge.

When he did come home, he descended like a Bedouin. He would open his duffel bag and unfurl his gifts for her—a copper bracelet, a rope of hand-painted African beads, a matchbox of tiny voodoo dolls, an antique glass-stoppered bottle of myrrh—and she would sit cross-legged on the bed and let him woo her with his stories. His life was thrilling, his stories dwarfed everything she had ever known or imagined. Her world stopped when Mark was home. It was not that he demanded her full attention, it was that she offered it up unasked.

He took her to rural Connecticut for the weekend. He had been in Afghanistan for two months, promising to be home at the end of every week. They stayed in a tiny, beautiful hotel, barely speaking. They drank whiskey in the bar until they were numb and went to bed. They fucked, then fought, and fucked again. They ordered room service and played chess in bed, and when she queened her pawn he reached under the pillow and slipped a ring on the little black chess piece. She touched the ring as though it might bite. It was a single brilliant sapphire, fiery and fierce on a clean gold band. She looked at him, eyes wide.

"Is this...?"

"If you want it to be."

"Do you want it to be?"

"If you do."

"I do."

"You do?"

"I do."

She called her mother to tell her the news. Bluey sounded pleased, but no more than if Annie had told her she'd enjoyed a book. The truth was, Bluey understood very little about her daughter's life. It was a foreign land and her mother did not care for travel. She ignored whatever she did not immediately understand. Annie listened to her prattle about her lost library card and the new family who had moved in next door. She was glad her mother did not ask for wedding details. She had none to give except the certain knowledge that the wedding would not be taking place in Australia. She did not mention her father, because they never did. They flowed around him like a river skirts an islet. Annie sometimes longed to ask her mother if she was safe, if he still hit her, but since they had never discussed it, she did not know how to begin now. Bluey mentioned that she'd run into Sam.

"Bente's ill."

Annie called Sam.

"It's everywhere, babes. She says she doesn't want all that junk in her veins, so we're just keeping her company now. She's slowing down, but there's no stopping her."

"How long do they think?"

"Who knows, darlin'? We're just taking it one day at a time over here. Anyway, how are you? You hanging in the Met yet? When's the wedding?"

The wedding became an unspeakable subject. Mark dodged the topic and she grew ashamed of asking him. She took to wearing the ring on her other hand. She hated herself for caring. She had never fantasized about being married, but this winking blue ring on her finger felt like a constant provocation, an unfinished sentence. She quit working for the well-known artist after he grabbed her ass while she washed his brushes. She slapped his face and the sapphire left a tiny cut just below his left eye. She did not wait to be fired. She asked the gallery if they needed her full-time, but they told her they really didn't need her at all. She had no money. She thought about selling the ring. Mark, on a crackly line from Lebanon, told her to focus on her own work and he'd take care of her. She flicked through the bridal magazines that Candace insisted on bringing over. She cut out brides and bouquets and sunset cruises and pasted them onto blood-red canvases. She spattered them with black ink, turning them into dark Venuses and Charons. She hated everything she touched. None of it made sense.

Miriam offered to host the wedding at her home in the Hamptons. Mark groaned and shot it down, leaving Annie with the awkward task of politely declining while not being able to explain why. She broke up with Mark over and over. She grew tired of going to openings and parties and dinners alone, tired of making excuses for his unpredictable absences, and tired of his bullish refusal to brook a single word of reproach. His sudden returns seemed less like miracles and more like assaults. She felt her love dwindle to hurt, then curdle to scorn. She grew disdainful of him, hating the callousness in her own voice as she shut down his excuses. One night, phone squeezed to her ear, she elbowed her fury past guests into a dank alleyway behind a fellow student's gallery opening.

"I don't care why you're not here. I just care that you're not here. Everyone else manages to show up."

"Annie, everyone else does regular jobs."

"What's wrong with a regular job? You make it sound like a death sentence."

"To me it is."

"How am I supposed to live like this?"

"You knew what you were getting into. I have never pretended to be anyone different."

There was no answer to this. She felt nauseous.

"What is the ring even for? What is it supposed to mean?"

"It means we belong to each other. It means you are who I come home to."

"It doesn't mean we're getting married?"

"Do you even want to be married to me?"

She didn't know. But she refused to gift him her uncertainty.

"I can't keep living like this."

He sighed. This fight was as familiar to him as his own hands. He knew all the parts, could rehearse both sides. Every woman, including his own mother, had spoken these words to him, with varying degrees of rage and grief. Annie caught a glimpse of her reflection in a window. Her face was blotched, her red dress was stained dark beneath her armpits, her hair clung to her neck like black rope. Through the open fire door she could see people drinking, laughing, buying her friend's art. She called Candace as she walked home.

"He'd rather take a bullet than a vow."

"I think he'd rather dodge both."

He came home from an extended trip to Beirut to find his loft stripped of her paintings, her clothes, and her sketchbooks. The ring glittered like an evil eye in a white saucer on the table. Affixed to one of the vast industrial windows was a paper bird. He approached it. It was composed of minutely torn paper feathers, covered in type. He squinted. They were the ripped-up pages of every article he had ever written.

Annie refused to take his calls. Candace was in London, fundraising for a film, so Annie let herself back into her old apartment and crawled into her friend's bed, where she sobbed herself to sleep. She got a job in a bar, painted a mural for a friend of Miriam's, told her mother the engagement was off, and felt like nothing good would ever happen to her again. She realized it was not Mark she missed, she was used to that, she had been missing him for years, but the phantasm of an imagined future. She felt soluble, an aspirin in a glass, as though she could disappear without trace in this city.

There was nothing to keep her in New York, but she had nowhere else to go. A few months later Miriam put her in touch with a producer who was making a movie about an artist and needed some original work to fill the character's studio. The producer agreed to look at her portfolio. Annie spent her last dollars on a flight to Los Angeles.

She is at the turnoff for the school. She has no memory of getting here. A queue of cars is backed up the school driveway, engines idling, a line of mothers sealed in their machinery, on phones, fixing hair, making appointments, improving themselves, their families, tethered by invisible threads to the school gate.

The passenger doors fly open, the car is suddenly full of noise and smells and children. She is immediately irritated. Vita turns on the radio, Jackson launches into an involved discussion about some card he traded at recess. Vita yawns.

"What's for dinner?"

"I don't know."

"Can it not be pizza?"

"What does that mean?"

"It means we've had either pizza or pasta for days now, and I'd like an actual vegetable."

"Then you do the shopping and make an actual meal."

"Fine. Stop at the store, and I will."

Annie pulls over at the local market, hands her daughter her wallet without looking at her. Vita stalks into the store. Jackson breathes on the window and draws stick figures with his finger.

"You okay, Mom?"

She looks at him in the rearview mirror. His face is perfect, open, full of solicitude. She takes a deep breath.

"I'm tired. That's all. Tired of doing everything on my own."

She is surprised at what she has said. She wonders if it is true.

"Oh."

He goes back to drawing.

She snaps off the radio. She is fed up with doing it all. Hector has always expected too much of her. He has never spared a thought about what she might want or need. He has always left her behind to manage everything while he enjoys his career and his hotel rooms. And he gets to say he's doing it all for his family. He has made himself bulletproof. She frowns, taps the steering wheel. Her phone buzzes and she grabs it as if someone might snatch it from her. It is Patti sending photos of another house. Annie feels oppressed. She doesn't have time for this job anymore. She corrects herself. She has spent all week daydreaming, ignoring her inbox and staring out of windows, and imagining herself in the arms of a man likely young enough to be her son. There is plenty of time for this job now that she has been rejected. She snorts. Rejected. She sounds fourteen.

"What, Mom?"

"What what?"

"You laughed."

"Did I?"

Vita huffs into the front seat, bearing a brown paper bag with an ostentatious head of cauliflower bobbing on the top.

Annie reaches her hand over, palm open, a peace offering, hoping her daughter will take it. Vita slaps the wallet into her hand and snaps at her mother, "I wasn't going to keep it!"

"I didn't think you... oh for fuck's sake."

"Mom!"

Jackson's eyes widen. Annie drives them home in silence.

CHAPTER 25

HECTOR UNBUTTONS THE CAREFULLY STAINED SHIRT HE HAS WORN on set all day. There is a knock at the door of his trailer. It is the director. She is holding out a DVD.

"Did you watch this yet?"

It is one of the films she recommended. He shakes his head (he lost the list, never watched any of them) and his shirt falls open. She tries to look away, brushes her hand across her face.

"You're busy, I'll come back."

He tucks himself in, a flash of pleasure at how discomfited he has made her. He takes the DVD and smiles.

"Can we watch it together? You can explain it to a dumb American."

Her apartment is in the northern part of the city, named for the jaguars that used to roam there. He comes, after much deliberation, empty-handed. Wine, flowers, chocolate—all send the wrong message. He regrets it in the elevator, contemplates going back to the street level to find a bottle, a book, something. Too late: The elevator doors slide open directly into her apartment. She stands in the doorway, barefoot in a loose dress. Her apartment is small, modern, open plan, with glass doors that open onto a balcony overlooking the river. Candles flicker. She is relaxed, casual. He knows he should not have come. He turns to hide his discomfort and admire the view, the dark snaking river, the glittering city. The wide windows reflect his pale face. The director opens wine, makes a salad. The dining table is covered in two laptops, papers, sketches, lists. One of the screens is frozen on a frame of a scene they shot earlier that week. He is suddenly aware of how little he knows about this woman with whom he spends his days. He struggles for small talk, gestures at the screen.

"How is the movie going? For you, I mean? How are you feeling about it?"

She shrugs, drizzling oil.

"Let's just say I look forward to making a movie for Argentines again. The US producers, US market... I'm not sure our tastes are... how you say... compatible." Hector has seen the American producers, a blond with an unreadable smile and a twitchy youth with a fledgling beard, making whispered phone calls behind the camera truck and once leaving the director's trailer red-faced (the blond) and tearful (the youth). He assumed the usual birth pains of moviemaking, the timeworn tussle between the creatives and the money.

"Artistic differences?"

"It's because I'm a woman," she says flatly, handing him a bowl. "No one believes women can make action movies. We're supposed to do rom-coms. We are only supposed to do feelings, intimacy, vulnerability. You know I had to storyboard this entire movie to even be given the job? They had to know every single frame of every single angle. Every day, I have to fight for the scene I want to shoot. Because you know how it is: You get to the location, and nothing is how you planned it, and the clouds come in, so you have to change your shots, and maybe, when I see the scene on its feet, in the space, maybe I decide after all I need a big wide, I want to see the horizon, and they say no, no, get tight, get close, see the blood spurt, the teeth, the rubber tires, like we planned, and I say, yes, yes, of course, *obvio*, but can we see the sky as well? Can we widen out as well as push in? What if I want to see more, not less? Last week, there was a kid in a field watching us, and he was just watching, not moving in the grass.

'Quick,' I said, 'throw up a lens, and let's grab it,' but they wouldn't let me. Everything must be known. There is nothing left to chance. I tell them, you will be sad, you will be sorry when you see this thing we are making. It will be just like all the other ones."

In her passion, her English becomes less fluent. He chides her, laughing.

"And you're surprised that the producers aren't behaving like artists? Come on. This isn't your first rodeo."

"No, it's not. Of course, the fight is always the same, always. But this is different. I come from a *machista* country, but I see it is much worse what your women are dealing with in America. Because here in Argentina, they either give you control or they don't, but our women here are not puppets. We are ferocious. Jaguars. We let our women become president in this country. But with this movie I have only the illusion of control. I am the director, but only because they will like to say to the press that a woman made this movie. These producers, they don't say it, but they want me to feel grateful for this opportunity. And I am, but they are also lucky to have me. You Americans, you keep your women prisoners, but you tell them they are free."

She finishes her wine.

"Let's watch."

They sit side by side on the sofa in the dark, twirling spaghettini. The movie is subtitled, written and shot by a woman, set in a tiny town in the southernmost tip of Argentina. Hector cannot concentrate. The director's feet are tucked beneath her, her knees just barely grazing the side of his thigh. She sits quite still, not moving, as though it were her first time seeing the film. Annie does not sit like this. She is always hovering, coming in and out, forgetting something. It drives him insane. But this woman's stillness is equally unnerving. He has no idea what is happening either in the movie or in this room. He has lost the plot. He wonders what will happen when the movie ends, whether he will, after all, hold her slender, tanned, naked body against his own, or whether he will ride the elevator back down to the street, clothes and integrity intact. He wonders how he has found himself—no, put himself—in this situation. He has done so well, avoiding these moments. He has no desire for them, really, for other women.

Hector does not look elsewhere because he is still possessed by his wife. She is his and yet not quite utterly. She is unknowable to him in ways he prefers not to enumerate to himself. She is always just slightly out of reach. In recent years she has replaced her aloofness with busyness but he suspects they are branches of the same tree. A part of her is observing, from a distance, not always quite there with them in the room. There have been many months in their marriage when she held herself utterly apart from him, remote and unreachable. There were days after Vita's birth when she could not even account for her time. Then there were the days when she sat in the tub and told him all the local gossip as he came and went across the bathroom. Nights when he looked at her from across a noisy candlelit table or crowded room and he felt his stomach clench knowing that she was his, that at the end of the night, she would go home with him. She is mysterious to him, his own wife, and in her secrecy lies the key to his own enthrallment.

The movie ends. A light flickers on overhead. The director stretches.

"So?"

"It was great. Beautifully shot."

"She is one of my heroes, this woman."

"I can see why."

She studies him for a moment. He wonders if she knows he didn't follow a word. She stands up, smooths her dress.

"I have to work. Are we fucking or no?"

He blinks.

"Uh . . ."

She laughs.

"I'm kidding. But not about the work."

She walks over to the entryway. He gets to his feet.

"Thank you for a lovely evening."

She nods, gracious, holding open the door.

"Of course."

He hears her close and bolt her front door as the elevator slides shut and drops him down to the street. He feels wrong-footed. Deflated.

Like he has both succeeded and failed.

CHAPTER 26

WEEKS PASS. ANNIE LETS THE CHILDREN ANSWER HECTOR'S CALLS. She drives miles to estate sales, bids half-heartedly on items she does not need and cannot afford, drives home with a truckful of old mirrors, weathered copper pans, ornamental urns. She eats when she remembers to. She snaps at the children, apologizes, snaps again. She forgets appointments, reschedules, forgets them again. She wonders what is happening to her. She wonders if she has ever been happy. She wonders if she dreamt it all, her astonishing nakedness on the kitchen floor. She is angry, always. She does not blame Thierry for her rage. This darkness is her fault, hers and Hector's. She empties the dishwasher, her enemy. There is no wine in the house because she has drunk it all. She buys a case. She books their flights to Argentina. She has left it so late that they are preposterously, laughably expensive. She tells Hector off-handedly, already resigned to his outrage.

"I told you not to leave it so late. Fuck. Alright. It's done. You'll love it here. So will the kids."

She does not want to go. She does not want to do anything but sleep. She contemplates sending the children to visit their father on their own but knows she cannot. She deletes Thierry from her phone but it is pointless because she has already memorized his number. Overhearing Remy in the back of the car telling Jackson he can't play video games because he has French this afternoon, she feels a stab of anger. She smashes a bowl of rice on the table and downs a glass of wine. At bedtime Vita shuts herself in her room with a derisive click.

Annie tries to lie down beside her son, to take refuge in his softness. He kisses her, then turns his back. She rises, leaves his room.

She must do better. This morning she saw Jackson flinch as she told him to pick up his backpack, caught Vita laying a protective hand on his shoulder. This is all wrong, she thinks. They should not startle when I speak. I am supposed to protect them from the world, not they protect each other from me. She rifles through the drawers of Hector's bedside table, searching for a pill that will drown her shame with sleep. She lies in bed, waiting for liberation, rehearsing Thierry's hands on her, the weight of him, the smell. She plays with forbidden worlds, one where they share a bed and he brings her coffee and there is no one to get up for or make food for or drive anywhere. The illicitness of this fantasy is so much more treacherous than the sharing of her body.

She gropes for her phone in the dark, finds a podcast to drown out her thoughts. The host of a news review show tells a story about a group of tourists on a guided tour bus in Iceland who got off at a rest stop to stretch their legs and take in the scenery. One female traveler decided to change her clothes before getting back on the bus. When it was time to leave, the passengers boarded the bus, and one of them alerted the driver that they were missing a passenger—a woman in black who had been sitting by the window. The driver agreed to wait, and they all sat on the bus, patiently awaiting this woman's return. Eventually, when she did not appear, they decided to get out and search for her. The female traveler joined in the search. Local police were summoned, the fire department deployed, all beginning an increasingly frantic search for a missing woman in a black jacket. It was many, many hours before the female traveler realized that she was, in fact, the person for whom they were searching. She informed the authorities, and the search was called off. The host laughs as he tells the story.

Annie is wide awake now. She pictures this woman, trudging through the tundra, searching for the missing tourist. She wonders how long it took her to realize her mistake. She wonders how long it took her to admit to it. Did she hesitate, Annie wonders, did she for one wild moment wonder what would happen if she never owned her mistake but allowed that other self to vanish into that treeless horizon? Did she, for a moment, hover on the threshold of becoming someone new, someone naked, reborn, free?

Annie stares at the darkness. She, too, is walking in the wrong direction, knowing full well that she is the one who is missing.

CHAPTER 27

IT IS FALL IN BUENOS AIRES. THE DAYS ARE YELLOW AND WARM, THE evenings crisp and cloudless. From their high-rise hotel Annie can see the wide brown river, like a vast muddied whale plowing its way to the ocean, Uruguay invisible on its far bank. She would like to lie on her side on the bed and just watch long tankers slide slowly up and down it like children's toys. But she cannot. Hector is working and the children want to go out. Jackson immediately loves the city, the mayhem of traffic, the ubiquity of ice cream, the friendliness of every waiter. He watches a low-slung yellow sports car explode through a city park.

"Let's move here, Mom!"

Vita is watchful but engaged. She likes the babies with their pierced ears, the creamy Art Nouveau buildings, the haughty girls and the way the men look at them. She takes photographs everywhere, of the multicolored houses stacked like bright cardboard boxes in the old port, the swaying string lights and the tourist-drenched tango dancers, the silent ombu trees. She visits Evita's grave with quiet solemnity and returns the next day, this time with flowers. The children squabble incessantly. The age gap makes it impossible to find activities that will entertain them both and Annie is exhausted from curating their days. Vita wants to wander the city alone, which she is too young for. Jackson wants to squat on his haunches in the Ferrari showroom that is across from the hotel. Annie shuttles between them both, following Vita at a discreet distance along cobbled streets buckled with erupting pipes, Jackson whining beside her, or waiting outside glittering car showrooms, watching the city pass her by, Vita staring balefully at her phone as Jackson sits behind the wheel of yet another parked sports car. Annie is surprised by how often she wishes she could call her mother. Her phone buzzes constantly. It is never Thierry.

They live on gelato and steak. Vita declares herself a vegetarian. They live on pasta and *dulce de leche*. The hotel rents bicycles but the streets are too dangerous to ride them in. The sidewalks are brown with fallen leaves and pulverized jacaranda blossoms. The walls are high and elegant or tumbled and gashed with graffiti. The city pulses with exhaust fumes and catcalls. There are cigarettes and beautiful women everywhere.

Hector is expansive with relief and reunion. He wrestles his son and squeezes his daughter and reaches for Annie with affection. She struggles not to recoil. She undresses in the bathroom, feigns sleep when he returns from filming, and rises early to breakfast with the kids. One evening, pulling his T-shirt over his head, he asks her what is wrong. His torso is sleek, tanned, sculpted for the screen; it repels her.

"Nothing."

"You seem pissed at everything. The kids. Me. All of it. What's going on?"

"Nothing."

She sounds sullen, she knows it. She feels caught out but also unable to articulate her emptiness. She tries.

"It's hard."

He looks surprised.

"Being here? I'm off all next week. Or do you mean at home?"

She feels ambushed by tears. She turns her face away. He puts a hand on her shoulder.

"Is it your mom? I'm sorry, my love."

She lets him comfort her. She feels both self-righteous and immolated with self-loathing. She lies down, hating everything.

They drive out to an estancia for the weekend. Hector fights off swerving cars that obey no discernible traffic laws while Annie tries to map read. Jackson occasionally asks about a word in his audiobook ("what's *comatose*?"); Vita stares rigid and unflinching out the window.

No one has been on speaking terms since early this morning, when Jackson burst sobbing into their room, a raised scratch mark livid across his skinny bare chest. Tiny crests of blood were forming.

"Vita scratched me! I'm bleeding! She scratched me with her nails!"

Hector scooted him to the bathroom to clean it up while Annie swept in to investigate. She found an indignant Vita in a baggy T-shirt, coiled by the window, clutching her phone to her chest.

"Jackson was looking at my texts. He was scrolling through my messages."

"That's no reason to scratch . . ."

"I woke up, and he was reading my messages!"

Jackson shrieked from the adjoining room.

"I was not! Anyway, you shouldn't write stuff you don't want people to see! She's got pictures of her boobs on there, Mom!"

"What?!"

"Bullshit, Jackson!"

"Vita, watch your language. What's he talking about?"

"He's lying!"

"I am not!"

"Vee, I need to see your phone."

"This is such double standards, Mom! You lose your mind if we go near your phone!"

"I don't know what you're talking about. I don't. And even if I do, I'm an adult." Vita ran into the bathroom and locked herself in. Annie banged on the door.

"Vita, come out and let me see your phone."

Jackson ran back into the room.

"She's gonna delete it all, Mom, but I saw it. There was, like, a whole bunch of boobs on her camera roll."

Annie banged harder on the door.

"Vita! Come out right now!"

Hector appeared behind her.

"Alright, alright, no need to kick it down. Vita, come out please."

Silence.

It took an hour for Vita to come out and thrust her phone at her mother, during which time Hector and Annie fought furiously in the other room. Hector was appalled at the very idea of his daughter's selfies, while Annie found herself irately defending Vita, saying it was normal, if not exactly desirable, to look for external validation.

"So, you think we should let her send naked images of herself into the world?"

"Of course I don't, and she didn't send them to anyone, she just took some photos of herself."

"Trust me, she was about to send them to someone."

"But she didn't."

Hector muttered something about things like this not happening on his watch and she told him he was welcome to come home whenever he liked and resume "his watch."

They waited in silence for the valet to bring their car around, Jackson enveloped in his headphones, Vita icy with indifference.

They are still not speaking by the time they bump down a sandy track and sweep into an oval driveway that skirts a colonnaded white house. Landscaped gardens wait patiently for someone to admire them. Hector filmed here a few weeks ago and charmed an invitation out of the owner, who now stands on the porch, tanned as a satchel, luminous in a sky-blue shirt, arms outstretched, hair oiled, an Argentine Gatsby, waiting to greet them.

"*Bienvenidos!* Welcome, my friends!"

His English is perfect, his accent delightful. They unfurl from the car, grateful to be apart. A peacock stalks up to inspect them, turns tail, disappointed, dragging its skirts. The owner pulls Annie into his scented chest, throws a casual linen arm around Jackson. His suede moccasins make no sound as he ushers them into the cool, quiet hallway. Jackson's headphones slip onto his shoulders as he turns around to take in the grand entry hall, the faded tapestries, the worn marble floors. Even Vita is awed. Jackson's eyes widen as an elderly maid in a frilled white apron reaches to take his stained hoodie. He clutches it to his chest, whispers to Annie.

"Is this his actual house?"

They drink tea from fragile porcelain cups, delicate as the tiny butter cookies that emerge plated and still warm from a swinging kitchen door. The maid, it appears, is partially deaf; the owner raises his voice to ask her for more hot water. She nods, wordless, returns to the kitchen. With the casual ease of generational wealth, he tells Annie that the maid, like him, was born on the property. He tells her about his great-great-grandfather who, fresh off the boat from Bilbao, made his first fortune by selling corrugated iron, then invested his money in the railroads that were beginning to thread this vast country. With his second fortune he built this house.

The children, bored, drift away into unseen rooms. Hector, who heard it all on his last visit, has disappeared upstairs with the bags. Annie longs to escape but is trapped, deadened by politeness. Vita, mercifully, appears in the doorway.

"Mom, you need to see this."

Annie makes her excuses, follows her daughter, grateful for the rescue. She wonders if this means she is forgiven. There is more to say, but it can wait. At least they are speaking. She rubs her upper arms for warmth. She wonders what it costs to heat this place, or if they even do. She follows her daughter down a long corridor.

The library is paneled in golden oak, lined with leather-bound, gold-embossed books from the floor to the high ceiling. A wheeled ladder surveys the upper stacks. The shutters are half closed in here, the filtered light striping the leather armchairs. Dust dances in strips of sunlight and settles across the saddle sofas worn supple and bowed with use. A delicate writing desk sits in one window, surveying the lawn. The room smells faintly of dying flowers. The rugs are French, heavy and good. Vita flops down on the couch.

"This place is insane."

On the low coffee table sits a silver cigarette box. She flips it open with her toe. It is packed with cigarettes, neatly stacked, ready for a party. Beside it a silver cigarette lighter, shaped like a shell, heavy as a fist. Stacks of photo books, ringed with glass stains, on landscaping, architecture, art, fashion. Vita tries to open one, but the pages are stuck together with something sticky.

Annie runs her hand along the bookcases, surprised to find how many volumes are written in English. She pulls one off the shelf. The pages are yellow and stiff, the spine uncracked. She goes over to the writing desk, which houses a collection of silver photo frames. Vita joins her. Elegant women step out of fast cars, tousled men in grass-stained white pants lean expensively on sweating ponies, mallets propped beneath their flinty forearms. Annie raises an eyebrow.

"They don't look like a bunch of readers, do they?"

Vita laughs.

Annie's phone buzzes, she answers without looking. A man speaks.

"Annie."

She does not move.

He says her name again. Vita glances over. Annie takes a step toward the window.

"It's Thierry."

"Hi."

"I...where are you? Are you back in Australia?"

"I'm in Argentina."

"Oh. Right. Sorry. I never heard from you. I wanted to...I wondered if everything was okay..."

"Everything's great. I'll call you once we're home."

She hangs up. The library seems brighter. She feels giddy, absurdly animated. She smiles at Vita.

"Patti. She forgot I was here."

She takes Vita's hand and kisses it.

"I love you, Vee."

Vita looks at her with surprise. She gives her mother a brief hug. Annie's eyes fill. She has not held her daughter's slender body in a while.

That night, Annie is electric, beautiful. She wears a white dress and a sweater of Hector's slung over her shoulders. She is funny, charming more stories out of their host, who leans in to refill her glass. Vita teaches Jackson backgammon. Hector relaxes, appreciative. Annie is proud of her family. She is her best self. Her arms are slim, chiming with silver bracelets, her lips are flecked with red wine.

The next morning Annie wakes early. She is impatient for the day to begin, as though urgency will bring her closer to returning home. She dresses quietly, slips downstairs. She finds breakfast laid out on a white cloth, thick black coffee and steaming hot milk in silver thermoses. Their host, slick from the stables, greets her, offers to show her the grounds. Here are the guest cottages, there is the vast chilly swimming pool, here are more peacocks, horses, dogs. Suddenly there is a church, flanked by twisted cypress trees, exquisite, ornate, a cuckoo clock nestling in the grass. Bosky ivy drapes the narthex.

"You have your own church?"

He shrugs.

"A chapel. We don't use it anymore. Except for weddings."

"But not yours."

"No, no, I never married."

"Why not?"

He laughs, his eyes dancing.

"In Spanish, we have the same word for handcuffs as we have for wife. *Esposas*, we call them."

"And what do you call husbands?"

"*Maridos*. Married men."

"Got it. And all this? Who do you share it with?"

He shrugs.

"Myself. My friends. I entertain. I am not lonely."

"What will happen to this place?"

"My sister's children will inherit it one day. There are six of them; they will share it."

He looks at her.

"It is okay, you know, to be alone."

The last few days of the trip pass peacefully. Annie resolves to enjoy everything. They ride horses, swim, play tennis on a buckled court, croquet on the bumpy lawn with worn mallets. On the terrace, the elderly maid lays out tea, curled toast in linen-lined baskets, homemade jam in chipped porcelain jars with silver spoons. The owner and Hector compare notes on the expense of property upkeep. The days dissolve into one another. The city recedes, fades into memory. The owner tells impossibly lavish stories of a faded past. It is like living in a Chekhov play, says Hector, clapping his hands in delight. Annie is sick of Chekhov, but even this does not bother her.

Eventually Hector is called to work and they return to the city. On their last day they visit him on set. The movie star smiles benignly at the children, a pope bestowing indulgences. She touches Jackson's hair, lays a hand on Vita's cheek. "So beautiful."

She murmurs herself back to her trailer. They do not see her again. The female director is polite but barely lifts her gaze from the bank of monitors. The producers buzz her like wasps. The children sit with headphones, snapping bubblegum that the movie star's makeup artist has palmed them.

That night, Annie and Hector are in the hotel bathroom. She packs her toiletry bag, he flosses his teeth. She screws the lid onto her face cream.

"Does she have a crush on you?"

"Who?"

"Your director."

"No. Why do you ask?"

"I wondered. She wasn't that friendly."

"Are you jealous?"

She laughs.

"No."

She zips the bag, taps him gently on the shoulder as she passes by. They have sex that night, silent, in the dark. She keeps her eyes closed throughout.

They part at the airport. She kisses Hector quickly while he hugs the children.

"See you in a month."

They stare in the dark at flickering screens in the airplane until they reach New York, then stumble into the dark house, reviving their former personalities now that they are home. Jackson forgets the wide avenues zigzagged with fast cars as soon as he sees his hermit crabs; Vita sighs with relief as she closes the door to her own bedroom, the first privacy she's had in weeks. Annie waits until the children are asleep, and then she texts Thierry. It feels like the few times she took cocaine with Candace, the mounting excitement, the impatience of having it near, the animal longing for another snort. She savors the moment of power as she types the message she has spent days crafting, shudders with the comedown the moment she has sent it. The rush is over. She switches off her phone.

CHAPTER 28

THEY LIE NAKED, SPRAWLED ON HER LIVING ROOM FLOOR. THE FIREplace is dull with ash. Annie's feet rest between his, her legs draped over his thighs. He runs his hand across her hair.

"It is nice to see you."

"It is nice to be seen."

He runs his hands across her waist, gently cups her buttocks. She feels smaller than when he saw her last. Slighter. Her legs are smooth, her hair glossy. She has prepared herself for him. He is stirred by this. He had felt nervous on the drive over, uncertain. Apprehensive in a way he was not used to.

"How was the trip?"

"Good. Weird. It's a beautiful country. I was glad to come home. But it was good for the kids to see their dad."

"Is he... is your husband, is he down with this?"

She laughs.

"'Down with this'? No. He's not. He doesn't know. We're not like that."

"I didn't know whether you had an arrangement or something... So, he... doesn't have anyone...?"

"No. Not that I know of. I mean, he's a flirt. Or at least everyone flirts with him. Men and women. They can't help themselves, it's almost rude not to. But I think that does it for Hector."

Thierry feels a spur of jealousy, a new sensation.

"He's never?"

She reflects. She has never worried about Hector's fidelity. She knows he loves her, but she also knows that what he really loves is his life, the stability of it, his place in it. It is not that she presumes his monogamy but rather his love of the predictable. Perhaps he has strayed, perhaps, but her instincts tell her that he would have no appetite for the work involved, for the mysterious contours of an unfamiliar person, for the precariousness of a fledgling intimacy. No. She knows. He has not strayed. She flashes for a moment on that director, her headphones pulled over her ears, not looking at Annie, at the children.

"I don't think so."

She shifts her weight, rolls onto her back. Her breasts are heavy, her stomach creased. She looks magnificent, open.

"What about you? Are you with anyone?"

He shakes his head.

"I like my freedom."

He stares at the ceiling.

"I'm not great at meeting other people's expectations."

She sighs.

"Oh God, is anyone?"

CHAPTER 29

SNAP. VITA TAKES PHOTOGRAPHS ON THE EDGE OF THE SCHOOL SOCcer pitch. Boys strip off their tracksuits, stretch their hamstrings. They look ridiculous, white mice in shorts. Snap. Martin throws his head back, laughing with some other kid. Snap. She hates him. Vita regrets offering to be school photographer. She only volunteered for the job so she could keep an eye on Martin. She is supposed to be gathering images for the yearbook. In reality, she has four hundred photos of him on the soccer pitch. It is an odd mixture of pleasure and pain to be near him. Zoe says a girl in their grade, Kylie, has been cutting her arms, something Vita does not understand, but she wonders if maybe this is what Kylie is seeking, this serrated edge of agony and anticipation. Martin has not looked her way once since she let him put his hand up her skirt at the welcome-back pizza party. Half the girls in her year have slept with a boy already. Vita's virginity is an iron padlock around her waist that clinks as she walks the school corridors. There is no one to confide in since Zoe, who is not a slut, just always ahead of the game, lost hers last year to some kid at sleepaway camp. Zoe was offhand about it, didn't seem to want to discuss it much. Vita yawns. She has not been sleeping well, not since Zoe told her she is leaving. Her father is moving back to the city, wants the children to move closer so he can still see them regularly. Zoe shrugged, resigned, when she told Vita.

"Divorce sucks."

Vita is gutted. She cannot imagine school without her. Everyone except Zoe is trivial. Vita has not even told her mother about her friend's imminent departure because her mother is barely home these days. And even when she is home, she is not really there; she's on her phone or locked inside herself. In some ways Annie's distraction is preferable since Vita prefers to live without interference. She worries about Jackson though. Lately her mother has been forgetting to feed them. Yesterday she forgot to pick them up from school. She arrived an hour late, flushed and full of excuses, claiming traffic, but there is no traffic in the countryside: She just forgot them. Vita wishes her father would come home so things would run smoothly again. It feels like he's been gone a year. Martin turns, glances up at her. Snap.

Jackson waits to feel the teacher standing behind him, then moves his rook. He likes it when she watches him. She pulls up a stool. He waits for the other kid to move. Chess club is his favorite hour of the week. He wonders if his mother will be on time today. In his pocket, Jackson rubs his thumb over the tip of the paper knife. He brought it to school to show Luke, who will love the way it pops out of the handle. Click. But Luke isn't at school today so it will have to wait.

Click. He likes the sound it makes. So satisfying. His mom said it was his grandpa's. She never talks about him, so Jackson doesn't know much, but he's pretty sure he was in the war and this was part of his uniform or something. That's what he's telling Luke, anyway. The knife's not that sharp. But it looks it. Click.

CHAPTER 30

ANNIE FEELS THIN AS AN OLD QUILT. HER WATCH DANGLES FROM her wrist. She looks at a set of dining room chairs but her heart is not in it. Her phone sits heavy and silent in her pocket. He is supposed to call her when he finishes his shift. She is supposed to be buying for a new client, a referral from Candace (Candace, she owes her a call, many calls, but she does not want to speak to her, to anyone): some couple who have moved into a beautiful Georgian estate near the river and need help finding "pieces." They have nothing but money. She will furnish them with taste. The store owner, a sour man in a lumpy cardigan, shows her a pair of armchairs. She is naked on all fours on her kitchen floor, Thierry moving behind her, holding her waist, toast crumbs graveled into her knees. She nods, barely listening to the store owner as he tells her the provenance and, finally, the price. She is everywhere and nowhere, unless she is with him. She forgets everything: to return calls, to reply to emails, to open the mail. She feels no compunction about any of it. Her life seems absurd, irrelevant, the tasks arbitrary, the agreements preposterous. Nothing matters. Her phone rings. She steps outside, smiling.

"Annie."

"Oh, it's you."

"Christ, you're hard to get hold of. Everything okay? Kids alright? Vee left me a message last night saying you'd left them at school, forgotten to pick them up or something?"

"She is such a drama queen. I was with clients, and it went late. No child left behind."

"My mom said she's left you messages. They want to come and stay, see the kids."

"Oh God. Does she have to?"

"I thought it might help. With pickup, driving? I thought you could use a hand."

"Your mother doesn't count as help. Your mother coming is like me losing a hand. Tell her I don't need any help."

She is distracted by a ping on her phone.

"I have to go."

"Will you call her?"

She has already gone.

"Le doigt."

"Le doigt."

"La main."

"La main."

"Les bras."

"Les bras."

"Les seins."

Silence. Lips on breasts. Tongue, teeth, sweat.

"L'estomac."

"L'estomac. I hate my accent."

"It's sexy."

"It is not."

"Some French people actually like French with an American accent."

"Nobody likes French with an Australian one. That's just weird."

"I think it's sexy."

"Now you're sweet-talking me."

"So?"

"Makes me feel old. Like you're doing me a favor. Taking care of an old lady."

"You know my roommate works in a retirement home."

"That's quite the pivot."

"I'm saying I know what it looks like to take care of old people. And it doesn't look like this."

Laughter. Silence.

Lips, tongue, thighs.

"I have to go."

"Not yet."

Sweat, fingers, breath.

"I'll be late for my shift."

Tongue, thighs, lips.

"Don't go."

"I must."

Silence.

"Again."

CHAPTER 31

HECTOR IS LONELY. HE HAS EXHAUSTED ALL THE EXHIBITIONS THERE are to see in this city, which feels small and provincial now and not as cosmopolitan as it once did. The director has not invited him to dinner again, nor knocked at his trailer. There is a splinter of coolness between them since his family visited that he wonders if he is inventing but suspects he is not. She is running a movie, he tells himself. The producers are killing her by inches. The film keeps running into delays; he has more days off than he knows what to do with. The production office sounds harried whenever he calls to ask for an update. But he is only a few weeks from being done now. He rereads *The Cherry Orchard* but it brings no comfort. He lies in bed, watching the news and documentaries about serial killers. He works out every day for a couple of focused hours.

Hector likes to get to the gym early. He is irritated to find someone already there; at this hour he usually has the place to himself. The man on the running machine seems familiar. Hector stretches his hamstrings, surreptitiously checking him out. The man's gray hair is scraped high into a top knot, below which he wears huge padded headphones. He walks at a steep incline, gripping the running machine with leather-braceleted arms. He turns to wipe his face on a towel and Hector realizes who it is. It is a face he has seen on album covers, cassette boxes, magazine spreads; a voice he has listened to since he was a teenager. Hector surreptitiously looks him up on his phone. The rock star is on the South American leg of his world tour. He is only eighteen years older than Hector but looks a century more. He strides up the steep hill with energy and yet there is a tender frailty to his body.

Hector joins him on the neighboring machine and they nod at each other briefly in the way of men at the gym. The man's face looks like a fallen soufflé. Hector wonders for a fleeting moment if the rock star has recognized him.

Hector's is the kind of face people know they know but can never quite place. He and Annie went to see a play in the city a few years back, and while she was in the restroom a Japanese couple approached him tentatively. The woman held up her camera questioningly. He smiled, broad, dazzling, threw his arm around her husband and posed. She hesitated, then took a picture. The woman held the camera out again.

"Now take picture of us?"

He flushed, laughed, and took a photograph of the couple just as Annie returned. Hector tells this story everywhere, always quick to laugh at himself before anyone else can.

He tells Annie about seeing the rock star when they speak that evening. She sounds unimpressed.

"Christ, is he still alive?"

Hector is surprised when, sitting at the hotel bar later that night, eating olives, reading the short stories, he looks up and finds the barman sliding a martini in front of him.

"Oh, I didn't . . ."

The barman nods to the other end of the bar, where the rock star raises his glass in salutation.

"Burden of fuckin' proof, man."

Hector is stunned. This is (almost) the catchphrase from the legal show he starred in years ago, back when Vita was born. It seems impossible that he is hearing it spoken in the gravelly Cockney tones of a man whom he, Hector, has grown up worshipping. The rock star shambles over with his glass.

"Fuckin' loved that show."

Hector shakes his head, eyes wide.

"You watched it?"

"Every single episode."

They talk for three hours. The rock star has eyes like a hamster, black beads that glint from within the deep recesses of his face. He tells stories from the road, of the good old days, of drugs and booze and his three ex-wives and four estranged children, of the new girlfriend awaiting him in Rio. He laughs often, listens never. His wrists are slender as a woman's, his hand trembles slightly as he sets his glass of ginger beer ("I quit the hard stuff after the last heart attack") on the table. His tone is confiding, conspiratorial: He assumes an immediate intimacy with Hector, addresses him as a fellow adventurer, a lover of romance and excess. Hector does not disabuse him but nods knowingly, smiling encouragement, committing every moment to memory, already dining out on this encounter for years to come. At ten thirty the rock star glances at his phone.

"Bedtime. You should come to the show. Ellie will leave you a ticket at the front desk."

"That sounds amazing. Thank you for the drink. And for the stories."

"I owe you, man. Life on the road gets lonely. You kept me company in a hundred fuckin' hotel rooms."

Hector rides the mirrored elevator back up to his hotel room. He is moved, oddly proud, that he should have touched this icon's life. That legal show was a job he took as a concession to fatherhood. It shot twenty-two episodes a year in a studio in the Valley eighteen minutes from his front door. It was the opposite of being a rock star. A network show is the actor's version of settling down. It is a way of staying in one place with the family while making steady money. For Hector it managed to be simultaneously a coup and the death of his movie career. He told himself it was worth it. While he missed the intensity of moviemaking, he liked the domesticity of television, the steady metronome it lent to life. He liked coming home to his family in the evenings. He waited to hear if the show was renewed every year, dreading the loss of income and the free fall of unemployment. Unemployment at his age felt undignified. He talked about doing a movie while on hiatus between seasons, but never did. He steered clear of the competitive gossip of the cast, hoping to position himself above the fray, but instead often found himself lonely, isolated, and ill at ease. He talked about directing an episode, spent time at the monitors chatting with the visiting directors about camera angles and lens sizes. The directors were encouraging, generous, the producers open to the idea. But a director's hours are grueling, and if he was serious about directing, he was required to shadow them all, to attend every production meeting, location scout, casting call. This unpaid time was an internship, spent watching and learning. It meant moving from actor to audience. Hector did not enjoy being in the audience because in his heart, he did not enjoy learning. He disliked feeling lesser than whoever was teaching him. He liked the unassailable authority of the actor's role, whose mastery of the character was rarely questioned. He liked the idea of directing, or rather the idea of having directed. He was not, in truth, suited to the discipline of marshaling other people and their ideas, was not patient enough to endure the tedium of meetings, nor adept at braiding the needs and desires of others into a single vision of his own. In theory, Hector could envisage himself in a production meeting, nodding thoughtfully while people pitched him ideas and an assistant handed him an espresso, but privately he knew he was not cut out for this kind of collaboration. He liked his own way and struggled to even pretend to listen to another's point of view. It was this, although he only hazily apprehended it, that made him only a mediocre actor. A serviceable one, employable, reliable. But never mesmerizing. Because he did not listen. And because he could not listen, he could not let himself be affected by what he heard. He could only imitate. There were no surprises in Hector's work, no unexpected curves revealing unlooked-for vistas. He was excellent at not letting his feelings get the better of him because he was not really on listening terms with his quieter, more vulnerable self. Hector gained a snake charmer's reputation for being skilled with older actresses; his silky ways were soothing to their brittle entitlement. He attended the premieres of his more successful friends, smiling bravely on red carpets that Annie refused to patronize. It was easier without her, but he found he missed her and her all-but-imperceptibly-raised eyebrow.

When Annie pitched leaving the city, Hector had been surprised by how open to the idea he was. He realized he had long exhausted the possibilities of the legal show. The guest stars got the good plotlines, did all the real acting. He was the background. He felt invisible to all, not least his wife, who had not watched the show for years. He returned late from set one night and, finding himself unable to sleep, had channel-surfed and stumbled on a rerun of a past season. He watched it, appalled. It managed to be both banal and preposterous. He barely remembered filming it. He poured himself a stiff drink and forced himself to keep watching. He had not watched his own work for years, he realized, and now he found himself looking at a man he recognized but did not know. He saw jowls and furrows and a permanently creased brow. He saw a limited range of overwrought responses. He saw a man who was better than the role he was playing. It was time for a change. Annie was right. He would move to rural Connecticut, repair outbuildings, grow calluses, drink homemade wine with a local farmer. He would learn about diesel and weed killer and squirrels. He would feel restored, in some inchoate way, to his virility. There was a dignity to hard labor that was elusive on a television set, where everyone handed you everything. It was easy to become effete. He would take the early train into the city for meetings, do a play again, perhaps make a well-written low-budget independent movie and win a minor award for his role. He would become interesting again, to himself and to the world.

Hector lets himself into his room, adjusts the air-conditioning, kicks off his shoes. He misses his home. He finds himself even missing the show, or rather not the show but the feeling of belonging. He is adrift on this movie. There is no camaraderie. He sighs. He will be with his family soon. That is where he truly belongs. Not in a folding chair with his name on it.

Two nights later Hector stands in a box overlooking thirty thousand screaming fans and a strutting silhouette on a white stage. He is surrounded by Argentine celebrities: a soccer star whose bullet head he vaguely recognizes and a model he sees on the back of every bus. All the men are his age, the women look barely older than Vita. Their bodies nod and sway like the silken tails of ponies. They keep their eyes on their men. The rock star is projected high above them all, vast and pixelated, and is just a few hundred feet away, a tiny human in black leather with a guitar. He is as animated as a puppet. He owns the stage like no actor Hector has ever seen. The little man engulfs them with his presence. Theater does not allow for this kind of possession. He struts, he holds the mic like a cock he is trying not to swallow. The crowd shrieks, groans, embraces him. He loves them. He is unearthly, a messiah, a gift to them. They are his congregation; this is his church.

He wheedles, seduces, demands their love. It is ecstatic, exhausting, immense. The vast stadium roars, the place is lit with the little screens of thirty thousand cell phones and the flames of ten thousand illegal lighters. The rock star unleashes his most famous anthem and they rise as one, radiating love, delight. One of the ponytails flickers Hector a smile, shouts something at him in Spanish, and he nods, not understanding a word, but beaming, bouncing, drenched in the music. He is happier than he has been in months, years probably. He undoes one more button of his linen shirt.

Backstage, the show over, Hector and a handful of others from the VIP box are escorted through a series of underground tunnels to a large dressing room. Hector is keen to go home, he is tired, he films the next day, but he does not want to appear ungrateful. They all wait, not quite together, not quite apart, no longer united by the glorious democracy of sound but by the uneasy competitiveness of adjacency to fame. The men seem unused to paying court, while the women patiently adjust their hair, eying each other or disappearing into their phones.

Bottled water and ginger beer gleam in ice buckets and a platter of untouched exotic fruits sits on the sideboard. A side door opens and the rock star emerges, downing a bottle of green juice, escorted by two men with dangling earpieces. The room ripples, applauds. He looks glitteringly tired, desiccated, smaller than ever. He raises his hands in greeting. People course toward him and he presses their hands like a politician, always moving through the room. His hair is wet, he has already showered, his eyes are darting, connecting. Hector hovers near the back and the rock star spots him, heads over to him.

"Whadja think?"

Hector stammers.

"It was... incredible, extraordinary... your energy is..."

"Yeah, but what about my pipes? They gave out in the last half. You guys sang the last songs for me. Was I okay?"

Hector is astonished that the rock star cares what he thinks, that he is still looking for affirmation after all that oceanic love. It flashes across his brain that there is no dignity in this, that he must not end up like this, a parched lizard craving water.

"You were amazing, man. It was a privilege to be here. Thank you."

The rock star clamps Hector's triceps with a fierce grip and then is gone.

Hector walks through the city back to the hotel. The streets are pulsing, thronging with concertgoers singing, drinking, tugging at one another's hoodies, leaping on each other's shoulders. He is alone in their midst. He almost collides with a couple who stop without warning to wrap themselves around each other's faces and kiss in the middle of the street. He veers around them and turns back to glimpse their young bodies, their oblivion to the world around them. He has a sudden memory of himself and Annie on an early date on a sheltered beach in Malibu, beneath a tangle of bougainvillea, of their sandy bodies and salt and her beautiful mouth beneath his and the feeling that nothing, nothing would ever be as exactly right as this woman again. He had known it when he kissed her that day, and he had felt her knowing it too. They had felt inevitable.

He wants to share this with her, this moment, this memory, this concert, this happiness. He pulls out his phone, dials. Her phone is off. He hesitates, readying to leave a message, and is jostled by a passing group of tumbling, laughing teenagers. Irritation flickers. The moment is gone. He hangs up. He will tell her in the morning.

CHAPTER 32

SUMMER NUDGES THE TREES. RICH LIGHT FLOODS THE TRUCK. THE sweet smell of meadow grass rushes through the open windows. Thierry is driving. He lights a joint and hands it to her. She takes it, holds the smoke in her mouth, her lungs, and closes her eyes. She has not been high in years. She has rented them a cottage for the weekend, a few hours' drive away. She has called Hector's mother, ignored her barrage of questions, and invited her in-laws to stay, leaving Jackson to stay with them and Vita to stay with Zoe, thereby killing multiple birds with one stone. She has told everyone that she is going on a silent retreat at a nearby meditation center. The unlikely excuse offers the double convenience of allowing her to avoid answering the phone for the entire weekend and being the most unappealing destination she can think of, effectively guaranteeing that Candace will not invite herself along. She had sounded shocked when Annie told her.

"That place? What on earth are you doing that for? Are you okay? I haven't heard from you for weeks."

"I'm fine. I just need some peace and quiet."

Thierry has told Maya he is going camping for the weekend. She raised an eyebrow and zipped up her bike bag. (She recently found a pair of clean wine glasses in the drying rack and an expensive lip balm rolled beneath the bathroom sink. She suspects an older woman but, true to their unspoken agreement, says nothing.)

* * *

Annie exhales. Already she can feel the nudge of time at their back, of every hour circling away from them, a dandelion clock born on the wind. She drags on the joint again, hoping to slow everything down.

The rental is preposterously enchanting. A cottage deep in the woods, three miles off the main road, striplings thicketing the narrow driveway. A pale blue front door nooked beneath a shingled porch, and through the birches a glimmer of the reservoir. They fall into the house, suddenly shy of their confinement and astonishing intimacy. Annie unpacks the groceries they stopped for on the way, grateful for a chore. She has brought bread, nuts, wine, chocolate, raspberries, eggs, and good butter. He has brought weed, condoms, and a frisbee they will never use. They make love immediately, as though to establish themselves, in the white bedroom with its vacant fireplace, white curtains fluttering in the breeze of the ceiling fan.

They lie naked, skin cooling, recovering themselves in this new space. She feels the pull of the domestic, the impulse to plan, to feed. She sits up. He touches her back.

"Where are you going?"

This will not do. She refuses this role, here, with this man. Perhaps she will never make another meal ever again. She lies back down.

They walk into the woods, drinking wine from tumblers they find in the kitchen. They puddle under an oak tree, sun-hazed, loose-limbed, drenched in sex and wine. Annie's hair is piled high; she wears a blue dress with nothing underneath. She lays her head in her lover's lap.

"There was this tree back home. A huge twisted old blue gum tree with a hollow in its trunk. It was right at the end of my road. Everyone knew it for miles. It was old, people said hundreds of years.

We used to hide our smokes in it—once, we found a bag of weed stuffed in there. It was everyone's stash. Sam and I used it as our message board; we'd leave each other notes in there. This was before cell phones."

"Ah, the Pleistocene."

"The night before I left for New York, I went back to my parents' house. I was living with Sam, but Mum wanted to see me before I left. I cut through the park and saw someone had painted a white line the whole way around the trunk, about the height of my thigh. The paint was fresh, still tacky. It was weird. I remember thinking it must have been a city thing, to make it visible for cyclists or something. The next morning, I took the bus to the airport. There was a ton of traffic, and the bus inched past this huddle of people and all these cop cars gathered around the end of my street. People were crying. The tree was there, lying on its side, cut clean through. It was huge, lying across the edge of the park and into the street. You could see the clean yellow circle of a stump. Someone had taken a chain saw to it in the night, cut it down, and walked away. It had been windy that night, noisy, so no one heard it. No one saw it happen. No one knew anything about it until it was too late."

"Who did it? Why would someone do that?"

"Turned out to be some crazy kid, not from the area, nineteen years old. He never said why. Told the court he just needed to get it done. He said he painted that line first to make sure he held the saw steady. That paint I touched was wet. I must have walked right past him. I cried for most of that flight."

He strokes her hair.

"That's the painting in your hallway."

She glances up at him.

"Vita told me that you painted it."

"What else did she tell you?"

"She said you didn't paint anymore. She said it used to hang in her bedroom."

He does not tell her that Vita had escorted him to the door of the bathroom, reached past him to point at it, and inclined her heart-shaped face so close to his that he could smell the berry of her lip gloss.

"I didn't know she remembered that."

She fights the urge to ask if Vita flirted with him because she does not want to imagine it and because he will lie to her anyway.

"Why did you stop?"

"I don't know. Babies, travel, life. It was never...a vocation. The whole world of it was, is, so cutthroat. I didn't want it badly enough, I guess. I didn't know how to make it happen. I just gave up."

She shakes her head.

"Oh God, I think if I'm being really honest, it gave me up long before I gave it up. I'd like to blame the family, but I can't."

He finishes his wine.

"How did you meet? You and Hector?"

She looks up at him.

"Do you want to know this?"

"Would you rather I didn't?"

"We met at a party in L.A."

"What brought you east?"

"We thought life in the countryside would be better for the kids. Although now, I don't know. Vita is so restless. I wonder if she'd be happier in a city. How was it for you, growing up out here? Did you wish you were in New York?"

"The city never featured that much for me. I didn't like leaving my mom alone after my dad left. I've always thought I'd end up in a European city rather than in New York."

"A corner table at Les Deux Magots?"

"Don't mock."

"I'm not. You still get to dream when you're thirty."
"Twenty-six."
She looks at him.
"You're twenty-six?"
"You sound shocked."
"Jesus Christ."
"Is it worse than thirty?"
"Much, much worse."
She closes her eyes.
"Whatever. It's all a disaster anyway."
She sighs, rolls her neck in his lap.
"Let's just pretend you're thirty."
"Fine by me. How old are you?"
"Forty-five. When can I read something of yours?"
"Eventually."
"I won't stop asking."
She stretches, reaching for the leaves, the soft scattered sky.
"This is heaven."
He leans down and kisses her.
"You are."
He runs his fingers beneath her dress.

They do not leave the cottage again. He runs her a bath, dries her afterward, drips oil over her naked body, leaving her slick and writhing and craving satisfaction. He feeds her wine and weed and raspberries. The bedsheets are ruined but they do not care. They eat everything they brought with them, and when they wake ravenous at 3:00 a.m., they ransack the kitchen cupboards and find an old bag of rice, which Thierry steams and laces with salt and yellow butter. They eat it with spoons straight from the battered saucepan, naked at the wobbly kitchen table.

"Read me something you wrote."

He shakes his head.

"Please."

She will not be dissuaded. He sighs and fetches his laptop. He sifts and clicks for a while in silence, hesitates, and then begins to read aloud. It is a story set in London after the war, about a group of young boys who decide to pull down a bomb-damaged house in which an old man is still living. They trap him in his outhouse, and he listens to the vandals working their destruction in the dark. He is powerless to stop the awful demolition of his own home.

"'They worked with the seriousness of creators—and destruction after all is a form of creation. A kind of imagination had seen this house as it had now become.'"

She listens, astonished. She cannot believe how little she knows him. He reads quickly, simply, without affectation. Hector does not read like this. He finishes, closes the laptop. She waits.

"You wrote that?"

He shrugs, puts the laptop away.

"I...don't know what to say."

He shakes his head.

"Your tree story made me think of it."

"Come here."

She pulls herself into his lap, takes his face in her hands. He closes his eyes as she kisses his forehead, his cheeks, his eyelashes, his mouth.

Hector's mother tuts as she closes the fridge.

"Everything in here has expired. I don't know how you kids have survived. Annie didn't leave us a thing to eat. What do you usually have for dinner, Jacko?" Jackson is slumped at the kitchen table, reading. His grandmother insists on his being downstairs all the time. He is counting down the hours until his mother will be home.

"Pizza."

"We had that last night. Shall we make a cake? Where does your mother keep her cookbooks? I don't know most of these. Jacko, which one of these does your mother actually use?"

He makes no reply because he does not know and does not care. He does not want to make a cake. Bryony picks one with a famous actress who is wearing a straw hat on the cover. Hazy fields stretch out behind her and a perfect sun burnishes her perfectly flyaway hair. Bryony clucks approvingly and begins perusing the pages. A small frown creases the space between her eyebrows. Jackson glances over at her. The furrow deepens. She studies a page, then another, muttering to herself, then closes the book with a snap. She looks at him.

"I'll order pizza."

Later that night, once she has made sure Jackson is asleep, Hector's mother slaps the open cookbook down in front of her husband. Derek, who is reading an old fitness magazine of Hector's, is startled.

"What?"

She jabs at the page. It is a double-page photo of the actress-chef bicycling beside a glowing cornfield. In place of her eyes are two dark holes, and an elaborate death's head is tattooed across her glowing face. Dark and exquisitely detailed wings sprout from her back, and inky vines snap at her ankles. Derek frowns, unsure of what is expected of him. Bryony pages through the book, a prosecutor before a bewildered jury.

"Look at this. All of them. Every. Single. One."

Every photograph has been illustrated. In every photograph the actress sprouts dark horns, spidery arms, Día de los Muertos cheekbones, and skull's head teeth. The bucolic landscape grows witchy, beaded with black ink. It is a psalter, a hymnal to the chaos that lurks behind perfection.

Hector's father frowns.

"Odd."

"Not just odd, Derek. This is the occult. She's lost her mind. This is not normal, not normal at all. This retreat she's on where we can't get hold of her, it must all be part of it."

"Part of what?"

She stabs the page with her red nail.

"This is not the sign of a sound mind! This is not what you want the mother of your grandchildren to be doing with her time!"

"Isn't it just... doodling?"

Hector's mother whirls to the bookcase, grabs another stack of cookbooks, and piles them on the table. She opens one at random, flings it at him. It is a book of Christmas recipes. The pages are lumpy, rippled with ink and dried water. A photograph of a festive kitchen has been embellished with drawings of dozens of dead roosters suspended from rafters; on the next page, an entire smiling family has been tattooed with face art. A crown of thorns sits atop a swollen fruitcake; two shadowy elephants hulk unnoticed among the guests seated at a Christmas table.

"My poor, darling Hector. His wife is mentally unwell."

Annie and Thierry sleep like voles in a burrow, huddled into one another. The fan cools their bodies; the sheets grow sticky all the same. She wakes, sheets drenched around her collarbone, her breasts slick with sweat. She goes to the bathroom and wets a facecloth, drapes it over her neck. She checks her phone in the dark. There is one hissed outraged message from Jackson.

"When are you coming home? Grandma won't let me play video games in the morning. She says I can only play in the afternoon because I have to be outside all day. She doesn't understand anything, Mom! Can you tell her? When are you back?"

She comes back to bed. Thierry does not stir. He sleeps the sleep of the young: flung, expansive, a felled tree. Hector sleeps on his back, away from her, tidy as a pharaoh. She wishes she could stop comparing them. Hector will be home in a few weeks. She thinks about what she told Thierry about how they met, at how much history is compacted in those few short words. She marvels at how long it will take to tell him who she is.

CHAPTER 33

THE HILL WAS STEEP AND WINDING. A LINE OF CARS PURRED IN THE heat. Annie paid the cab at the last curve near the brow of the hill, wedged her portfolio under her arm, and walked toward the house the cabbie had pointed at. The driveway was packed with expensive cars; the lacquered black front door stood ajar, flanked by tall pots of bright white hydrangeas. Women in little heels and fluttering dresses laughed as they walked inside. She checked the address. There was no mistake. On the phone earlier that week, the producer had invited her to lunch. She'd been waiting all week for his call and had assumed she should bring her work. She had not thought she was coming to a party. Too late, she wondered how to get the taxi back. A pretty girl with bitten nails offered her a glass of something sparkling. She took it and wandered into the house, past the flickering glances of couples, the trembling jasmine, the fragile canapés. The view wrapped itself around the hills of Bel Air. Clusters of people stood in the garden, chattering, clinking. The pool was pale and dazzlingly still. She fumbled for her sunglasses, downed the sticky sweet drink, stopped a passing waiter, and asked him if he could point out her host. He shook his head politely and turned indoors. A voice behind her spoke.

"The orange one."

She turned around. The man who had spoken smiled at her, easy as breathing, and pointed out the host, a small man with feathered white hair and an improbable tan, with his arm around one woman while talking animatedly to another.

"Thank you."

"How do you know him? Or, rather, not know him?"

"I'm supposed to be working with him."

"With him?"

"For him. He looks like the kind of person you probably work *for*."

"Definitely. You're an actress?"

"God, no. I'm an artist. He needs artwork for his next movie, and a mutual friend put us in touch. He hasn't seen my paintings, and when he invited me to lunch, I thought—"

"You thought this was your audition?"

"I'm an idiot. I didn't realize *lunch* meant *lunch*."

He smiled again. Annie liked that smile. She liked how steadily he looked at her, although for a fleeting moment she wondered if he was looking at his own reflection in her sunglasses. He introduced himself.

Hector made sure she got a drink and an introduction to the producer. He told her about the show he'd just finished shooting in New Orleans, how he'd fallen in love with the city, the drifting music in the cobbled streets, the shuttered afternoons. He asked her questions about her art, about how she made it and why. He asked about Melbourne and what she missed about it. She felt his attention drape across her shoulders. She left her paintings, at Hector's insistence, on the producer's bed.

She spent the next few days in his company, in his open-topped car, driving through streets snarled with bougainvillea and traffic, laughing at his stories. He told wonderful stories. He made her laugh. He did not rush her. The producer called and gave her the job, asked for eight canvases and as many sketches as she could produce. Hector took her to the beach to celebrate. In the ocean, finally, he kissed her. His body was impossible; she would like to have sketched him, but she said nothing. She flew home with sand in her hair. Her lips were swollen with kissing, her tongue full of his mouth. There was a message waiting for her when she landed.

He flew to New York a week later. She was startled by his alacrity, unused to this kind of attentiveness. She now had a volume of work to produce and felt nervous about making time for him, but he kept his distance during the day, appearing on her doorstep at night with Vietnamese food, a book of tinted lithographs, a perfectly ripe mango. He took her to see plays in tiny theaters she'd never heard of. He introduced her to his friends, actors all, well-spoken people with stylish coats, a gift for attention, and accents. He could not wait to fold her into his world. She let herself immerse, felt the waters close over her head. When they had sex, it was like they had done it all their lives. He felt familiar, known. Safe.

"He's so beautiful."

Lying on Candace's floor, she spread her arms wide. Candace tidied a line of coke on the Louise Bourgeois art book Miriam had given Annie for Christmas.

"He must be. I haven't seen you for a month."

Hector was offered a part in a movie about World War I. It filmed at a studio outside London. He asked her to come with him. She had never felt so powerful, so necessary. She shipped her canvases off to Los Angeles and flew to London, planning to stay a week. She stayed three months, ignoring the leathery producer's repeated invitations to come to L.A. and supervise the floundering actor in his make-believe studio. She loved London, the little galleries and echoing museums, a city made up of intersecting villages ribboned by the gray river. She loved the unexpected parks and secret greens, the walled gardens and generous squares.

Hector left for set early in the mornings, kissing her where she lay sprawled across the hotel bed and disappearing into a waiting car. She found a life-drawing class in a freezing studio where a cold man with long balls stood on a dais rinsed by the winter light and seven of them drew in charcoal silence, scratching his hidden penis on their white pads. She turned down invitations to drink with her fellow students in order to be back at the hotel in time for Hector, so she could lie with him in the bathtub and hear about his day or help him learn his lines. She was surprised by how seriously he took his work, bit back the urge to tease him, and chose to bask instead in the novelty of feeling essential to someone else's happiness. She could not believe how free Hector was with his love, how readily he shared his delight in her. It startled her. He, this long lean man with dark eyes and the profile of a minor god, could not wait to see her every day. She waited for him to tire of her. She wondered if she would tire of him. She was impatient to get to the bad times.

"Why do you love me?"

"Your fancy accent."

"Fuck off."

"Your exquisite cuisine."

She punched him.

"Your fabulous wealth."

She punched him again.

"Because you refuse to fall at my feet. Because you are immune to my charms. Because you, my love, could take me or leave me."

He came back from set one evening, tired. He'd crept out in the dark morning and now it was dark again and he was home and ready to collapse. He pushed open the hotel door and heard a rustling sound, felt a dragging resistance as he pushed it. The blue carpet was covered with torn paper, tiny white slips and shreds and feathers and leaves of paper that fluttered up as he entered, like ash in a grate. He felt irritated. Annie came out of the bathroom, wearing the T-shirt he had left her in that morning. He frowned.

"What's all this?"

"Fuck!"

"Fuck what?"

She pointed, frustrated.

"Those were all in place."

"Annie, I live here, I need to be able to walk in when I get home."

"I can't believe it. I finally got back to work . . ."

"I just spent all day at work. I don't want to have to tiptoe through another minefield when I get home."

"What do you mean 'another' minefield?"

"I mean I've spent all day running through trenches, and I just want . . ."

"They're not real trenches. You're not actually at war. They're not real grenades."

"Thank God you told me. I do realize I am not actually at war. I am not, unlike your last boyfriend, a war hero, who, incidentally, was just there writing things down, not engaged in military action, but I digress. Grenades or no, it was a tiring day at work."

Hector's command of language intensified as he grew angrier. His voice grew clipped, his words precise as bullets. She had never heard him like this.

"I didn't mean . . ."

"And I don't think it unreasonable to want to be able to cross the floor of my own hotel room."

"I don't have anywhere else to go!"

"I don't want a fight. I want a shower."

She gathered up her papers, swooping them into her arms recklessly, hurling them all like a snow flurry into the corner of the room. He walked past her into the bathroom and closed the door behind him. Later he lay in the bath, staring at nothing. She came in, sat on the toilet seat, looked at her hands.

"I'm pregnant."

They got married four months later at the City Hall in West Hollywood and drank champagne and ginger ale in the courtyard garden of a famous hotel perched high against the hills. Hector called his parents from the lobby. His mother tried unsuccessfully to hide her dismay. She was only grateful Annie was not an actress. No one could remember what Derek said. Afterward, Hector handed his wife the phone.

"Your turn."

She looked confused.

"Aren't you going to tell your parents?"

She struggled to explain.

"They're not really like parents. They're more like... the people I was born to."

She had never known how to speak about the violence. It was not something she had words for. Her mother had told her a few months back that her father had had a stroke, was different now.

Hector kissed her forehead.

"Let's tell them in person."

They spent a week in Melbourne. Annie had not been home for nearly ten years. Her mother's bright blue irises were cloudy now, the whites yellowed, faintly traced with capillaries; the backs of her hands, the ones Annie had drawn as a child, bore dark stains. Her teeth were longer, yellower, the lower ones jumbled, sloping into one another like old gravestones. Her father was suddenly old, hoarse, his face slumped. He said little. He sat in his armchair, one half of his face crumpled, his unclenched fists slack and trembling. He nodded at Hector, who sat and talked to him about cricket scores, a sport he'd diligently researched on the flight over. It was hard to know if her father could hear them, if he understood anything. Bluey wiped a little speck of saliva off his chin with her cuff, adjusted the net curtains so the sunlight didn't fall on his sunken face. She looked at Annie with her round belly.

"He's so pleased to see you, love."

His hand was a claw in his lap, trembling slightly.

Vita was three weeks old when Annie's mother called to tell her that her father had died in his sleep. Annie was silent. The baby slept in her bassinet on the tiled kitchen floor, her mouth pursed in a kiss. Annie did not know what to say.

"Oh Mum."

Her mother prattled on about the funeral, about neighbors, about what everyone would eat afterward. Neither of them cried. Neither of them mentioned Annie's attendance. They both knew it was impossible, that Annie could not leave the baby, nor the baby travel so young, and that it suited them all this way. She was still dry-eyed when she told Hector that night. He held her tight, released her when he felt her unbending body.

"Are you okay?"

She nodded, dried a plate.

And later that night, in the dark, his hands on her face, she whispered to him about the thuds and the fists and her mother's bruises and he listened and he wondered at the many worlds his wife kept within her.

* * *

Thierry rolls on his side. He had not meant to pass off another man's writing as his own, least of all a famous Graham Greene short story. When Annie insisted that he read her something, he had wanted to show her the kinds of stories he intended to write, the kinds of prose that inspired him. "This," he had wanted to say, "this. I am not this, but I will be. One day." He had pulled up "The Destructors" and begun to read. And as he glanced at her rapt face, he found he could not find the right moment to stop and to tell her the truth. The next paragraph, he thought. And then the next. And before he knew it the story was done. Now he lies restless, feeling like the house in the story and its owner, trapped inside and gutted from within. He resolves to come clean the next day. But when he wakes in the morning, she is on top of him, and it is not the moment.

Thierry drives them home. He rests one hand on her knee in between gear changes. She likes its weight. It feels like they have been away for a month. She feels the rising tide of anxiety as they near home, the ribbon of responsibility tightening about her neck. She fights off the urge to check her phone. They stop for gas. She goes inside to buy water while he tends to the truck. The day is breathless; the heat seems made of felt. Inside it is cool and electric. She grabs water, coffees, and a couple of rubbery-looking pastries, pays at the counter, and turns, almost colliding with a mother from Vita's class.

"Sorry...Annie, hi! What are you doing in this neck of the woods? Hector still away?"

"Yes. I'm on my way to see a house. Realtor's waiting. Sorry, I'll call you!"

"Yes, yes, run. I do want to talk about summer camps for the girls, shall we—"

"Yes! Call me. Bye."

She feels the eyes of the mother on her hands, conspicuously laden with snacks and two coffees. She barrels out of the service station. She prays Thierry is back inside the truck. He has moved over to the passenger seat now, checking his phone. He glances at her.

"All okay?"

She grinds the gears and backs out with a jolt.

CHAPTER 34

JACKSON IS WAITING FOR HER IN THE DRIVEWAY, HIS MOUTH AN O OF distress. He flings himself at her truck, wrenches open the door. He is sobbing, incoherent.

"What is it? Jackson, what happened?"

"She...she..."

"Jackson, what happened?"

"She's going to throw my iPad in the pond."

Before Annie can reply, Hector's mother appears on the doorstep. She looks flustered and suddenly old.

"There you are, Jacko. I've been searching everywhere for you. Hello, Annie, how was your weekend?"

"What's going on?"

"We were just having a discussion about his screen time..."

"It was NOT a discussion! You just snatched it out of my hands and said you were going to throw it in the pond!"

"I did not, Jacko, I asked you to give it to me and..."

"You LIAR! And don't call me Jacko!"

Annie places her hands on her son's shoulders. He is trembling.

"That's enough. Go inside, my love. Let me talk to Grandma."

Jackson buries his head in Annie's waist and refuses to move.

"He needs a break from those electronics. He has a real addiction going, if you ask me."

"I didn't."

"What?"

"I didn't ask you. I didn't ask you to police his screen time. I asked you to look after him while I went away for the weekend."

"Well, I hope it was a good break for you."

"Thank you. It was."

"You seem a little overwhelmed."

"Overwhelmed?"

"Mom, come on, let's go inside."

"It's not surprising. It's hard to give children the attention they need. What with your mom, Hector away, the house. You've been dealing with a lot. That's why we're here. We're all a little concerned."

Annie feels her pulse in her neck. She wants to throw stones at this woman. She wants to open her mouth and say it is too late for help, that everything is collapsing. She feels exhilarated, on the threshold of confessing everything right there on her driveway. She opens her mouth. A loud horn makes them all turn around.

A moving truck lumbers down the driveway. Hector's mother squints into the evening glow. Derek, beery in a mustard sweater, appears in the doorway of the house. Jackson, outrage forgotten, runs to investigate.

"Are we moving, Mom?"

"No."

The truck lumbers to a halt and a man slowly dismounts. He wears a black sweatshirt with the company logo on the chest. His face is pitted with acne scars, his sunglasses perched high on his forehead. He brandishes a clipboard with the air of someone who expects trouble.

"Are you Weymouth? Annie Weymouth?"

Annie nods, astonished to hear her name in this man's mouth.

"Been trying to get hold of you for three weeks now. You already owe a penalty for storage, but boss says we just gotta deliver this now cos we got a big shipment coming next week, and we need the floor space. Sign here, and we can start unloading. We only do on-site, no stairs."

"Unloading what? I didn't order anything."

He shrugs, gestures back to a shadowy guy inside the cab of the truck to get out and start unloading.

"Twenty-two boxes."

From the rear of the truck, they hear the sound of a lowering ramp. Annie feels a wave of panic.

"What... where did this all come from?"

He checks the clipboard.

"Melbourne."

CHAPTER 35

"Hello, darling."

"Hi, Mom. Can I call you back? I'm walking to set."

"Your father and I are in the car. We're heading home."

"Already? I thought you were staying a week."

"So did we. It seems Annie has other plans."

"What does that mean?"

"It means we looked after Jackson all weekend, but now she's home and says she doesn't need us."

"Oh, I'm sure she's . . ."

"We don't care, darling. It's not for us, you understand. We only want to help. But you know Annie. She beats to her own drum. And she more or less threw us out, so here we are, driving home."

"Threw you out? I'll call her."

"No, no. She was quite clear, she doesn't want our help. Which is fine. I mean, I think she could *use* some help, especially now with all those boxes, but you'll work it out when you get home. Jackson's fine, slightly feral, but that's to be expected with you gone. No, it's Annie we're concerned about. She's . . . she's been painting."

"You say that like it's a bad thing."

"I'm sure it's nothing to worry about. You'll be home soon enough. Everyone's longing to see you."

"What's wrong with her painting? And what boxes?"

"Darling, do you think it's possible she's in some kind of cult?"

"Annie? In a cult?"

"Well, the silent retreat. And the drawings. Something's not right, is it, Derek?"

A grunt from the passenger seat.

"Anyway, just wanted to give you an update. All is well. Bye."

His mother is gone. The phone rings again. He answers immediately. It is the blond producer. In her rasping voice she tells him that the movie is shutting down for a few days. When he asks why, she tells him smoothly, as though she were putting a child to bed, that they have fired the director and hired a new one who is arriving that evening. He hangs up and calls his agent.

"I was about to call. I just heard. They fired your director."

"I know. Some guy I've never heard of is flying in to finish the movie."

The agent reassures him. The new guy is a hotshot, they're lucky to have him, he'll get it wrapped up.

"But prepare for reshoots. We'll try to cap the extra days."

Hector slumps in his chair. He stares at the calendar Jackson made for him. It is stuck to the mirror with Band-Aids. He has crossed out every day as it passes. He calls Annie.

"Bad news."

"What?"

"I'm stuck here. They're saying at least another two weeks."

"Oh."

"They fired the director. I can't believe it. No warning."

"Jesus."

She sounds odd. He tells her the name of the new director, lists his blockbuster movies. It is not clear which of them he is trying to impress.

"Maybe it's a blessing?"

"How was it?"

"What?"

"The retreat thing."

"Oh. Good. Peaceful. In fact, it feels kinda weird to be talking. Can we speak later?"

"Everything okay with my parents?"

"Ugh. Your mum drove Jackson insane, but what's new?"

"Will you tell the kids?"

"What?"

"That I won't be home for another few weeks?"

"Yes, of course. Sorry. They'll be bummed. We'll manage. It will fly by."

She hangs up. He wonders, briefly, if she is relieved that he is delayed. He detected something, some catch in her voice he could not identify. He dismisses it. He walks to the hotel window. He is suspended over the city, an animal in a high glass cage. He pulls out his phone and tries the director. Her phone is switched off. He does not leave a message.

He returns to work a few days later. The blond producer introduces him to a skinny man in a black baseball cap and expensively scuffed sneakers. The man offers Hector his fist to bump.

"Dude. Let's do this. Psyched."

The director's breath is pernicious, as though something inside him has been dead for a while. Hector leans back as the director sketches out his vision for the remainder of the movie. He uses only active verbs and single-syllable nouns.

Everything about him smacks of efficiencies. Hector does not once see him sit down in three weeks. The producers lounge like cats now.

CHAPTER 36

A SINGLE DOGWOOD BLOSSOM CIRCLES IN A WIDENING GYRE AND lands on Bluey's dressing table, which sits beneath the flowering tree. The matching bench seat is neatly tucked beneath it and a bound blind mirror reflects nothing at all. The faded upholstered skirts, lightly drenched with dew, graze the grass. A rook perches on the glass, surveys the lawn, and takes off again. A box of saucepans rests on the grass; a colander drops slotted shadows on the lawn. More boxes lie piled about, bulging, stuffed on armchairs, propped on a bookcase, stacked on an old stereo.

Three mattresses lean against Hector's workout shed, like men smoking on a break. A plastic laundry basket full of assorted shoes sits on the kitchen table, nested between four upturned chairs. It looks like the set of a dream, thinks Annie, standing at her bedroom window. It looks like a bunch of junk, thinks Vita, pulling a sweater over her head. It looks like an awesome scavenger hunt, thinks Jackson, letting himself out the back door.

Annie calls Sam.

"You could have warned me."

"I emailed and left messages, doll. You never answer your phone. I didn't know what else to do. It sold faster than anyone thought it would, $30K over asking. They asked for the curtains, I didn't think you cared about them, and the chooks, but we'd promised them to Helen—what does everyone want with fuckin' bantams these days?—so I paid the movers to pack up the rest and ship it over. That way, you can decide what you want to keep. Did it all make it okay? Breakages?"

"No, no. It's all here."

"You'll have the money in your account in the next couple of weeks, I reckon, sans shipping."

"The money?"

"They wanted to pay with wampum, but I wouldn't let them."

"How much?"

Sam says a number. It is more than Annie has ever earned in her life. She is silent.

"You okay?"

"Yep. Thank you, Sam. For dealing with it all."

"How you doing, babe?"

"You know, same old."

"He home yet?"

"Hector? No. He's delayed. He'll be back in a few weeks."

"You managing?"

"Yes. We're great. I must go, Jackson's yelling. Love you."

Vita comes home from school to find her mother sitting on the grass with a bunch of photo albums in her lap and an empty bottle of white wine lolling in the grass. Vita stands, one hand on her hip. She waves her hand across the littered lawn.

"So, are we just living like this now?"

Her mother does not answer. Vita goes inside and calls her father.

Annie is asleep. A sound awakes her. She is downstairs at the back door, and there is Thierry like an emergency, his face on hers, his mouth at her neck, her lips. He says nothing, buries his face in hers and she turns her face up to his, and now they are silent, wrestling with clothing, only breath and arms and urgency and the ache of the other. She cannot tell where she begins or ends. The terror of discovery is overwhelming. She peels her body away. He kisses her once more and then is gone. She walks upstairs, her skin on fire, and does not sleep again.

The children are at school. Annie looks up from her laptop to see Brian's truck pull up in her driveway. There is a large empty trailer hitched to the back. She is surprised; she does not remember calling him. Brian, on crutches, hauls himself from the passenger seat. His nephew, Ricky, emerges from the driver's seat and lets out a whistle. They survey the cluttered garden, muttering. Annie sighs.

She calls a storage facility that is an hour away. As Brian directs, she and Ricky load up the furniture and boxes, hauling them off the lawn and onto the truck, back and forth, back and forth. Obeying some instinct she cannot articulate, Annie keeps pulling certain boxes off the trailer and carrying them back inside the house. There are certain things she wants near her, and others she is willing to store, and that is all she knows.

Three abreast, they drive an hour south to a windowless cement monolith just off the freeway. There they heft her parents' belongings onto a flatbed trolley, trundle them into a clinking freight elevator, and then pack them into the climate-controlled storage unit that she has rented. She shutters it with finality.

The garden looks bereft. For days the grass is creased with pale oblongs and tiny rectangles, holding the ghost furniture, until with one heavy dew, it releases, springing back to itself.

She thinks about Thierry all the time. He is part of her now. She cannot imagine a time when he was not her waking thought. He is sewn into her body. They meet in snatched makeshift moments to feast on one another, but even when they are together, she dreads their parting. She avoids mention of her family so as not to remind him of their existence, as though he might forget about her situation, as though he might not notice the multiple calls on her time and attention.

The weeks race by; every day they cannot manage to see each other feels like a gold coin dropped down a gutter. She scrabbles for time but they have so little. Thierry has his pupils and his shifts at the hotel bar, Annie her children and her clients. Weekends are an impossibility, as are the evenings. Maya is on night shifts and sleeps at the apartment all day. So they meet for pilfered hours in the afternoons in a field on the outskirts of town and lay a rug on the hard rippled surface of the truck bed. She feels the ridges ache between her shoulder blades. Afterward his kneecaps are indented with wide white stripes.

One time a black-and-white dog tries to mount the rear fender to see what is happening. Its barking is sharp and relentless. They stifle laughter and long for privacy.

Thierry sits at Candace's dining room table, teaching Remy irregular verbs. In the kitchen, construction workers heft slabs of marble. He hears Annie's voice before he sees her. She is talking to Candace, laughing. She hovers in the doorway. Candace smiles.

"How's it going, guys? Annie, how is your French coming along? I keep forgetting to ask. *Parlez-vous?*"

"I had to give up. Too much going on. Hi, Thierry."

He nods in greeting and corrects something on Remy's page.

"*Quel dommage.* Thierry's the best."

"Wish I could give up," says Remy.

"Well, *mon cheri*, when you're a grown-up, you can."

Annie stands behind Remy, as though to inspect his work. She runs a fingernail up the back of Thierry's neck as she looks at Remy's page. Thierry shifts in his seat. He does not like this game.

Annie turns to Candace.

"I brought you a bench."

She makes sure her departure coincides with his. They bid their farewells and drive half a mile down the road in their separate cars, before she pulls off sharply at a turnoff and gestures at him to follow her. They make out for four furious minutes in his back seat. She tucks her shirt back into her jeans and gets into her car.

He is left breathless, disheveled, a torn printout of the subjunctive trampled on the floor. He feels inexplicably furious. He drives to the bar and pours angry drinks till his shift ends. He comes home and drinks three beers. He finds himself swaying in Maya's doorway. She turns to him, pulls back her duvet. And he lifts her faded T-shirt over her head and pulls her soft, dark body to him. Because she is not Annie. Because she is familiar, safe, and circumscribed.

He lies here now in the darkness, feeling the light stubble of her calves, her beaded braids pressing into his biceps. He does not know what to do about Annie. He feels unsure, precarious. He dislikes feeling at a disadvantage. And yet he cannot wait to see her, to feel the solidity of her flesh again beneath his fingers.

Only in her presence does he feel assured, in charge. It is her absence that unmoors him. Thoughts of her distract him as he tries to write, to correct homework, to wipe down the bar. Is this love, he wonders, with Maya heavy on his arm, this uneasy mixture of longing and dread? He has swum farther out than he intended.

CHAPTER 37

THE DAY BEFORE HECTOR LANDS, ANNIE BOOKS A ROOM AT A NEARBY bed-and-breakfast. She asks Candace to keep the kids. She will need to pick them up later; she can think of no excuse for staying out late on a school night. Thierry has swapped his shifts at the bar and rescheduled two students. Nothing is easy, nothing, but they have procured themselves an entire afternoon of sex on a hard bed. Now she lies in the bathtub in the narrow bathroom. Thierry leans naked on the basin, smoking a joint. He watches her submerge and return silvered to the surface.

"What will you do?"
"When he's back?"
"Yes."
"Meaning what will *we* do?"
"Yes."
"I want to keep seeing you."
"I want that too."
"Then somehow, we will manage it. I will manage it."
"How?"
"I don't know."

They stare at each other for a long moment. They are trapped beneath the bell jar of each other's gaze.

"I love you."
"I love you."

The water sloshes over the tiled floor.

Later the dismayed owner will cluck at the soaked bathroom, the number of damp towels, the stained sheets, the faint smell of lingering smoke. Carrying an armful of sodden towels past the office, she will mutter to her husband.

"Does this place look like some kind of sex hotel?"

And he will shake his newspaper and remember his first love.

CHAPTER 38

HECTOR KEEPS BUMPING INTO THINGS. HIS HOUSE IS NOT AS HE LEFT it. Chairs have sprouted in the upstairs corridor; boxes are stacked beside the washing machine. The house feels saturated, as though there were no room for him. He is used to Annie's furniture habit. But these pieces are not vintage, not elegant, not even chosen by her. They are flotsam from the shipwreck of her family home, a home she did not cherish and whose aesthetic, if you could call it that, she never embraced. This unexpected sentimentality jars him. It is like stumbling across a new room in a house you have lived in for years.

He says nothing for the first few days, knowing from experience that reentry is bumpy, that helpful suggestions about domestic arrangements are not welcomed by the one who has managed them all single-handedly for months on end. They have lived through this before, have staggered their way through this dance. It is just another of the many and minute adjustments that are made in the reaccommodation of the interloper. He feels irritated at the faint smell of resentment that seems to pervade the house. It is like mold. Almost undetectable and yet unmistakably there. He feels like reminding everyone that the only reason he left was to keep paying for the lives that they have enjoyed with unbroken ease in his absence, that it is not as though he left to lie on a beach for four months. But this will not end well. The fight over who has had it hardest is not a fight worth waging, or winning. Annie seems at best distracted, at worst irritable. She barely broke stride to greet him when he arrived home (a dry peck on the cheek and a pat on the shoulder on her way up the stairs), did not even offer to fetch him from the airport ("Doesn't production send a car?"). He had not expected a banner, but a welcome-home dinner would have been nice, instead of hastily assembled Indian takeout fanned out on greasy, flimsy plastic bags. Only Jackson met him with enthusiasm. Vita seemed relieved that he was back but soon retreated to her bedroom, where she now lives, it appears, texting thoughts she refuses to speak.

He senses a general wariness in the house. The children glance at their mother as though she were a weather system in need of constant surveillance. Hector says nothing. He does not feel welcomed. He does not feel cherished.

He opens his gym, discovers another stack of bulging cardboard boxes. His jaw sets. He finds Annie in the kitchen on her laptop.

"What's happening with all the boxes?"

"What do you mean?"

"I mean, why are they in my gym? What's the plan here?"

"I don't have a plan."

"Annie, I can't live like this, tripping over stuff, unable to move for crap you've squirreled away around the house. I thought you rented a storage unit?"

"I did."

"So, why are we drowning in fucking boxes?"

"I need to go through them. But I can't do that if they're not in the house."

"There's not going to be anything in them that you want."

"How could you possibly know that?"

"Because you hated everything to do with that place! I don't know why now suddenly we're all supposed to treat the contents of your childhood home as a bunch of precious artifacts."

"Fuck you, Hector. I'm so over you deciding for me what it is that I want."

"Woah. No one's deciding anything for you. I'm just asking—"

"You always do this. You always override me—"

"What's wrong with the garage?"

"There's no room. It's full of my inventory."

"Then they can live outside."

"I can't leave them outdoors, they're full of books and photos," she lies, not knowing what is in them, nor why she is keeping them.

"Then store them in the unit and sort through them there. Just get them out of my fucking gym."

Annie feels herself slipping. She wants to settle back into her role but it keeps snagging on things, the way a baggy pocket catches on a door handle. She resolves again to fasten herself to the family. She will make dinner. She goes to the market, buys vegetables, ground pork, noodles. She slices and steams. She marinades, chops, sautés. The children come and go around her, comforted by her presence in the kitchen. Vita coils on the window seat, Jackson runs in and out searching for his trading cards. Hector is reassured by her presence at the stove. He was surprised and grateful to see Brian appear in the afternoon and helped him load more boxes into his truck. Annie has made no mention of it, so now he keeps quiet, rallies Vita to help him set the table. The kitchen smells rich, exotic. Annie, flushed, serves them steaming bowls of silky noodles, sticky with dark sauce and nuggets of gleaming pork, hidden bright vegetables, a sharp scattering of scallions, green herbs, sesame seeds. Jackson wrinkles his nose.

"What is this?"

"Just try it, will you?"

"What are all the bits?"

Hector puts a hand on Jackson's.

"Try it, little guy. Your mom made it specially."

"Why?"

"Because she wanted to make us something nice, right, Mom?" says Hector. Annie winces. She hates being called Mom by anyone other than the children. She nods, twists her fork.

Jackson points at the bean sprouts.

"Ugh, what are these? I'm not eating this. Mom, you should stick to pizza."

"Jackson, stop it."

"Dad, you weren't here. We ate frozen pizza for, like, four months, and now you're home, she's making fancy food to pretend like this is how life was, but it wasn't, and anyway, I like the frozen stuff."

"Jackson, that's enough."

"Dad, you don't know."

Annie reaches across to Jackson's bowl and turns it upside down on the table in front of him. The noodles sprawl in a gelatinous nest, treacly soy sauce oozes down the table leg, pork crumbles onto the floor. He looks at her, wide-eyed.

"What the?"

Annie lifts the upturned bowl and drops it on the floor, where it breaks neatly into two, a pair of shuddering crescent moons. Vita pushes her chair back in disgust.

"Jesus, Mom."

Hector rises to restrain his wife.

"Annie, calm down."

But Annie is perfectly calm. She walks out of the kitchen, out of the house, and onto the driveway. Behind her she hears the raised voices of her family, but they are at her back, they cannot reach her, they must not reach her. She has no idea where she is going but she knows she cannot go back inside that house. She walks to the truck, where the keys sway in the ignition, waiting for her hand. She drives into the evening light, the gravel harsh beneath her wheels.

The house is dark when she climbs the stairs. She slips inside the bedroom. Hector lies on the bed, not sleeping, facing the ceiling. He does not turn to her. She walks into the bathroom, locks the door. When she emerges, she is scented, clean, a rustle in the darkness. She slides into her side of the bed, lies on her side, rests her head on her pressed palms like a child. Her hands are ragged, the nails torn, the wedding ring worn to a thin dull band. The hands of a slave, she thinks. She wonders if she is going mad.

Hector looks at her pale spine, her shoulder blades like little wings at rest beneath her rinsed skin.

"What is going on?"

She opens her mouth, waiting for everything to fall out of it. Nothing comes.

CHAPTER 39

THE PAPER KNIFE LOOKS SO SMALL ON THE PRINCIPAL'S DESK. IT IS strange seeing it there. Annie has only ever seen it among her father's papers, lying at right angles to the chipped commemoration mug celebrating some faded royal wedding, now full of leaky pens. The principal keeps gesturing at it with the back of her veiny hand, as though it were a murder weapon.

She has been talking for a while. Annie can feel Hector growing impatient beside her. He is nodding but she knows he does not agree with whatever the woman is saying. His right knee is vibrating. Words drift across her like dust in sunlight. The principal has a tiny speck of raspberry lipstick on her tooth. It is distracting. Annie wants to reach over with a tissue and wipe it for her. Hector pushes his chair back.

"We need to get home."

The principal looks affronted, perplexed. Hector stands up.

"Right now, I'm paying school fees and a sitter so that you can tell us that my eight-year-old needs to stay at home because he is a danger to society because he showed his friend a blunt paper knife—a knife that is not a knife at all, in fact, it is more of a brass leaf. He did not, by your own admission, brandish this thing, harm anyone, even threaten to. He did not use it or attempt to. He showed his friend a memento that belonged to his grandmother, who recently passed away. My son is no threat to you or your school. He will be back in class tomorrow, and you will continue to teach him. Come on, Annie."

They drive home in silence. Annie clicks and unclicks the paper knife in her lap.

"Why did you give it to him?"

"What?"

"Can you stop doing that?"

"How is this my fault?"

"I just don't understand why you would give our son a knife."

"You said yourself it isn't a knife. It couldn't cut a grape. It can barely rip an envelope. You literally just said so yourself."

"I'm just curious, what was your thinking behind giving it to him?"

"There was no 'thinking.' It was just a keepsake."

"Ah."

"What is that supposed to mean?"

"It means something is off. It means you haven't been thinking like a parent, Annie. You're somewhere else. It's like you're just clocking in."

She hurls herself out of the car and tumbles out onto the asphalt and feels the grit of the road on her palms, her cheek, the shriek of pain in her ribs. She shifts in the seat. She rests her head in Thierry's lap. She presses her thumb into the paper knife. She presses it so hard that she feels it puncture the pad of her thumb, a dark bead of blood opening beneath its dull point. She inhales sharply. Hector glances over. She buries her thumb in her lap and watches the beeches, the birches, the world whirl past her.

CHAPTER 40

THEIR CLOTHES LIE TANGLED ON HER MOTHER'S DRESSING TABLE. The storage center is silent, dark, long since closed. It was the only place she could think of to come. Annie brought a blanket and sheets and made up her parents' bed while Thierry restacked boxes and piled furniture, clearing an island of space around them. She plugged in an old standing lamp from her parents' living room. Together they made a tiny iron bedroom. Mid-sex they clutched each other, burying laughter as the overhead lights turned off with a metallic clang, as the gates shuttered closed below them.

"How will we get out?"

"We won't. We live here now."

Now they lie, sweat-slicked on the bed.

"Where does everyone think you are?"

"Here."

"Here?"

"It was Hector's idea to get the unit. I told him I still have to go through all the boxes. So, now I have an excuse for being gone all hours."

"What will you do with all this stuff?"

"I don't know. I should just burn it. I don't know why I'm hanging on to any of it. It's hideous, most of it. And hardly filled with great memories."

She nods at a faded armchair wedged in one corner.

"That was Dad's throne. No one else was allowed to sit in it.

He'd come home from work and turn on the telly and yell for Mum to bring him his beer. Beers. She had to sit on the couch and pretend to be interested in his drunken politics, his sports, his police dramas. I said I had homework so I could stay in my room."

"He sounds fun."

"He was a drunk. He came from a long line of them. I don't think he knew any other way. We all turn into our parents in the end."

"I hope not."

"You set out with the best of intentions. I had all these high-minded ideas about what kind of mother I would be. And I guess some of them I've managed to live up to. Until you don't. But then one of them locks your keys in the car or floods the bathroom, and it's all over. Next thing you know, you're just another ape murdering its young."

He laughs.

"I bet you're a great mom."

She looks at him

"Do you want kids?"

He is careful.

"I can't imagine myself as a father. But I don't know. It seems like later life could be pretty empty without them. But I'm not sure you should have kids just to give yourself a sense of purpose. That feels like it might backfire."

She stares up at the ceiling.

"You should have to pass an exam to become a parent. It should be like your driver's license. You should have to keep reapplying every five years to make sure you're still up to the job. They just send you home with a baby, no questions asked."

"And they take your kid away if you fail your test?"

"Sure. Give it to someone better equipped."

He lifts her chin to better look at her face.

"What's going on?"

"I don't know. I feel...desolate. Is that the same as *desolée*?"

He touches her cheek. Her voice trembles. Tears spill.

"I can't keep doing this. It's killing me. I am ruining everything, everyone."

He waits.

"My life doesn't feel like it belongs to me anymore. I mean, it looks exactly like mine, but everything in it feels off. And all this stuff...feels so oppressive. I'm holding on to it out of some loyalty to a family I never actually had. But I don't know how to let go of it. Any of it. I don't know how to break it all up."

She shakes her head. Wet drops fall on his chest.

"I know I'm supposed to stop seeing you, I know you're not helping, but I also know you're not the problem. And I don't know how to give you up. I want to be with you. All the time."

She turns to look at him, her face wet, undone.

"Does that terrify you? That I say that? Is it too much? Am *I* too much? I don't know what else to say. I don't know how to do this well. I've never done this before. What I'm trying to say is that this isn't your fault. It's not because of you. I mean it is, but it isn't. I have been hurtling toward this for years, but so slowly I couldn't see it. I can't end up like Mum, waiting till the very end of her life to be happy. I refuse to wait that long."

She is shaking now, her words ragged. He holds her close to him. He has no idea if he is ready for this, if knows how to bear the weight of her. He does not know how to let her down. He does not know if he even wants to.

CHAPTER 41

"YOU NEED A BREAK."

Candace takes her friend's hand. Annie nods, sips her iced tea. She has forgotten what food tastes like.

"Let's go on a trip. For your birthday. Hector can manage the kids, God knows it's his turn. I'll look into some hotels."

Candace does not tell Annie about the call she had from Hector two nights ago, ostensibly to discuss Annie's birthday, but ending with his too casual inquiry about whether Annie happened to be with her. It was ten o'clock at night. She does not tell her friend because Annie has not mentioned it, and with uncharacteristic discretion, Candace assumes Annie must not be ready to talk about whatever fight she and her husband had. The thought flickers across Candace's mind that perhaps Hector has had an affair while he was away, but she dismisses it like a moth. He is discreet enough, surely, to have hidden that. Hector is vain, but not stupid.

"I need a break."

Annie and Hector sit side by side at Vita's dance recital. Jackson's face is buried in the program, searching for his sister's bio. A supermarket bouquet of roses the color of Pepto-Bismol sits in Hector's lap. They fought in the car over whose responsibility it was to remember to buy Vita flowers, with Annie fiercely defending her right to forget. Hector pulled over, furious, stormed into the nearest gas station, and yanked the last bunch from a dry bucket. The flowers now lie, defeated, plastic-frilled, in his lap. He looks at his wife.

"I think it's a good idea."

"Candace suggested it."

"Where are you thinking?"

"I don't know. Maybe London."

"London?"

"I don't know."

"Oh. I thought a spa weekend?"

"I don't want to go away with Candace."

He waits. She goes on, looking straight ahead at the blank stage.

"I want to go to London."

"Who with?"

"Alone. Who would I go with?"

He pulls at one of the roses. It collapses immediately in his lap, littering his pants with petals. Jackson looks up from the program. She puts her hand on her son's knee.

"Did you find her photo?"

"No. What are you two talking about?"

"Nothing," says Hector.

"Going away," says Annie.

The room goes dark. The curtain rises.

BOOK FOUR
FALL

CHAPTER 42

SHE CRIES FOR THE ENTIRE CAB RIDE INTO NEW YORK. SHE LEANS her head on the window and behind dark glasses she does not see the yellowing fields rise and fall and yield to grimy clapboard, to four lanes of tarmac, to steaming redbrick and graffitied high-rise buildings; she sees only her children's bewildered faces. Jackson holding on to her thighs, dragging her back inside, like he did when he was little when they used to go out to dinner, pleading with her not to go, unselfconscious, as though he knew, as though he alone understood what was happening in that moment, as though he were begging on behalf of them all. She peeled his arms from her legs and held him, his heart beating like a bird in her arms, and she almost collapsed there on the driveway. She knelt down and kissed his hot wet face. Vita refused to come outside, only offered her cool cheek in the kitchen and turned back upstairs to her bedroom, not meeting her mother's eye. Hector carried Annie's suitcase outside for her, ignoring the unraveling of the suspension bridge between them, the slow collapse into the ravine. He closed her into the cab.

"Have fun. Call us when you land."

She checks in to a Midtown hotel. It feels like nowhere she knows. The room is anonymous, hostilely clean. Two plastic bottles of water sit on the cold windowsill, and a wafer of soap on the sink. She lies on the bed. Her flight left an hour ago.

She rebooks it for the following day. She wonders if she will actually get on that one. Her stomach growls. She goes in search of food. She is unfamiliar with this part of town. It is early evening; people are beginning to cluster outside the theaters, adjusting their ties and skirts. She stands beneath some scaffolding, trying not to call Thierry. She calls Sam. It is very early there but Sam answers on the second ring. It is a relief to finally tell someone the truth. Sam listens, unsurprised. They both fall silent. Annie watches a couple bickering over a lost ticket.

"I don't know what to do."

Sam sighs.

"Get your ass to London. You can't know what you want, being so close to everything. You need to get away from Hector and the kid."

"Kids."

"I meant the French guy."

"He's not a kid."

"Whatever. Leave them all behind. You need to be on your own for a bit. You do you, babes."

She does not know how to tell Sam that she has no idea what this means.

She walks uptown, brushing past people brimming with urgency, with a sense that their lives are waiting for them, just around the next block or sitting at the next bar. She wonders, again, what Thierry is doing. She will not call him. She must try being alone. The day turns suddenly cloudy, the temperature drops, and a sharp wind chisels the avenues. She slips into a store with huge glass windows, where a bored liveried security guard holds open the door. She buys herself an expensive coat. She has no idea what color it is. She pays for it and wears it out. She walks without seeing, just to move now, just to feel her feet on the sidewalk. She is aimless, restless. There is no one she wants to see. On an impulse, before she can stop herself, she finds herself calling Mark. She expects a foreign ringtone, a standardized voicemail, and is surprised to suddenly hear his voice. He is in town. He can meet her in an hour. She heads toward Central Park. She glimpses herself in the glittering windows, a middle-aged woman with windswept hair in a dark coat. She makes no attempt to tidy herself.

An elegant pianist dips over the keys in the velvety darkness of the hotel bar; peanuts glimmer in tiny dishes. Mark sips his martini. He looks fat.

"You look beautiful."

She feels like gossamer, like a spider's web suspended over a foxhole, like a breath could bring her down.

"What's going on?"

She tells him about the children, about a play she saw months ago, about Hector's movie. She tells him nothing at all. He tells her about his girlfriend, an architect who commutes between Berlin and New York, and shows her a photograph of a beautiful woman with a blunt bob. He grubs peanuts out of the dish and tells her about his recent trip to Russia and the former spy he interviewed there who answered his questions while facing the wall in a darkened hotel room, and she remembers all the years she spent feeling invisible by his side. Her life is so small. She cannot think why she called him. When the bill comes, they both reach for it. Mark places his hand over hers and squeezes. His pressure is firm, insistent. He pays. He places her new coat lightly on her shoulders and kisses her too close to her mouth. She shudders, feels the martini like a silverfish jumping in her veins.

She climbs into a cab, promising to stay in touch, and calls Thierry before she has rounded the park. She hangs up before he can answer. She switches off her phone.

* * *

"The children will be fine," she tells herself the next day as she fastens her seat belt for takeoff.

"They are better off without me. At least for a while. I am doing more harm than good by staying," she tells herself as she stares unseeing at the page of her book. (She will not let herself see Jackson turning in his bed, turning and turning and waiting for her footfall in the hallway. She refuses to see Vita alone downstairs, making her meager meals in the silent kitchen.)

"It is just for a week or two," she tells herself as the clouds scud beneath her, as the drink shudders untouched on her drop-down table and the man beside her laughs at his screen.

"Just till I figure out what I'm doing," she repeats as she unlocks the door to a studio apartment in Earl's Court, a rental she found online that morning that seemed cheap and central. Sam recommended the area ("full of Aussies") and it had the added merit of being an area of London in which she had never spent any time with Hector.

The flat is light, airy, white, full of cheap Scandinavian furniture. She feels dizzy with rootlessness. She dumps her bag, walks back onto the street to buy provisions from the local corner shop. A girl wearing a headscarf and glued-on eyelashes waves away her crisp new note.

"Card only, love."

Annie tries her credit card but it is declined. She tries another. Even her bank does not want her to be here. She looks in despair at the girl, who shrugs and points at a tiny fruit stand on the corner.

"Try him."

She buys overpriced, overripe strawberries and a coconut and carries them back to the studio. She lies on the couch, eating the strawberries and studying her new home. The cornice on the ceiling is ornate, like the frosting on an old-fashioned wedding cake. It stops abruptly halfway across the living room. The room has been sliced in half, a cheap partition thrown up to create the bedroom. Every room has been carved out, as though someone has excavated as many dwellings from the building as they legally can. It overlooks a leafy square to which she has no access, but the presence of green is reassuring. She reads the laminated card of fire instructions that is studded to the wall, leafs through the plastic folder of house rules and local restaurants. She tries unsuccessfully to break open the coconut with a fork and her shoe.

She lasts exactly half an hour before she calls Thierry. He answers immediately.

"I miss you."

"I miss you."

"How long has it been?"

"Years."

"I can't do this."

"Where are you?"

"London."

"London?"

"I don't know. It seemed like a good idea at the time."

"Is it?"

"A good idea?"

"Yes."

"If you come."

"To London?"

"To me. Will you come to me?"

He arrives a day later. His duffel bag sits untouched in the narrow hallway. For a day and a night they do not leave the bedroom except to find food and bring it back to bed. They feed each other, touch each other, bask in the sheer permission of each other. Annie forgets who she is, where she has come from. She wonders how

Hector ever came home to them after being away. She marvels at how trusting she has been. The children call and leave her messages. Hector texts and receives no reply. She is underwater. She cannot be reached. She can hear no one down here.

Eventually they run out of milk. Thierry gets dressed and leaves for groceries. It takes him twenty minutes to get out the door. She stands naked in the window, watching him walk down the street, in love with his broad back, his stubbled head, the cut of his triceps beneath his T-shirt sleeves. He smiles as he passes an old lady almost bent double walking her small white dog, who yaps at him. He bends down and scruffs it under the chin and it whines with pleasure. And the old lady smiles, suddenly young, and Annie touches her own throat, smiling to see it.

She dresses, sits on the sofa, rests her head on her arm. She video calls Vita, but Jackson answers in a rush. She is flooded with love for this pale insistent face. She can barely speak for the immediacy with which she misses him. Now she is her old self in this new place.

"Mom! Tell Vita she can't use my iPad!"

"Hi, love. What am I telling her?"

"She takes my iPad to listen to her music when she can't find hers, and now mine's all filled up with her lame music, so can you just tell her?"

"Aren't you on her phone right now?"

"Yeah, but only cos I saw it was you calling. I don't know where she is. Are you in London now? Vitaaaaa...I think she's outside or something."

"How are you, baby?"

"Fine. When are you coming home?"

"Not yet. I just got here."

"What's the place like?"

"It's nice."

"Show me?"

Annie gives the phone a quick flash around the room.

"How far away is the London Eye? I really wanna go there. Luke says there's a racetrack there where they actually let you drive Ferraris. Can you find out?"

"I'll see what I can find out, my love."

"Jackson! Give me back my phone!"

Vita snatches the phone. She looks aggrieved.

"Hi, Vee."

In the background Jackson protests.

"It's Mom. I only picked it up cos it was Mom."

"How's London?"

"It's nice. Sunny. I haven't been out much, but I can see people wearing shorts."

"Mom, do I have to keep going to camp? I'm too old for it. It's just so embarrassing being there."

"I don't know. What does Dad say?"

"He says if I don't go, I have to get a job, but what job am I supposed to get? We live in the middle of fucking nowhere."

"Don't swear. We talked about you babysitting."

"Can't I just go and stay with Zoe? She's in the city with her dad. It's so boring here."

Annie feels irritated. She does not want to hold this responsibility from here.

"You and Dad can work this out."

"Dad says you're not answering his calls. Did you get a new coat?"

"What?"

Vita points behind Annie's shoulder. She turns.

"I did. In New York. I'll call Dad."

She can see Thierry walking back to the apartment, swinging plastic bags. She watches him, smiling. Nothing matters now.

"Let's speak tomorrow. Love you."

CHAPTER 43

ANNIE CANNOT SLEEP. AT FIRST, SHE THINKS IT IS JET LAG, THEN THE time difference, but as the days become weeks she can no longer blame the clock. She is awake all night. There are no drugs that can tame her mind or the heat of her body. She tries all the local pharmacy can offer but nothing is strong enough. She has no doctor here to prescribe, nor Hector's stash to raid. Wine makes her sleepy but wakes her with a jolt two hours later, weed (a thumb-sized bud Thierry scores from a dreadlocked white kid outside the Tube) makes her suspicious and hungry and if she does sleep, still she wakes, doused in sweat, thrumming like a harp string. She wonders if it is perimenopause, or guilt, or if they are in fact the same thing: the revolt of the feminine, the abdication of a former role, and now the uneasy interregnum. Her periods visit her like estranged relatives, unpredictable and demanding. Everything feels tentative, provisional. Nothing in this rented space is her own. The bed cannot hold her. She gets up and walks the city, leaving Thierry asleep like the child she fears he is. She walks through sleeping streets, quiet with domesticity, past furniture and lighting shops full of darkened lamps, sixteen-wheelers and garbage trucks lurching past her. No one slows down. No one looks at her, a restless woman alone under a streaked sky. She walks to the ropey river and the bridges that look like castles and touches the rough pebbled wall of the river walk. She turns and walks back the way she came, past shuttered markets and the neon flicker of the gas station. She lets herself in to the silent flat and collapses, finally, finally into sleep.

Their days settle into a rhythm. She sleeps as late as her body will let her and Thierry reads or writes while he waits for her to wake. He brings her coffee and she pulls him into her and they have sex, devour each other as though it were the first time. Later they walk the city, hand in hand. He has never been to London. They use the river as their artery, meandering the double life of both its banks, crisscrossing bridges, pushing deeper into the heart of the city. They drift into museums, float through parks. They watch silent rowers silking the water and motorboats rocking with music and string lights, dark swaying barges, and listing deserted yachts. Memories of London flutter her: a glimpsed storefront, a remembered restaurant. She skims the city, neither needing nor daring to plumb its depths but only skittering its bright surface. She has been here several times with her husband, was last here for a premiere of his some years ago. She skirts the parts of town that feel too saturated with her past.

In the early afternoons they go back to their flat, making dinner plans on the way. Thierry writes every afternoon, sitting in the pale wood Scandi armchair, a battered water bottle wedged beside him, laptop balanced on his thighs, cushioned earphones over his skull, oblivious to her and to what city he is in. He is withdrawn, thoughtful. He tells her not to take it personally. It is how he gets when he's writing. She lets him be. She lacks all industry and all drive toward it. Her former busyness feels like a mirage. She basks in the sheer absence of obligation. It is both wonderful and paralyzing. She ignores her phone, leaving it switched off for hours at a time, turning it on only to ring her children. She steps out into the street, preferring to be alone for these calls. She buys books to read but cannot concentrate for long. She sketches a little but it brings her no pleasure. She naps in the afternoons and wakes creased and uncertain to find Thierry frowning at his screen. She kisses his neck, and they make love again.

Sometimes she goes out to walk alone in the afternoons, watching the city surrender itself to fall. Sometimes down to the river again, sometimes to the little graveyard a half mile away, an old cloistered space tucked between two main roads, littered with mossy headstones and forgotten graves. Sometimes she takes her sketchbook there, or a book. On the way home she stops for a cup of milky tea in the local café, retrieves their laundry from the nearby launderette, gathers ingredients for their evening meal. The fruit guy knows her by name now. They have divided their meager tasks (she shops, Thierry cooks, she retrieves laundry, he cleans, although she noticed the bathroom floor was gritty this morning). One afternoon she checks her bank balance, is startled to see the sum of money that is in there. It is a number she has never seen in any of their accounts. The funds from the sale of her mother's house must have cleared. She feels panicked, unsure if she can trust herself not to accidentally spend it all on something absurd: a rope of pearls, a vintage car. She does not tell Thierry. She likes the budget they live on, the parity it gives them. It reminds her of being a student. They live frugally on pasta and vegetables, soup, rice. It is delightful to be cooked for. One night they buy kebabs from outside the Tube station and walk home eating them, the oily meat tumbling out of the warm pita bread, rich gravy trickling down their fingers. They pass a beer back and forth. Thierry marvels.

"Is it legal to drink in the street here?"

"I think it's illegal *not* to."

At night they reach for each other in the dark. Afterward they lie draped across each other's bodies, listening to the noises of the building. Thierry invents stories for her, one for every sound they hear: a heavy step, a slammed door, the bump of a suitcase being dragged across the floor. He points at the ceiling.

"That's Lena. She and Matt got married three days ago in Boston City Hall. They met at her gym. She only invited her two best girlfriends to the wedding. She still hasn't figured out how to tell her mom; she's thinking of sending her a postcard from Buckingham Palace. They've only known each other five months, but she knows he's the one. He's a personal trainer."

"But I only hear one set of footsteps. Where is Matt?"

"That's the thing. They wouldn't let him on the plane because his passport had expired. He begged them, Lena cried and pleaded, they said it was their honeymoon, but it made no difference. So, she came on ahead."

"Without him?"

"He told her he'd stay and pay to get it expedited and that he'd be with her in a few days. But secretly, he's relieved. He can't afford the expediting fee. He could barely afford the flights; he took out two new credit cards just to cover them. He actually knew his passport had expired. He wants her to be here, though, to enjoy herself. He loves her. He just doesn't have any money. His brother told him to sit tight and take her to Miami for Christmas."

"So, Lena is on her honeymoon alone? This is such a sad story."

The suitcase rumbles to the other side of the room.

"She doesn't mind. She made friends on the Tube, and they're meeting up later at a nightclub in Tufnell Park."

Annie laughs, touches his cheek.

"I love you."

* * *

The chestnut trees beckon, forbidden in the secluded square. She manages to slip inside it once, after a young family let themselves in with a key. She helps them wrestle with the gate and their stroller and they smile as she slides in behind them and stretches herself out under the rich skirts of the generous trees. But this only happens once, and now she is used to the sooty tang of Earl's Court Road and the ripe smell of trash and transit and tourists. Everything about this place feels temporary. The flimsiness of the partition walls, the endless tread of backpackers up and down the corridors, wedged in the hallways, politely backing up, laden in the entryway early in the mornings, or late at night. Everyone is simply passing through. It is a corner of London dedicated to impermanence, to transit, to journeys not completed. Even the Tube station feels enthusiastically liminal. No haggard commuters here, no passive consumers of life's offerings, only young people, laden with backpacks and suitcases, excitably on the cusp of their lives, thresholding their future.

She feels old here. Living in Connecticut has sheltered her from this feeling. Everyone is middle-aged in the country. Here, for the first time, she feels self-conscious when she is out with Thierry, conspicuously older. They have not paraded themselves before, have not asked the world to hold them as a couple. She swallows her insecurity. She will not share this with him, will not ask him to reassure her, it will only draw more attention to what is inalterable. On a whim she gets a piercing, high in her left ear cartilage. It aches for weeks, this gold bead that catches her eye every time she sees her reflection; she cannot lie on that side, but the pain makes her feel alive and, somehow, younger.

Life is simple, as long as she looks no farther ahead than that afternoon. The children ask when she is coming home and she cannot tell them. Hector asks her nothing at all about her plans, as though fearing her answer. Thierry does not ask about her intentions nor offer his. They renew their flat on a weekly basis, taking it in turns to pay the rent. She wonders which will run out first, Thierry's money or his nerve.

For her birthday he buys them tickets to the theater. It is a new play, in a theater famous for new plays, on a leafy square opposite a department store. They can walk there, Thierry tells her, and have dinner afterward in a little brasserie he has booked for them. He is delighted with his plan. Annie does not know how to tell him that she does not know what she hates more, her birthday or live theater.

The last play she saw was one of Hector's. It was in New York; she had kept the kids out of school, driven hours into the city, fought for parking, bustled them into the auditorium, hissed explanations at them in the dark. He had been gone for months of rehearsal, coming home only on weekends. She had, as so often before, managed everything while he was gone. And now she sat in the theater, between her children, watching her husband, feeling only the wrongness of everything. He was not right up there. He was not himself. Or perhaps he was entirely himself and only this black stage and white light allowed her to see it. Perhaps it took seeing him in costume. Everything about him felt false and outsize. Even his feet looked too big, as though his shoes were a size too large. She could not stop looking at them. He stood on stage like a ballerina in third position, toes turned outward, one foot slightly ahead of the other, weight evenly distributed. She wondered if he stood like this in everyday life, if she had simply failed to notice. She found she could not watch the play, only his feet. No matter where he moved to on the stage, his feet resumed their stance, like a sailor on a tilting deck. She wondered if everyone stood like this, if she had simply never noticed how humans stand, and fought the urge to ask everyone to stand up so she could check and see for herself. It seemed to Annie that these feet of her husband's summed up all that was wrong with him—his need to present himself, best foot forward, at all times. He felt rehearsed, even in life, as though he had undergone extensive private coaching on how to be a better Hector. She had sensed this when she met him, of course, and then willfully, steadily, because that is what love demands, turned away from what she knew.

Later, Annie shepherded the children backstage. They were gleeful, proud, ready to lay claim to their father again. He was electric, fizzy with adrenalin and relief. She kissed him, hugged him, whispered in his ear.

"Well done."

And he had pulled away and studied her face.

"You hated it."

Jackson thrust his program in his father's face.

"Dad, can I get the autograph of the dude from the earthquake movie?"

"I didn't hate it! How could you say that? I just told you I—"

"No, what you said was 'Well done.' You didn't say you loved it. You said, 'Well done.'"

"Because I hadn't finished talking!"

"Dad? Can I?"

"What did you like about it?"

"Hector, I liked all of it. Can we not?"

"Has he left already? Dad, has he left? Vita, get off!"

"I thought you were amazing, Dad."

"Thank you, darling. At least my daughter liked it."

"Oh Christ, Hector, give me a break. I loved it. I told you. You were great."

"Your mother is a tough crowd, my kids, and don't you forget it."

Annie felt like throwing something. Hector smiled, cold.

"Kidding. Come on, let's get dinner."

They poked at steaks, spoke only to the children, avoided one another's gaze. He ordered one Manhattan and then another. They crowded into the cramped Chelsea apartment he was borrowing from a divorced school friend. They settled the kids on the pullout sofa, overriding Vita's complaints and Jackson's protests, and retreated to the bedroom. The bed dominated the room, there was barely room for them to stand on opposite sides, undressing. Hector flopped on the bed, eyes closed. Annie looked at him.

"I'm sorry."

"For what?"

"For not saying the right thing. I never know what I'm supposed to—"

"You're not *supposed* to say anything. You're *supposed* to enjoy my work, to feel proud of what I've been doing, to admire, if nothing else, the sheer fucking effort. You're supposed to take a fucking interest, not usher the kids backstage like a glazed au pair. Let's not pretend you don't have an opinion, Annie. You always have an opinion."

They fought with whispered intensity. She apologized again for not expressing herself correctly. She assured him she felt proud but sometimes found it hard to say. He was disbelieving of her reassurances. He confessed to the insecurity that drove him to make such demands of her, that it was perhaps outsize, but this was what made people into actors, what put them up there, in a dark room, in front of a hundred strangers.

"We do it because we need to be loved. And if you don't love it, love me, you, of all people, then what hope is there?"

The play opened to good reviews. Her husband was described as "the always reliable Hector Cass," an epithet she heard him on the phone repeating to friends with an eye roll, but Annie knew gave him deep satisfaction. She did not see the play again.

The play Thierry takes her to is unexpectedly good. She wonders if perhaps she does enjoy theater after all, if it was just her husband she did not like.

CHAPTER 44

ANNIE WAKES WITH A START AFTER DREAMING ABOUT HER CHILdren. For a moment she cannot remember why they are not with her. Thierry sleeps beside her, perfectly still. She drags herself to the bathroom, lays a cool, damp washcloth across her neck. She sits in the armchair that overlooks the street. The city is strangely quiet. Her phone tells her it is her mother's birthday. She is shocked that she almost forgot it. She has been so busy missing her children that she has forgotten to miss her mother. Or perhaps all the missings contain each other, like Russian dolls.

She waits for sunrise, dresses, quietly slips out, and buys a bunch of chrysanthemums from the flower stall outside the Tube station. She walks to the graveyard and lays them on the most neglected grave she can find. She sits on a nearby bench and waits to feel something. There is nothing. She dials her mother's number. She is barely breathing, suspended in the impossibility. The phone rings and rings. There is no reply. She hangs up.

Hector stops asking her when she is coming home. She tells him she is reading, walking, drawing, seeing plays. She tells herself she is being truthful. He asks if she is lonely and she tells him no one can be lonely in London. His calls are brief, as though he were cutting himself off. She wonders what he really thinks, or what he is refusing to know. She dismisses the thought, just as she dismisses the calls from Candace, the texts from Patti, the emails from the dentist, the school, the bank. She ignores everything and everyone who might ask anything of her.

* * *

She wakes one night unable to move her right arm. It is frozen and traced with hot rivers of pain that shoot through her back ribs when she tries to lift it. She stands under the shower, the water hot as she can stand it, but nothing shifts. In the morning Thierry rubs it with arnica cream, but to no avail. She swallows some ibuprofen; the pain abates a little, but still she cannot move. Thierry goes out, comes back with a small business card.

"This person is supposed to be great. Girl downstairs says she's been twice. I called, and they can take you in an hour."

Annie presents herself at a gray front door three blocks down the street. It is slivered between a betting shop and a convenience store. A slender, androgynous person answers. They are barefoot, dressed entirely in black, with a shaved head, an exquisite profile, a sleeveless T-shirt revealing muscular biceps.

"Annie?"

"Yes."

"I'm Jude. Come on in. Let's get you fixed up."

She is ushered up narrow stairs, into a darkened room, scented and flickering with candles and a massage table with a sheet neatly folded on it. Jude taps the bed. "Hop up, honey. Face down, clothes on. Let's see what's going on."

Jude's hands are confident, moving with gentle but unerring precision from place to place along Annie's spine. She winces in certain spots and Jude clicks knowingly. Annie closes her eyes. She has never enjoyed massages; they have always been Hector's thing. But necessity enjoins surrender and she lets the hands move and press. She closes her eyes. She breathes. Jude asks her to roll over, touches her belly.

"Here. Breathe here."

A hand is placed on her abdomen. She tries to move it with her breath. The hand moves, she follows it with breath. Lights dance behind her closed eyes. Her shoulder thrums. She wonders when Jude will get to it, but the rhythmic breathing is oddly enjoyable. A thumb moves deeply along the side of Annie's neck. The tendon feels tender, taut as a harp. Annie sighs in pain. Jude persists, gently, but insistently, pushing their thumb deeper into the slowly softening flesh. Jude steps away. Annie is surprised, abandoned. She can hear the sound of running water, cracks an eye to see Jude washing their hands in the tiny sink. They dry them on a paper towel, then return to the table, holding them high and upright like a surgeon.

"May I work in your mouth?"

"In my mouth?"

Jude nods, implacable.

"Uh, okay."

She opens, tentatively, and Jude places an index finger on her bottom lip, just touching her lower teeth. Jude leans in, sweet-breathed, and slowly slides their index finger inside Annie's open mouth. Annie keeps her eyes closed to avoid the unbearable intimacy. Improbable as it is, there is nothing sexual in this encounter. It is exploratory, probing, but not predatory. The finger slides across her molars to the far dark corner of the cave of her mouth. There the finger finds the ribbon of tight flesh that holds her upper and lower jaws apart. The finger presses firmly into the tendon. Slowly the finger slides, up and across, inside the slime of her cheek, back down to the ridge of her gums, loosening the muscle's grip on her jaw. Up and down, aching and firm, the finger insists its way around the back of the inside of her mouth. Annie slowly feels a widening, a spreading back there, like the unspooling of a thread. There is an infinitesimal amount more space in her mouth and yet it feels infinite. She is astonished to feel tears coursing down her cheeks.

She is weeping. Suddenly she feels as though she needs to bite down, as though she might choke if she does not close her mouth. She pulls Jude's finger from her mouth and rolls onto her side and sobs violently. She does not know how she will ever stop. Jude waits, stands at her feet, with one hand resting gently on Annie's bare ankle, a tether to the earth. Annie does not know how long she lies there. She takes slow deep breaths to calm herself. She wipes her eyes and sits up, shakes her head.

Jude nods.

"Drink a lot of water. Come back if you need to."

Annie walks back to the flat, swinging her arms. Her shoulders lie flat and free. Her mouth is a hydrangea in bloom. Her tongue lolls, a snake in a cave.

Thierry looks up from his laptop. Annie stands in front of him. He is worlds away, has been for hours. He has no idea how long she has been there.

"How was it?"

"I have to tell them."

"Tell who?"

"About us."

He blinks.

"I can't go on lying. I've been waiting to know what to say because I don't know what will become of us, and I wanted to know more definitely before I told them, whether we are just, you know, a fling, or if we are something more than that, and I...don't know what we are doing, but I can't keep waiting to find out."

She looks at him.

"Do you know what we are doing?"

He blinks, shifts his laptop.

"I know I want to be with you. And I want what's best for you. Which might not be the same thing."

"I want us to be together. I can't go back. I know that now. I can't."

She looks down at her hands.

"I won't be forgiven. But I won't forgive myself if I go back."

She gazes out at the dirty street. She thinks to herself what she cannot say out loud, what is inconceivable and yet she knows to be true. Hector must keep them, she thinks, my children. He must keep them in their home. I must be the one to leave so that they can stay in all that keeps them safe and anchored. I must go because I am being buried alive by the very things that keep them safe. I must lose them or I must lose myself. They will come to visit me, as they choose to, and it will be unbearable, it will be almost unendurable, until slowly it is not. It will be the end of everything and also the beginning.

She feels nauseous, vertiginous.

"I will tell them tomorrow."

CHAPTER 45

"SHE DID, DAD, I'M TELLING YOU."

Vita zooms in on a screenshot of her mother's face. She holds it up to her father, who is frying lamb chops while Jackson and Remy throw a tennis ball back and forth in the kitchen. They are weak with laughter, making up the words to an invented rap song. Hector is impatient, raises his voice over the whine of the extractor fan, flips a chop.

"Can this wait?"

"Look, you can see here."

Jackson and Remy whoop behind them. Jackson drops the ball, approaches.

"Can I see? Can I see?"

"Can we do this later, Vita?"

"Dad, look at her ear."

"So, she got another earring. Big deal."

"It's a mid-life crisis. She'll get a tattoo next, I'm telling you."

Remy, clutching the ball, pushes his way in to peer at the phone.

"Why's she got Thierry's laptop?"

Vita looks at him.

"What?"

He points.

"That's his laptop."

Hector frowns.

"Who's Thierry?"

"My French teacher."

Remy wriggles back to the game. Jackson joins him. Hector takes the phone and zooms in farther, beyond his wife's face, over her shoulder, to where an open laptop sits behind her on a bare table. It is decorated with the silhouette of a tree and a child with its outstretched arm.

CHAPTER 46

SHE IS ALREADY AWAKE WHEN HER PHONE RINGS. SHE HAS BEEN watching the gray light turn milky on the walls, rehearsing the phrases, unspooling the silk that will take her through the labyrinth of the call she knows she must make. She is surprised to see Vita's number. Her daughter never calls her. She answers immediately. But it is not her daughter. It is Hector. He spits her name. He does not let her speak. He runs out of things to call her. His disgust defies even his rich vocabulary. She can taste his revulsion in her own mouth. It is Hector as she has never known him. He is titanic in his rage, unreachable. He has searched the devices in the house, found texts, emails, photographs. He has dates. He is sickened by her. Her silk is useless to her now, snarled in her trembling hands. She pulls on clothes, shaking off Thierry's outstretched hand, and shivers into the pale street so they can talk.

Hector is shaking with clarity. He is an arrow poised in the bow, trembling with potential, the bull's-eye tingling in his fingertips. He would love to be wrong, and knows he is not. He has known, somewhere in the back of his skull, for months now, that this is what has happened, that there is some unknown shadowy figure helping himself to his life. He has not wanted to know. He has relied on time and space and discretion to save them. But now everything is glaring, neon as a streetlight, ineluctable. Now he is roaring at her, waiting for her to interrupt him, to plead with him. He dares her to correct him. She says nothing. She submits to his contempt. He is glad he cannot see her. He tells her he does not care about the act, but it is her deceit, the months of her duplicity he cannot stomach. He sneers at her choice of lover. He accuses her of cliché, falling for the children's tutor, like some nineteenth-century chatelaine. She has humiliated herself, humiliated them all, with this yokel, this child, this "Terry." She weeps. He feels himself rattling inside the cuckold's rusted armor. He does not care. He does not care about being original now. He cares only to wound her as he has been wounded. He waits for her to tell him he is mistaken, that he has misunderstood everything. She does not say these things. She does not tell him he is wrong.

Annie's chest aches, her breath comes in ragged strips. She waits for him to stop but he does not. She tells him she is so sorry, so very sorry. There should be a separate language for this kind of pain, one that we only use in extremis, she thinks. "I'm sorry" is what you say when you are late, when you spill milk on the rug. It cannot encompass this rupture. It is not big enough and yet it is all she has. She feels clammy with shame and the simultaneous impulse to peel it off her body and fling it back at him, to try to explain herself. She walks the dark streets, not knowing where she is going, not seeing the cold hard river, but hearing only the whip of Hector's voice and the cataclysm of her shattered world. She tries to tell him why, that she is in love, that she does not mean to hurt, that she has not been happy, not for a long time. She fumbles for purchase with words that have no teeth because in truth, she does not know why. She can hear his disbelief and slides down the icy face of it. She denies nothing. She admits everything. He asks her when she plans to come home. She has no reply to this question because there are too many assumptions in it.

Hector falls silent. He has no more words. He has lost her. He hangs up. Annie walks unseeing through the streets. Her mouth is full of blood. Her heart is wild. She cannot imagine how on earth she will ever stop walking. Thierry calls her. She turns off her phone. She cannot talk to him. She feels manic, deranged, drunk. She is out of her body, several strides ahead of it. It drags behind her, an exhausted dog. Deeper and deeper she strides into the stirring city. She must keep moving now. It is done.

Hector sits down on a low hard stool by the fireplace. The children are asleep. Earlier he had sat through dinner, eating nothing, enduring their chatter, their mindless, endless chatter, then, with Vita's help, corralled Jackson and an excitable Remy into showers, pajamas, and eventually sleep. He did not confide in his daughter, nor she in him. She shut herself in her bedroom and he was grateful for it. He waited until he could be sure the children were asleep, searched all the devices, found what he could not believe was not better hidden, and then, using his daughter's phone, he called his wife.

Now, he sits, spent, numb. He places the phone on the table and looks around the kitchen, at the chipped mugs on the shelf, the furled magazines in the basket, the faded cushions on the window seat. He wonders what it all means, what on earth it is all for. His mind goes instantly to division. He is not a man to beg, nor to plead. The banality of his wife's choice appalls him. Perhaps she will come to her senses. But nothing in the call indicated that outcome. He will not wait for her. There is nothing for him to cling to but the children. They are his. She will not leave them. She might leave him, but not them. He will keep them and she must live with the consequences of her choice. He will show her what it means to be a parent. He is full of contempt. He thinks of all the women he has turned from, gently rebuffed, in order to stay loyal to his wife, and to his own sense of self. He flashes on the slender ankle of the film director, the pressure of her knee on that couch.

It does not matter who this boy is, Hector tells himself. This stripling will not hold Annie's attention for long. She must know that. It is an infatuation. It will pass. But now he holds his head in his hands and asks himself how well he knows his wife, how well he has ever known her. Annie was never infatuated by him. She had always taken his love lightly, worn it over her shoulders like a summer jacket. And he had known this, privately admired her for it, and trusted the constancy of her delicate love. But now she has shrugged it off and left it in the street. Is she, who surrenders nothing, who gives so little of herself to anyone, is she now given over entirely to another? Images of her body, her dark nipples, her narrow waist flicker across his thoughts. He shakes them off. He refuses them. He has satisfied his wife, he knows that. He has given her everything. They have sex, they have children, there is enough money, usually. He loves her, she loves him. Has she forgotten this? He has no answers and she had none to give him. Over and over, she repeated, weeping, "I don't know, I don't know." He walks the house, mechanically turning off lights, picking a coat off the floor, locking the doors. Too late, he thinks, the intruder is already inside. I have already been robbed.

He goes upstairs and lies fully clothed on the bed. He stares at the ceiling. He knows sleep will not come. He fumbles for a sleeping pill, swallows it, bitter and whole. It will not sedate him, he will never sleep again. He wonders if she slept with her lover in their home. Did she fuck him in this bed? He picks up the phone to call her back and ask her. He puts the phone down. He cannot lie here. He takes his pillow and a blanket and goes downstairs to lie on the sofa. He will call Patti in the morning. He will put the house on the market. The kids will want to stay in their schools, but he cannot stay in this house, he will move them. They will stay in the area, but they must start over. There is no time to lose.

The fireplace is dirty; a film of ash breathes and shimmers as he flicks the blanket over him. The smells of charred lamb, woodsmoke, and his own animal sweat linger in the room. He pulls the blanket over his head.

CHAPTER 47

"IT'S A MID-LIFE CRISIS."

Hector's eyes are closed; he leans back on Candace's new marble kitchen countertop. Candace's eyes are wet, one palm to her cheek, her coffee untouched.

"This is what Annie does. She just leaves. It's what she did to her parents. It's what she did to her ex. Now it's our turn. It's what she's good at."

Candace is silent. She cannot believe that Annie has carried all this inside her, saying nothing, disclosing nothing. She is stunned, and beneath that, betrayed, wounded to have remained on the outskirts, uninvited to this intimacy, after so many years of sharing everything. She, too, must question everything now. She feels dizzy. She wonders what else Annie has never told her.

Hector showed up unannounced on her doorstep that morning, hair wild, the car door still open behind him.

"Did you know?"

His face had crumpled at her blank astonishment.

Candace had, of course, speculated about her friend's disappearance, her resolute refusal to communicate, but she had not imagined this. Never this. Annie had been depressed before, had withdrawn, retreated, but always returned, regrouped, armed with new resolve, new hobbies, a new version of her life. But this is a newness that Candace does not recognize. She wonders now if her friend has been slowly disappearing before her very eyes.

Hector looks terribly young, standing in her kitchen. He looks like he has not slept for days: His strong face is lined with pain. His mouth falters, his chin slackens, he turns his face away from her. He sobs, harsh and brief.

"I don't know what to tell the kids."

Later that night Candace stares at the ceiling.

"We haven't really spoken in so long, I realize. I mean, we used to see each other, talk about the house, the kids, our lives. But not for months now. And before that, too, now that I think about it. I mean, I thought we were sharing stories, I thought we were complaining, like women do. But that's all I thought we were doing. Just venting. I thought we were in the same boat. I didn't realize she'd capsized." Edouard looks up from his iPad, pushes his glasses up the bridge of his nose.

"It sounds like she didn't know either."

"I feel so guilty."

"I don't think this was your fault, *ma belle*."

"I introduced them! I literally paid Thierry to go over there."

"You gave her a gift, not a lover."

"I should have checked in on her more often."

"You've never stopped taking care of her. People have been rescuing Annie her whole life. For all her feistiness, has Annie ever really had to manage on her own? Maybe this is what she needs."

"I've left a million messages. She won't take my calls."

"She will."

"What will happen to her?"

"She'll have her fling and come to her senses, and then she and Hector will rebuild. You'll see."

Candace shakes her head, still troubled. She cannot imagine what Hector is telling the children.

* * *

Vita watches her father closely at dinner. He is unusually quiet, performing his interest in their days. She noticed a long call with her mother in her phone history a few days ago. She has seen the pillow on the couch, the folded blanket wedged in a basket. She does not want to ask him what it all means because it will require her father to look her in the eye and either lie or tell the truth, and both seem unbearable right now.

After dinner, he washes dishes at the sink. She puts a hand on his back.

"I'll do it."

He lets her. He is soft. His eyes are so tired. Behind them Jackson asks for chocolate ice cream and whether zero is a prime number.

Vita calls Zoe from her bedroom.

"I think my parents are getting divorced."

CHAPTER 48

IT RAINS FOR THE ENTIRE MONTH. THE FLAT FEELS CRAMPED AND airless; the noises from the floor above are oppressive now. The pavements outside are slick with sodden leaves and abandoned crisp packets, dog shit, and flyers for sex. The city feels tired and waterlogged.

Annie feels paralyzed. The phone calls are terrible but the dissolution of her family is only endurable from this distance. She cries all the time. Thierry wraps his arms around her but there is nothing he can say. Their sex becomes more intense, moves from animal to something more profound, emotional, and beyond words. She relies on him to restore her to her body, to her senses, to why she is here. She no longer walks, not wanting to be far from him, needing him in a way she has not before. It makes her feel nervous, this need, but there is nothing to be done. The rain is her excuse. She stays inside and weeps and reads. Behind her grief she feels the tremendous relief at no longer lying to everyone. She does not think she will be able to tell another lie in her life.

Thierry disappears into his writing. He feels her watching him from across the room but writing demands all his focus. This experience, of Annie and of London, has been a watershed for him, he knows it. He has crossed a threshold. He has always suspected that a richer, more exotic life awaited him, but has never quite understood how to access it. Now, this new life unscrolls before him. He tries to capture it on the page, to distill this woman, this city, these days into something he can use but he intuits it will take time to understand exactly what is happening to him. Nevertheless, he likes how his writing feels of late. It flows, he is scooping from a river in spate. His prose seems richer already. And at the same time he feels trapped by her steady gaze. He goes for long runs by the river in the rain. She hates it when he leaves but she does not stop him. He loves Annie. He is not sure what he has done but knows he must stand by it. So much destruction must be paid for. Every book he has ever read confirms this.

His mother calls him from Paris, demanding to know why he has not visited her. She knows he is in London. She does not know with whom. He has always kept his liaisons to himself; they have courteously skirted each other's private lives ever since she returned to France. He has withheld his relationship with Annie from his mother for good reason. He knows too well how his mother feels about parents who walk out on their families. She will not be kind to Annie.

Annie takes herself to a Gauguin exhibition. She waits in line for hours in the rain, then stands, damp and shivering, before his saturated canvases, feeling the heat of his tangerine skies and coral beaches leach into her body. She comes back to the flat, filled with colors and also with longing for something she cannot name. It is not home, because she does not know what that is now, and it is not her children, because Vita will not speak to her and Jackson is either subdued or reproachful. He wants to know when she is coming back, why she and Dad can't just make up, why she does not come right now. Hector calls drunk on a couple of occasions, once spitting invective, then, again, broken, derailed, incoherently apologizing for sins he cannot seem to enumerate but for which he is desperate to atone. She hangs up, walks to the bathroom, and vomits. He does not call again. He communicates now via text, essentials only: the orthodontist's phone number, where to find Jackson's shin guards.

She replies instantly, regardless of the hour, offering up her relentless attention as recompense for her absence. She is alert to everything. She is awake.

They have been inside all day, Thierry writing, Annie attempting to read. She cannot concentrate. She wishes they could have sex but he is writing now. She gets up to make lunch. They have barely spoken all morning. He looks up briefly when she hands him a bacon sandwich, smiles, and returns to his laptop. She wonders how long they will keep this up. She rereads the same page.

"Let's go to Paris."

Annie looks up, surprised.

"When?"

"Tomorrow?"

"Have you told your mother?"

"About you or that we are coming?"

"Both. Either."

"She'll be fine. She just needs to meet you. She'll love you."

"What if she doesn't?"

"She will."

"But what if she doesn't?"

"It won't matter."

Thierry searches online for an apartment to rent. He finds one, shows her the images on his laptop. It is in the far outskirts of Paris. The photos are grainy, cramped; a checkered towel hangs off the back of a door in a dark bathroom. She frowns.

"We'll end up killing ourselves. Or each other."

She books them into a beautiful tiny hotel cradled in a high-walled courtyard off the Left Bank.

"My treat."

She wonders how many times she will say that. She wonders whether she will come to be irritated by paying. She is unused to having her own money. Her mother's money. She wonders what her mother would make of her now, what she would say. She has no idea. As she makes the reservation her thoughts flicker to Vita. For years she has planned to bring her to Paris on a girls' trip, to this very hotel. She bookmarked it a year ago with Vita in mind. Vita will never want to do that with her now. Annie lays down her credit card and sobs. Thierry comes over, holds her, waiting. She cries these days as though she were sneezing. It is over so soon. She finishes the reservation.

"Let's go to the pub."

They order rounds of vodka and tonics and clink them back to their little table in the corner. The vodkas are small and warm. They have to ask for extra ice. They order more; they drink till they feel the heat of excitement. He lists all the places in Paris he cannot wait to take her: the flea market, the museum of salt, the football stadium, the tiny bookstore, the best falafel. He is buoyant, boyish with enthusiasm. She is giddy, enlivened, happy. The move to Paris is inspired. It is exactly what they both need to break their melancholy trance.

He gets up to use the restroom. She checks her phone. Calls from Candace, from Patti, from a mother in Vita's class. Texts from Candace, who does not give up, from the children's pediatrician, from a local antiques fair, from two friends she is not particularly close to, both asking how she is doing, which means they must have spoken to Hector. She does not blame him for spreading the news, although she is surprised at how far it has spread. There are so many people to avoid. She will get back to them from Paris, she tells herself. She stuffs the phone in her purse and realizes Thierry is not back. She scans the pub. There is no sign of him. She stands up, looks across to the bar, but he is not there. The pub is busy now, full of hovering couples hoping for a table. She sits, waits, drains her empty glass. She tells herself he must have received a call and stepped outside to take it. She waits. He does not come. She calls him, feeling foolish. His phone goes right to voicemail. She is suddenly terribly sober. She gets up, forfeiting their table, and hovers outside the men's restroom, but a different man walks out of what is clearly a single-stall room. She feels her pulse rise, her face flush. Perhaps he has gone back to the flat. Perhaps he has forgotten his wallet and run back for it. Or perhaps he has left her. He has grown tired of her weeping, of her grief-soaked shame. Who would blame him? She must get out of here, immediately. As she exits she glimpses another room, an annex off the main room, one she has not noticed. There is a pool table, and on the wall above it a vast glowing television screen showing a soccer game. A huddle of people with upturned faces, Thierry among them, holding two drinks, cheer and comment on the screen. Annie watches him, unseen. He is flushed, chatting, youthful. A girl turns to him, says something, and he replies without looking at her and she throws her head back and laughs, her chipped pastel nails like tiny Easter eggs at her face, her mouth full and wide and open, and now Thierry is looking at her, at how he has made her laugh, and he is smiling, laughing too. Annie walks up to him and slides her hand into his back pocket. He is surprised, pleased. She is not given to public displays of affection. She leans her body into his ribs. The Easter egg girl smiles, friendly. Annie smiles stiffly back.

 She watches the game, about which she cares nothing. Hector, mercifully, has never cared for sports. Perhaps, she thinks, perhaps one day Thierry will watch a game with Jackson, perhaps they will sit together on a sofa and yell and point at a screen, while she and Vita make snacks in a kitchen. The image comforts but refuses to stick. She nuzzles his shoulder and finishes his drink.

CHAPTER 49

VITA RINGS THE DOORBELL. DESPITE BEING NEIGHBORS, SHE'S NEVER actually seen this house. The driveways for their properties are separated by trees and a field. It takes only a few minutes to walk here but already it feels like she has stepped into a different world. This house looks newer than theirs. It is redbrick with some kind of weird bell tower jammed on the top. A clean yellow Jeep sits outside. Even their view is different: Like theirs, this house is surrounded by trees, but she can hear the road from here, the swish of passing cars. She wishes her dad had walked her over, but she knows she is too old for that. Plus, he's so out of it lately. A boy answers.

He looks older than Jackson, but younger than Vita. Maybe eleven. He peers at her.

"Are you the sitter?"

"Yes. Hi. I'm Vita."

He sticks his hand up in greeting, flat, like a stop sign.

"I'm Ezra. Come in."

He ushers her inside, pushes past a coatrack heaped with purses of all colors and shapes, cluttered with coats. Two small anoraks lie on the floor. The house smells of fresh paint. Boxes are stacked against the walls; a rail of clothes clutters the stairwell, and paintings lie propped against the brick fireplace. She tries to be polite.

"You guys still moving in?"

He frowns, shrugs.

"I guess."

He glances upstairs.

"I'll find Christy."

He disappears upstairs. She stands, uncertain. The television blares in the kitchen. Her phone buzzes. It is her mother. She declines the call and wanders into the kitchen. There is another boy, younger than the first, curled on the sofa, watching the television. His thumb is in his mouth but he removes it hastily when she walks in.

"Who are you?"

"I'm Vita. I'm your sitter. I live next door."

He looks her over and returns to the television, pulling a thin blanket over his knees.

"What are you watching?"

He does not answer, gestures with his chin.

She perches on the arm of the sofa, wishing she had not come, wishing her father had let her go and stay with Zoe in the Hamptons, wishing her mother would leave her disgusting boy toy and go back to being an actual mother again. She watches TV with the kid, holding her phone in her lap, wondering what to do.

The mother rushes into the kitchen in a cloud of something rich and musky. Vita vaguely recognizes her from the Christmas party. Her hair is frizzed and red with dark roots. She wears a bright green dress that is tight all the way down. She looks like a palm tree. She waves at Vita.

"Hiiii. Thanks for coming. Boys, did you say hi?"

She doesn't wait for an answer but places her foot on the kitchen counter to adjust her ankle strap. There is a glimpse of darkness at her crotch. Vita quickly turns away.

"How's your mom?"

"She's good."

"I haven't seen her around for a while."

"She's away. Traveling."

"Good for her. You gotta take breaks. Otherwise, they suck the life outta you."

She laughs. There is gold in the back of her mouth.

"Ezra, show her the fridge and the microwave. Help yourself to whatever. Won't be late. Be good everyone. Send them to bed at some point. Thank youuu."

She blows kisses to her sons, who do not respond, and then Vita hears the sound of the front door closing.

Ezra turns to Vita, points.

"Fridge. Microwave."

He disappears and Vita finds herself alone again with the other kid. It is definitely too late to ask his name now. She studies her phone. The kid glances over.

"Is that a 15?"

She frowns. He points.

"Your phone. Is that a 14 or a 15? The 14 has the best lens, but the 15 has more capacity."

"I don't know. It's an old one of my dad's."

The kid snorts, goes back to his incomprehensible show.

Vita explores the fridge. There is some fresh pasta and a tub of tomato sauce. She heats it up on the stove, finds a nub of cheese in the fridge drawer, and grates it. She calls upstairs to Ezra and is surprised when he comes down to join them. She sits with them, watches them slurp their noodles. She has brought a hard-boiled egg in her pocket that she will peel and eat later, when she is alone. She can feel the light weight of it in her pocket. A dating show blares behind them.

"Where do you guys go to school?"

The younger kid keeps eating. Ezra pushes his glasses up the bridge of his nose, mentions a nearby public school.

"How is it?"

Vita hates this kind of small talk but does not know what else to say. She is not cut out for this, she realizes. She does not even really like kids other than her brother. She only took up babysitting because her dad said she could skip camp as long as she got a job. She tries again.

"How long have you lived here?"

Ezra shrugs.

"I dunno. A year maybe?"

The younger one inhales a long strand of spaghetti.

"Where did Mom go?"

Ezra answers without looking up from his food.

"Dinner with her boyfriend."

"That's nice. Do you like him?" Vita asks.

The young kid nods.

"He has a Porsche."

"Oh, you're into cars? My brother likes cars too."

The kid looks appalled.

"I'm not into cars. A Porsche is not a car. It's a work of art."

"Oh, okay."

Ezra sighs.

"He thinks this guy's great because he drives a bunch of dumb cars and took us to a Knicks game last week. Floor seats."

"That sounds cool."

"I mean, if you don't mind being bought, sure. All Christy's boyfriends think they have to buy us stuff. I got a new laptop off the last one. This guy wants to take us to Maui for Christmas."

"You call your mom Christy?"

"That's her name."

The younger kid tips the last forkful in his mouth and goes back to the sofa to watch television. Ezra yells after him.

"You need to clear your plate."

Without turning round, the kid raises his middle finger.

"Clear your plate, douchebag. And it's your turn to do dishes."

"I did them last night."

"YOU DID NOT."

"Did too."

"YOU DID NOT—"

Vita interrupts.

"It's okay, it's okay. I got the dishes."

Ezra pays no attention. He stands in front of the television, blocking his brother's view.

"GET OFF THE FUCKING COUCH, DOUCHE."

"Ezra, there's no need... it's fine, I can handle the dishes."

"I SAID GET OFF THE—"

The younger kid lashes out, kicking Ezra in the groin with his heel. Ezra doubles up, groaning. Vita races over. The boy is on the floor, clutching himself. He moans at his younger sibling.

"You little fuck."

Vita bends over him, resting a hand on his back.

"Ezra, are you okay?"

The younger kid, untroubled, kneels up on the couch so he can keep watching the television over his prone brother's back. Vita tries again.

"Are you alright?"

He looks up, eyes wide, points to his crotch.

"Will you kiss it better?"

From the sofa, the younger kid explodes with laughter. Vita stands up, her face on fire.

"Fuck off."

Ezra feels for his glasses and smiles.

"Jeez, you freak out easy."

* * *

She spends the rest of the evening on her phone, texting Zoe, who is only half paying attention because she is at a party in the city. Vita wonders, again, what Martin is doing. She knows she should call her mother back but she does not want to. She has nothing to say to her, and unless her mother is calling to tell her that she is so sorry for her disgusting behavior and that she has made a terrible mistake and is coming home, there is nothing else she wants to hear from her. Ezra disappears upstairs. The dating show ends and a news program begins but the other kid shows no sign of caring what he watches; it is all the same to him. At ten o'clock she tells him it is bedtime and is surprised when he gets up without a word, leaving the television on, and heads upstairs. She cannot find the remote so she leaves the television blaring and calls up to Ezra from the foot of the stairs.

"Guys, brush your teeth. You need to go to bed now."

She hears some to and fro in the passageway, bickering, laughter. She does not want to go up and check on them, wary of walking into an ambush or some kind of nakedness. Instead, she waits, calling up from time to time. Eventually the footsteps stop, doors close, and the upstairs rooms fall silent. She sits at the bottom of the stairs, not wanting to be in the bright kitchen with the chattering television, nor alone in the dark living room.

She waits another half an hour, then tiptoes upstairs to make sure the kids' lights are off. The corridor is silent and dark. All the doors except one are closed. The door is ajar, the light still on. Vita taps on the door, then pushes it open. High heels lie scattered on the carpet; bright bras and lacy underwear drift from drawers. The armoire bulges open, wedged full of patterned silky dresses. More dresses hang from the sagging door; several lie crumpled and pooled around the unmade bed. Her mother's closet has not one of these colors in it. The bed is vast; pill bottles loll on the bedside table, next to flattened books, dark-rimmed mugs, half-empty blister packs, and a tube of something prescription. White lights pass on the road.

She walks into the mother's bathroom. The tap drips; there is a brown circle in the bottom of the basin. A pair of crumpled underpants sits on the floor, and makeup bottles lie open and scattered across the marble countertop. She inspects the brands. Vita has been playing around with her mother's makeup lately, experimenting in the mornings with her eye shadows and blush while her father makes breakfast. Last week she stole three lip glosses from the drugstore in town, slipping the bright tubes in her pocket before she even knew what she was doing. Her heart pounded all the way to the parking lot, where she slid in beside her father and didn't breathe again until they pulled up in their own driveway. The lip glosses roll in the back of the drawer of her bedside table. She doesn't even like lip gloss. There is a mini screwdriver, a key ring, two lined notebooks, an upholstered wallet, and a pair of heart-shaped earrings in that drawer as well. She has stolen all of these things over the span of a few months without knowing quite why. She has no use for any of them but stuffed them all in a pocket of her backpack and brought them home.

She touches the mother's highlighter stick, pearly and smudged. She wipes it over her eyelids, uses her finger to blend it, turns her head to see how it catches the light. A lipstick rolls on the counter. She tries it on. She looks like a clown. Her teeth look yellow. She is wiping it off with a tissue when she hears a sound in the doorway. The younger kid is standing there in his pajama bottoms, watching her. His bare chest rises and falls and his mouth is open.

"What are you doing?"

She wipes her mouth calmly.

"Why are you out of bed?"

"Are you allowed to be in here?"

She throws the tissue in the trash.

"Do you need something? A glass of water?"

She walks toward him, puts a hand on his shoulder. His skin feels cool, clammy to the touch.

"I heard noises. Is Mom home?"

"Not yet. Come on, I'll walk you back to bed."

His bedroom is dimly lit by a moon-shaped night-light. In the darkness she can make out the outline of giant LEGO structures, a city of buildings spread out across the floor. He climbs into bed. She hovers by the door.

"Good night."

"Will you stay for a bit?"

"In here?"

"Till I fall asleep?"

"Um, okay."

She is wary, expecting a prank, or to be laughed at. But he lies on his side, eyes wide in the dark.

"Did Mom say when she'd be home?"

"She said she wouldn't be late."

"She's always late."

"Yeah, mine too."

"Where's your mom?"

"In London."

"Does she live there?"

"No. She's just visiting."

"Does she live with you?"

"I guess."

"Does your dad?"

"Yeah, we live next door to you."

"My dad lives in California."

"Do you get to see him?"

"Mom got a restraining order because she says he's batshit."

"Oh wow. That's intense."

"He just loves us too much. That's what he says. We have our own phones that he gave us so he can talk to us and that way Mom doesn't have to deal with him. He's gonna come and get us, he says."

"To go live with him?"

"Yep."

"Do you want to?"

The kid blinks.

"I dunno."

He rolls away from her.

"You can go now."

As she walks out, he calls out.

"I won't tell Christy you were in her bathroom."

The kitchen is streaked with gray light when Vita wakes to the sound of the doorbell. She has fallen asleep on the sofa in the kitchen. After a fruitless search for the remote she resorted to unplugging the television from its socket in the wall. She was sure this was not optimal but she had been all out of ideas. Blearily she stumbles to the front door. There is a strange man there. He is small, paunchy, stubbled. A gold chain glints at his neck.

"I forgot my key."

"Oh."

"Sorry. I didn't mean to scare you."

"Where's Christy?"

"She's on her way. She stopped for gas. We're in separate cars. She asked me to run you home."

He gestures behind him, a sleek gray car parked in the driveway. She holds the door, uncertain. She has no idea what she is supposed to do. Her heart feels like a fist.

"It's okay. I can walk home."

"If you're sure."

He takes a step toward her. She shrinks back, reluctantly letting the door open. He brushes past her into the hallway. Now he is inside and she is the one in the doorway. She takes her time sliding on her sneakers. He seems at home, dumping his car key on the hall table, slipping his shoes off at the bottom of the stairs. He does not seem batshit. She sees him glance upstairs.

"Boys okay?"

"Uh, yes."

"Good."

He chuckles. She feels certain she should wait for Christy but does not know how to do that. She hesitates in the doorway. The man pulls out a thick black wallet and withdraws some crisp bills.

"Does this cover it?"

She takes the bills, feeling certain she is being paid off. It is much more than she was expecting.

"That's fine."

"You sure you don't want a ride?"

She shakes her head. She opens her mouth. He smiles.

"Thanks for coming."

He closes the door in her face.

The trees are black sticks, the moon a feather in a slurried sky. A gray Mercedes sits parked outside the house. She walks slowly down the driveway back to the main road, hoping to see Christy's yellow Jeep, but the road is dark and empty. She walks the few hundred yards along the main road, then down the lane that leads home. She glimpses the roof of her house when she remembers the boys telling her that Christy's boyfriend drives a Porsche. She stops. Her chest feels tight. She does not know what to do. She had one job, to look after the boys, and she failed at it. She feels sick to her stomach. She turns back, runs along the road back to the house. She has no plan but knows she must go back. The Mercedes is still parked in the driveway. She crouches behind the trash cans and takes a photograph of the license plate. At least the police will be able to track him. A stocky silhouette appears at the window of Christy's bedroom. She holds her breath. He draws the curtains. The light stays on behind them. She waits, scarcely breathing. She is so cold, her teeth chatter. Still no sign of Christy's Jeep. She imagines hurling herself at the front door. She throws a brick through the Mercedes windshield. She sets fire to the hedge. She turns and runs home again, her breath tearing at her chest.

Her father is asleep on the couch again. She stands over him, wanting to wake him, to ask his advice. But he looks old in his sleep, his face crinkled and hollow. The blanket has slipped from his shoulders. She pulls it over his chest. She can smell the tang of whiskey on his breath.

She calls her mother from her bedroom. Annie answers immediately.

"Vee?"

"Hi."

"I'm so glad you called."

"Yeah."

"Is everything okay?"

"Yeah."

"You sure?"

"Mom."

"Yes, love?"

"Are you ever coming home? Like, coming back to the US?"

"Of course. Of course I am. I just need... a little time."

Vita waits.

"I love you so much, Vee. You know that."

She nods, furls and unfurls the label inside her coat on her lap.

"It's late there, love. Did you need something or… are you just calling?"

"Just calling."

"Where are you?"

"Home."

"How was your day?"

"I babysat. For Christy next door."

"How was it?"

"Weird."

"She seems weird."

"It wasn't her. It was the guy."

"What guy?"

"Her boyfriend. Or maybe her husband. I don't know. He was weird."

"Vita, what happened? Did he try anything?"

"God, Mom. No. Nothing like that. Don't be gross."

"Is your dad there?"

"Yes. I don't need Dad. It wasn't that. I just don't know who he was. I feel bad because I left."

"If it felt weird, then you did the right thing. You got out of there."

"You don't feel bad for leaving us?"

"What?"

"Never mind."

"I don't want you sitting for them again."

"Mom. Stop."

"Vee, did he touch you?"

"Ugh. My God. You always freak out about the wrong shit."

Vita hangs up. She throws her coat on the bed. Something falls with a gentle thud. It is the hard-boiled egg, which has tumbled from her pocket. It rolls along the bedroom floor and comes to rest next to her desk. Its brown shell is crackled with tiny white fissures. She throws it in the trash.

The next morning her father asks her how it went. She shrugs, sips her scalding black coffee.

"Fine."

He drives her into town, and she cranes her neck to peer down the neighbor's driveway, glimpses a flash of yellow. A few days later they pass the boys walking along the main road. They are bickering, swinging water bottles and tennis rackets. She slinks down in the passenger seat. They do not see her.

CHAPTER 50

PARIS IS FREEZING. THE WIND BITES AT THEIR ANKLES. THE HOTEL IS even smaller than pictured. Their bedroom is on the top floor, a garret with sloping ceilings and a slanted wooden floor. The heat from the entire building gathers beneath the rafters, so their room is stuffy, oppressively hot. They sleep with the dormer windows flung open. They go downstairs for breakfast, which is included in the price of the room. The dining room is all glass, a modern addition, with uncomfortable molded chairs. The orange juice is thin, acidic; the croissants are chewy. Nothing is quite as advertised. Thierry stands in the courtyard, hunched against the wind, talking to his mother on the phone. He has been there a while. His smile is tight.

He joins her at the table, scraping his chair.

"I'll go and see her on my own today."

"Oh?"

"We'll all have lunch tomorrow."

Annie waits.

"I think it will be easier."

"She doesn't want to meet me."

"She does. She just wants to see me on her own first. We haven't seen each other for almost a year."

"She does know about me?"

"Of course."

"But...?"

"She's protective."

"Of you?"

"Of course."

Annie stirs her coffee.

"Because I'm married?"

He shrugs, nods.

"She knows about the kids?"

"She knows you have kids, yes."

"Maybe we shouldn't meet after all."

"We came to Paris to see her."

"You did. I just came to Paris to visit Paris."

"Don't be like this. I want you to get to know each other."

"Why? She already knows what she thinks of me."

It is their first fight. Thierry leaves, coat flapping.

Annie sits, her coffee filmy, the city gray beyond the glass window. She has never felt so alone. Paris feels secretive after London. It feels walled up, enclosed, private. It is beautiful and inaccessible, a duchess glimpsed in the back of her carriage. London is a bawd in the street, her muddied bloomers on display for all. She has only been here once with Hector. They took the train from London for a weekend one summer, drank wine in Les Jardin des Tuileries, sunbathed by the river. It feels like a lifetime ago. It seems impossible that it was ever sunny here.

Annie takes herself to a famous flea market and shivers through the stalls of exquisite junk. She wanders, aimless, unmoored. She cannot communicate with anyone. She has no one to buy for. She has no home to buy for. She buys a vintage neck scarf for Vita; it is heavy cream silk with a red border. For Jackson she finds an old microscope complete with antique slides of bone, moss, blood that she knows he will love. She will ship it home. She fingers linen sheets, embroidered tablecloths, a set of silver teaspoons, but for the first time in her life nothing holds her, she cannot imagine what any of it is for, nor where any of it will go. Candace calls, again. Annie sends the call to voicemail. She no longer bothers listening to any of her messages. There is no point in calling anyone back. She has nothing to say. Her life is unrecognizable to herself, she has no way of making it scrutable to others. Her life is a new language, as faltering as the little French Thierry has taught her. It is unintelligible to anyone but herself and him.

She drifts into a restaurant, orders an aniseed drink that turns cloudy with water. She wonders what Thierry is doing. She wonders where her children are. They are back at school, the metronome has resumed, they are immersed in their dramas and homework. Hector will be picking them up from school in a few hours. She knows those drives too well, the children noisy with petty slights and victories, discarding their armor with their hoodies and backpacks, scattering it around the house, taking all evening to wind down and return to their soft selves. She does not miss the stooping to gather up. She does not miss yelling up the stairs for shoes, for dinner, for a sign of recognition that she exists. She does not miss the listless planning of an eternity of meals, nor the Sisyphean laundry. She misses none of this. She misses her children, their bodies in space, the smell of their hair, the weight of their arms around her neck.

An older man and his wife sit at a nearby table. They are elegant, sedate, undeniably French. They are studying the menu with occasional comment. The man leans forward and unhooks his wife's glasses from her unresisting face. He pulls a pale blue handkerchief from his pocket and cleans the lenses thoroughly, scrupulously, without comment or censure. Naked-faced, the woman waits, looks out the window. He places them back on her face, like a kiss. They both return to their menus. Annie bows her head to hide her tears.

As she is paying, Thierry calls. His voice is high, excited.

"Guess what?"

"What?"

"I'm getting published!"

"Thierry, that's wonderful! Congratulations! Which story?"

"The one about the guy and the dead mother."

He mentions a magazine she has never heard of. He tells her he will be back soon, he is just finishing up with his mother. He will see her back at the hotel. It is as though their fight never happened. He sounds giddy, full of plans for getting an agent, for his next submission. She hangs up. Her palms tingle. He has never mentioned this story.

Annie sits on the hotel bed, sifting through Thierry's laptop. She glances at his emails. They are mostly bills, spam, literary newsletters, some in French from his mother, one from Maya asking when he's coming home and whether he's paid the cable. She sees the email from the literary review congratulating him on their acceptance of his submission, "Rest in Peace." She does a search for the title and finds the story immediately.

It is a story about a young man, a telemarketer who sells home security systems. He is given an ultimatum by his boss to make a sale that day or lose his job. He has been working at a call center for three months and has yet to close a single sale. He cannot afford to get fired. His fourth call of the morning is to a woman who answers the phone with a curious "Hello?" From the upward inflection, he knows he is in with a chance. She is "timid as a flightless bird." He introduces himself and the company he works for. She does not tell him to get lost. He asks her how her day is going. She thanks him for asking, says she is a little busy at the moment. He asks what she is up to. He is butter-smooth. She tells him it is nice to talk to someone. She tells him that her mother died a few hours ago and she is here, in her mother's room, trying to figure out what to dress her in before they take her away. She would like her mother to be buried in a dress, not the velour tracksuits the old woman lived in for the last years of her life. He listens, waiting for his chance. The noise of the floor fades out behind him. He knows that this is the one. He will have to be patient. He flashes on the floor manager telling the new recruits to "tickle 'em first" before reeling them in. He offers his condolences. He asks about the mother. The woman tells him her mother was eighty-three and mad as a rat. She tells him that her mother was a shut-in, that a car crash as a kid left the mother with a lifelong terror of motorized vehicles, so she refused to get in a car again. The mother's entire life—and, by extension, the daughter's—has taken place within a ten-block radius. The woman is weepy. The young man listens, alert. He comforts her. He knows he is close. He establishes that the woman lives alone now. He would like her to feel safe; a security system will help with that. She is distracted, uncertain about which dress to bury her mother in. He tells her to send him a photo so he can help. He gives her his cell phone number. He knows it's forbidden, but he is close, so close. A bleary image of two flowered dresses hanging on the door of an armoire appears on his screen. He tells her the blue one is perfect. He tells her she deserves a life of her own now, a life of freedom and possibility. He believes what he is saying. He is offering deliverance, in the form of cameras, an alarm, and an app. He is gliding toward a sale, he can feel it. He tells her it was fate that he called this morning. "Seems like it's your turn now, Miss. It's never too late to change your life." He mentions travel, adventure, and security, all in the same sentence. She sighs. He tells her she sounds like a nice person. He bets she has a beautiful smile. She giggles, delighted. But she must go. The undertaker will be here soon. Can he call her back later? He squeezes his forehead. He has spent too long on this call already. He tells her he cannot, that he is only authorized to offer this deal at this price right now, that he cannot vouch for how much it will go up should he call back. She is perplexed, reluctant, even petulant, but then, astonishingly, she agrees. He takes down her credit card details hurriedly before she can change her mind, before any interruption can snatch his prize away from him. He is giddy. He thanks her for her time, tells her someone—no, he—will follow up in a week to make sure she's happy with her system. He assures her that her life is about to change. He hangs up and throws his fist in the air. An approving nod from his supervisor across the floor. He calls his girlfriend from a stall in the men's room. The baby is screaming in the background, but he can tell she is relieved.

Later that evening, forking ramen in his mouth as he reads the basketball scores, his phone pings. It is a text from a number he does not recognize. It is a photograph of a woman asleep. He looks more closely. He recognizes the blue dress. The woman is dead, not asleep. She is lying in a coffin, hands clasped. He whistles, shows his girlfriend the photo. His girlfriend shudders. A new message comes in. "Don't she look pretty?" He wonders what to text back. The girlfriend tells him he shouldn't have taken advantage of a crazy lady. He tells her he doesn't see it that way, that he gave her what she needed. They whisper so as not to wake the baby asleep in the hallway. She tells him just to block the woman's number. He tells her he can't. He needs to guarantee his commission; if the woman backs out before installation, he won't get a dime. His girlfriend tells him to send her a photo of her fine ass, then goes to bed. He hovers over the phone, then types, "rest in peace." It seems exactly right. It covers all the bases. He has sex with his girlfriend and falls asleep. He is woken by the sound of his phone ringing. His girlfriend stirs. The baby yelps. He silences it and rolls over. The phone lights up again. All night long, and for days after, the phone lights up.

* * *

Annie closes the laptop. Her heart is pounding. She feels plundered. It is like waking up in a strange room with no memory of getting there. The story he has written is not theirs, of course, but it carries so many echoes of her life, faint drifts of responsibility, a theme of deadening commitment, of obligations seen through to the bitter end. Is this what he thinks of her? Is she that lonely woman, unhinged by her dead mother? Is she the insistently ringing phone? She resolves never to ask him, nor to admit she has read the story.

She does not last long.

He laughs, setting down the bottle of champagne he bought on his way home.

"You are hilarious."

"I don't feel hilarious. I feel unsettled."

"By my short story? I guess I should be flattered. Did you like it?"

"Of course."

"You forgot to mention that part."

"I'm terrible at praise."

"But you liked it?"

"I can't separate from it. I think so. It's so different from the other one."

"Which one?"

"The Blitz one."

"Oh. Yes."

"Do you feel sorry for me? Or did you? Is that why we are here?"

"What? Of course not."

"Is this you 'tickling' me?"

"Annie. I'm not writing about you. Or at least, it's not only you. I write about what interests me. You interest me. Your world interests me. But so does selling things on the telephone for a living. It's all just a place to start. This isn't wish fulfillment or exorcism. It's a way of rearranging the familiar to arrive, hopefully, at something new. You're no more a lonely shut-in than I am a cynical telemarketer. They're all me, I suppose. Or they're all parts of me."

"She's pitiful, that woman. And timid. That's not me."

"Of course it's not you."

He feels impatient with her, irritated that the celebration of his success is attendant on this fixation of hers.

"I can't believe this is what we're fighting about. I thought I was coming home to celebrate."

"See, it is like your story."

He laughs and shakes his head.

"Which makes you the fine-ass girlfriend."

He kisses her hard on the mouth. They have sex, but for the first time they are both somewhere else.

That evening they meet Thierry's cousin Ludo in a bar in Montmartre. The hill is precipitous, the bar low-ceilinged and crowded, people in thick coats spilling onto the steep sidewalk, laughing. A cluster of German tourists sit at a spindly wrought iron table, trying to fit in. Annie overhears them, guttural over their beers, their neon fanny packs cluttering the tiny table.

Ludo is compact, tight as a wrapped stone. He wears a silky T-shirt the color of apricots and his hair slicked back. His front tooth is slightly chipped and his forearms laced with faded tattoos. Ludo kisses Annie on both cheeks and casually checks her out. He gives Thierry a broad grin and runs his hand briskly over his cousin's shaved head. He introduces them to his son, Mael, a sulky eight-year-old in a soccer shirt who is watching something on a smeary cell phone. Mael does not take his eyes off his screen. Annie leans over to see what he's watching. Mael glances at her, distrustful. She asks him, in her halting French, what it is. He tells her. It is a series she knows, one that Jackson likes, about zombies. She tries to communicate this but the boy does not care, has gone back to his show. Like a stiletto in the rib, she misses her son.

In his scattered English, Ludo tells Annie about his job (selling motorbikes from his workshop near Versailles), his girlfriend (a real estate agent from Algiers), his ex-wife (a "Breton whore"). He asks Annie nothing. Thierry and his cousin laugh, drink, shout in one another's ear. Annie understands not a word that they are saying. Thierry is loud, extravagant, full of gestures. He likes making Ludo laugh. He forgets to translate for her. It is strange to watch his body speak since she cannot understand his words. She feels so distant from him. He feels foreign to her, and yet he seems entirely at home. He is lost in his storytelling. Annie finishes her drink. The bar is too noisy and the street too cold to stand in. She tells Thierry that she's heading home, that he should stay, and stuffing her hands in her pockets, she walks the narrow streets back to the hotel.

Lying in bed, waiting for sleep, it occurs to her that if she is not already a character in one of Thierry's stories, she is destined to become one. This is what lies at the root of her fear. That he will sit naked in a bed, somewhere, someday, with some young woman in his lap, and will tell her about the affair he once had with a woman twice his age. Annie will become an anecdote. The discovery of his short story was only a rehearsal for the story she knows she will one day become.

Later Thierry slides into bed beside her, alcoholic, apologetic.

"You okay?"

She pretends to be asleep.

They sit in a half-empty Moroccan restaurant in the northern part of town, waiting to meet Thierry's mother for lunch. A waiter brings them a carafe of red wine. Thierry and Annie sit side by side on the banquette. He checks his phone, rubs his newly shaved chin. She doesn't like it when he's clean-shaven, it makes him look too young, but she says nothing. He pours Annie a glass of wine, checks his phone again. Outside, the street is streaked with slanting people, angling themselves against the wind.

"You know my mother speaks almost no English."

Annie looks at him in surprise.

"But she lived in the US for twenty years?"

He shrugs, suddenly very French.

"I did most of the talking for her. Or my dad did."

"I can't believe you're only telling me this now."

"What difference would it have made?"

"This will be interesting."

A tiny woman appears in the doorway. She is dressed in a gray coat and carrying a woven bag full of groceries. She skirts through the tables and, placing a tiny hand on his massive shoulder, pecks Thierry on both cheeks. She does not greet or even look at Annie. Annie is so startled, she forgets to sit down. Thierry helps his mother with her coat and eases her into her chair. He seems nervous. He introduces them.

"*Maman, je te présente Annie*. Annie, this is Laure."

Annie takes her seat. Laure is so small that Annie wonders if her feet reach the floor when she sits. It seems impossible that she gave birth to this colossus. She is covered in freckles: They look like they have been hand-painted with a quill. She wears a thin gold cross at her neck. She is neat, as though she has tidied most of herself away. She hangs the grocery bag on the back of her seat. Oranges bulge and settle through the netting, parsnips claw at the string. Thierry offers to put the bag beside him but she shakes him off; they will stay where they are. His mother speaks crisply, still without looking at Annie. Thierry translates.

"She says she is sorry she was late; she was at the market, and the butcher always talks too much."

Annie suspects everyone talks too much for this woman, but she smiles and nods encouragingly.

"*Pas de problème, Laure.* I'm sorry... *je suis désolée... mon français n'est pas très bien...* is not very good. I've been learning, Thierry has been teaching me, but I haven't got very far."

Laure flicks a glance at her, then looks expectantly at Thierry, waiting for him to translate. He speaks swiftly. His mother nods, implacable, says something with a raised eyebrow into her water glass, and then gestures to the waiter to bring the menu. Annie leans over to Thierry.

"What did she say?"

He smiles, dry.

"She says I should stick to writing."

She directs the waiter to address her on the other side of the table so as not to bruise her hanging produce. The waiter accommodates. Annie wonders if this is standard French deference to the sovereignty of food or if this diminutive tyrant is always used to getting her own way.

Lunch is impossible. It is a series of stalled one-way conversations, Thierry trapped between them, ferrying Annie's attempts across to his mother, who neatly capsizes every effort. Laure addresses all her questions to her son, who attempts to translate them for Annie but is interrupted by another remark from his mother. Annie places a hand on his knee, unsure if she is giving or seeking reassurance. Laure is impassive, immutable as a god. She is a wren and a whale. She dilutes her wine with water, scoops tiny mouthfuls of couscous with her fork, clicks in disapproval at the quality of the bread. Annie tries again.

"How is it, living in Paris again after so long away?"

Thierry translates. His mother shrugs, replies to her son.

"Les gens sont les mêmes où que vous alliez."

"She says people are the same wherever you go."

"Does she... do you miss anything about America?"

He translates. She snorts. She looks at Annie for the first time. Her eyelashes are so pale, they are almost nonexistent. Her voice is hoarse.

"My son."

"She hates me."

"She doesn't hate you."

"She couldn't even look at me."

"She takes time. My friends were all terrified of her."

"I'm not surprised. How did you turn out so nice?"

"She was a good mom. She *is* a good mom."

"What does that even mean?"

"It means... oh, I don't know, she was there for me."

"Like how?"

"Like, there was this kid in third grade, Tom, who made fun of me for being tall. Normal kid stuff, but I hated him. He started calling me 'the Janitor,' said I should change light bulbs for a living. Soon, all the other kids were doing it. I came home one day and told my mom. And she got in the car and drove to where this kid lived. I crouched in the back seat so no one would see. The mother answered the door, and my mom asked to speak to Tom. Next thing I know, my mom and Tom are on the doorstep, and she's talking to him. I don't know what she's saying because, as you know, she doesn't really speak English, but whatever she is saying, he gets it. They're almost the same height, but she's jabbing him in the chest, and he's taking it. I can see him blushing, cringing at this tiny woman taking him down in her broken English. He never knew I was there, or I don't think it would have gone well for me. But no one called me 'the Janitor' after that."

They are lying in bed, fully clothed, facing each other. Outside it is raining. The room smells faintly of the Brie they ate with a spoon several days earlier. He rolls onto his back.

"Ludo has an apartment he wants to show us."

"We don't need an apartment."

"This hotel is so expensive. We could get somewhere great for half what this place costs."

"But we're not staying long enough . . ."

"But what if we do?"

"What do you mean?"

"I mean, what if we stay?"

He glances over at her.

"What if we spent some time here, some real time?"

She does not reply.

"Shall we take a look at this apartment? Just to see?"

"You want to live here now?"

"I could write, teach English, you could paint, learn French. Ludo will help me find work. It could be fun."

"But I can't."

"Why not?"

"Because I'm not French. I don't belong here. This isn't my home, it's your home."

"It's not my home either."

"I have to see my kids, I'm not moving to Paris."

"You can still see them. Fly back and forth."

"I don't... that's not what I want."

He nods, stares at the ceiling.

"Is it what you want?" she asks.

"I don't know. But I don't want to go back to before."

She has been waiting for this. It feels inevitable. He is expansive here in a way she has not seen him be anywhere else; he is chatty, excitable, making friends on the Métro, in the street, with the waiters. He is eager to belong here. He can imagine himself here. He has, in fact, always imagined himself here. London was their fever dream. He needed her to bring him here, to help him into his new life, just as she needed him to leave her old one. She does not know where she belongs, but it is not here. She has no home. And she cannot make him her home.

CHAPTER 51

SHE BUYS A BOX OF MACARONS AT THE AIRPORT. SHE HAS NO IDEA who they are for, but it seems negligent not to buy something for someone. Rain streaks the vast glass atrium. The flight is delayed. Everyone groans, reaches for their phones. She wonders who to call, who to tell. One by one she eats the macarons: vanilla, rose, coffee, violet, apricot, pistachio.

CHAPTER 52

HECTOR SITS AT THE HEAD OF THE TABLE. HIS FACE HAS MORE angles in it and there are deeper lines around his mouth, but he looks, if possible, more handsome than ever, his mother thinks as she enters from the kitchen, bearing the loin of roast beef. She rose early this morning, pulled it from the fridge, salted it, and let it sit at room temperature while she peeled and prepared the potatoes, the carrots, the brussels sprouts. She liked having the kitchen to herself. Annie never let her help, was always frazzled, but didn't know how to delegate, that was her problem. One of them, anyway. Vita set the table, Jackson managed to fold the napkins. Hector dug out the Christmas crackers from last year. Annie had texted, told them where to find them. Derek slept in, which was fine; he and Hector had stayed up late pulling down some string lights that seemed to be driving her son nuts. The house looks festive, she thinks, laying the beef in front of him. She had brought some decorations from home, and Hector had done well, getting the tree up and decorated, presents bought and wrapped. Well, she had done the wrapping, but that was to be expected. No, he is doing well, she thinks, managing these kids entirely on his own. They haven't missed a day of school, no bones broken, everyone seems to be doing fine as far as she can tell. Vita is morose, but that is the age. Jackson is his usual inscrutable self. Her son is proud and unwilling to confide in her but that is the man she raised. It is gallant of him to host this gathering, and to allow his estranged wife to join them. She can scarcely look down at the other end of the table. She chose her seat carefully, this end, next to her son, as far as possible from where her former daughter-in-law (she cannot bring herself to say her name anymore) sits, pale and listening, like a ghost almost. Here we all are, Bryony thinks, setting down the gravy, despite it all. She had known things were not right; hadn't she warned them all? It is so hard to always be right. Candace and Edouard are keeping things festive, even though Candace brought her spoiled stepmother along, but Derek is managing her; he doesn't mind, he's good with everyone.

Hector's mother takes her seat beside her son, satisfied. The beef is done to perfection. Hector should take a nap after lunch. He looks tired. You never stop worrying, she thinks, no matter how old they get. She wonders if Alexander will call from the Alps later. She puts a spoon in the broccoli. You are always a mother, always, she thinks, no matter where they are.

Candace grasps Hector's hand as she tells him a story about some tech giant she is trying to persuade to join one of her boards. He would like to shake it off so he can begin carving, but her grip is absolute, her focus not to be shifted, and she has been kind these last months. Deeply kind. She has listened to him, shaken her head, averted her eyes as he wept, kept the children for the nights when he could not face them. She has told him everything she knows, reported back on her few phone calls with Annie, shared her disapproval and disappointment. She has, in short, been a friend. He feels heavy with magnanimity as he looks down the table to the far end where his wife, his former wife, Annie sits. He does not know what to call her now. She is strange to him. She is both known and utterly foreign. She is here as a guest, as his guest, he supposes. Everyone is talking, everyone is smiling studiously, keeping themes light, keeping the conversation flowing so that nothing can actually be said. He glances at Annie, who is seated between Edouard and Miriam. She looks tired. And thin. But younger, somehow. Her eyes seem huge, as though she has dissolved herself in them. She is listening to Edouard but keeps flicking her gaze over to Vita, who is seated in her mother's former seat at the head of the table, and who, he notices, refuses to look at Annie. He feels for his daughter, for her brittle composure, for the membrane with which she has coated herself. He sees Annie's hopeful glances across the table and Vita's refusal to acknowledge them. He feels a flicker of compassion for his wife. But he shakes it off. This is not his cross to bear. This is not of his doing. They are here, assembled, as a family, at her request. Annie had asked if they could be together on Christmas Day and he, for the sake of the children—well, for Jackson, really—had finally agreed. But also he wants to see her up close. He wants to watch her witnessing what she has done, all that she has left behind. He wants to see for himself who she is now, what has become of her. He has barely seen her since she got back. He has not wanted to see her strangeness nor bear her familiarity. But this is the Christmas she wants, so this is the Christmas she will have.

He is to play Vanya in the new year. He will be extraordinary in the role. He will bring them all to their knees. He will never, ever get used to this. And he will never, ever take her back (she will not ask, he knows this). He will be dignified. He will behave perfectly. The cathedral is intact. But the crypt is in ruins.

Candace tosses up another story to distract Hector, to entertain him. She can tell he is barely listening to her, but she will not give up. She is good at this, at never letting the ball drop. She marvels at his strength, at all their strength, holding this table together, being so civilized. She wonders what she would do if Edouard left her. She cannot imagine it. And yet men do it all the time. Funny, she thinks, we are so used to men leaving their families, but not women. We roll our eyes and shake our heads. But mothers do not leave. Mothers we cannot forgive. She and Annie have spoken a few times on the phone. They both cried. Candace spoke her mind because someone had to. She told her that she loved her, and she understood, of course motherhood is hard, marriage is work, mistakes are made, but leaving? Walking out on the children? Was this the answer? And Annie had not replied, but only cried a little, and said she did not expect Candace to understand. Candace had not known whether to be flattered or insulted. She cannot imagine leaving her family. It would be like committing suicide. She wonders how Annie spends her days now. She must have so much time on her hands.

Candace is glad her stepmother is here. Miriam had gone very quiet when Candace had told her the news, and asked how Annie was doing, not Hector, which was strange. Miriam always loved an underdog. Candace glances down at her phone to make sure the surrogate has not called. The surrogate is eight months pregnant with their child; she has assured them she feels well and strong, and the doctor says this baby is not due for another six weeks, but still Candace cannot help but worry. She wakes in the night and checks her phone, over and over, compulsively, as though she might feel the baby kick there. She is frightened of what awaits her, the vigils, the exhaustion, managing Remy's inevitable jealousy, the depletion at her age, and yet she knows that they are doing the right thing. She cannot wait to smell her daughter's skull, to swaddle her against her empty breasts and know her baby for the first time. She feels giddy as a bride. She cannot believe her good fortune.

She drinks sparkling water; she has abjured alcohol ever since their surrogate confirmed she was pregnant so that she, too, could bring her cleansed, best self to this moment. Edouard is apprehensive, she knows this. But he will come around. Once he meets his daughter. He's a wonderful father. Like Hector. She glances down the table at her friend, who looks irritatingly thinner. Annie seems very quiet, but that seems appropriate. She's lucky to be here, thinks Candace. We should have lunch, thinks Candace. I miss her, thinks Candace.

Jackson is longing to get down from the table and play with his new snake. He can't believe he finally got one. Dad is a legend. Remy wants one now but Remy is getting a baby, so he definitely won't be getting a snake as well. He kicks his legs, accidentally kicking Vita, who snaps at him. She's mad all the time these days. His dad says it's hormones but she screams at him if he says that so he just whispers it to Jackson instead. But Vita lets Jackson sleep in her bed every night and does not tell anyone about it, so that is something. He wonders what his mother got him. She arrived in time for lunch and whispered in his ear that she'd give him his gift afterward, "when it's just us." He had kissed her cheek and squirmed off her lap to get back to his snake. One good thing about this new arrangement is double presents. He hadn't considered that. He wonders if he clears his plate whether they might not notice if he leaves the table.

Vita cannot wait for lunch to be over. Everything about this Christmas is off. The house is full of some lame tinsel that her grandmother has stuck everywhere. Jackson tore through his crappy stocking this morning before anyone else got downstairs and no one said a word about it. She never even got one, which was probably for the best. Her dad had obviously forgotten and bought whatever he could find at the gas station. They should have just canceled Christmas this year. She wishes her mother had stayed away. She does not know why they are all sitting there pretending everything is normal when normal disintegrated the day her mother left. Her mother has destroyed everything. She looks old, which serves her right for hooking up with a guy half her age. She checks her new watch. Ashley has sent her a bunch of festive emojis. Zoe waved from Antigua. A text from Martin. Her stomach flips. He's having friends over tomorrow, does she want to hang. Her head feels light. She needs to call Ash, she must wash her hair, she must get away from this table.

Miriam is just back from Aspen. She paid a small fortune to spend a week listening to global thought leaders present solutions to the world's problems. She is energized, full of stories of alternative fuel sources, education reform, universal health care. She is aware of how valuable her time is. She was diagnosed with late-stage cancer six weeks ago. There is nothing to be done. She has told no one. But she will waste nothing now. No breath, no opportunity. This table is soaked in grief. She can feel it. She wishes she could tell them all just to love and to love and to love. Annie rises. Miriam meets her in the kitchen, bearing plates.

"You okay?"

"Yes."

Miriam puts her hand to Annie's cheek.

"Live, my dear. You must live your life."

Annie is grateful to be here, with these people. She drove here from the small cottage that she has rented eight miles away. It is furnished simply. She sleeps in her mother's bed and wipes her face at her mother's dressing table. There are six plates on the shelf, six mugs, and a jam jar of winter roses. She has donated or sold everything else. She no longer stages houses for Patti, or for anyone. The freezer has two frozen pizzas in it in case the children come to stay. There are bunk beds in the second bedroom, although Jackson sleeps in her bed and Vita has yet to spend the night. She came once, descended like a visiting monarch, sipped black tea, and called a local cab to take her home. She will not let Annie do anything for her. One day she will come of her own accord. One day. She has her own key. Annie will have to wait for her daughter's grace.

She feels the heat of judgment coming off Candace, radiant as a gas. It is noxious to get too close so she keeps her distance, both missing her and not. Watching her friend struggle to make sense of her, to hide her palpable censure, is exhausting. Candace will support Hector because that is her way of showing her love; she will wrap herself around Annie's children, she will lead by example. She is grateful to her friend for buttressing her husband. Hector will always need someone to hold him up. He looks both frail and more himself than she remembers. The show is over. He will never forgive her. She knows this. There is nothing to be done.

She reads books, more than she has for years. She attends a life-drawing class in the evenings. She eats little, goes to the city less often than she had imagined. She speaks to Thierry, although less and less these days. The time difference does not help, but it is not that, they both know it.

He has another story published. She sends him a bottle of champagne to celebrate. He calls to thank her two days later. She has stopped waiting for him to tell her the truth about the story he read to her in the kitchen that night, a story she had been forced to study at high school, a story she knew almost by heart, had underlined and critiqued, a story he told her was his own. She had held her breath, waiting for the truth, wondering how to tell him that she knew he was lying, but in the end had tucked this knowledge away, holding it as tenderly as if it were one of her son's baby teeth placed beneath his pillow.

We all tell stories that are not ours to tell. He had wanted to dazzle her and she had wanted to be dazzled. And she had told him her untruth, that she was five years younger than she was. He would never know that she had turned fifty by his side.

There is no one to tell her stories now. And there is no one for whom she must make them up. She has a ticket booked for Paris for the new year but she wonders if she will use it.

* * *

Her life is small and quiet as an apple. It is the first time she has ever lived alone. Some nights she weeps and waits for the weeping to pass because it always does and nothing lasts. Some nights she sleeps sprawled across the entire bed, a starfish beached; others she lies awake and then gets up and makes herself tea and moves through the small cold house with warmth in her hands, turning on low lights, lighting a fire, disturbing no one and nothing, kindling the dark chill air as she moves like a candle from room to room with her own immense self.

TOPICS AND QUESTIONS FOR DISCUSSION

1. What do you think drew Annie to Thierry, beyond their initial physical attraction? Was it about what he represented to her? What do you think Thierry symbolized for Annie? Were they in love?

2. Did you sympathize more with Annie or Hector throughout? Did your loyalties shift at different points in the story—and why?

3. How did the alternating points of view in *Wifehouse* inform your understanding of Annie's choices throughout the novel?

4. Did Annie's life decisions resonate with you? Some? All? Discuss why or why not.

5. The book explores a woman navigating the multilayered roles of wife, mother, daughter, friend, and lover. Did you relate to Annie's often changeable feelings as she navigated these various roles? Which role do you think felt the most constricting for Annie? Which was the most liberating?

6. How does *Wifehouse* challenge or reinforce traditional ideas about marriage and fidelity? What are your thoughts on the tradition in today's society?

7. Is Annie's decision to leave her family for Thierry selfish and impulsive or daring and courageous? Or is it something more complex?

8. How is the relationship between Annie and Thierry shaped by their differences in age and stage of life? What are the power dynamics between them?

9. Annie gives up her nascent art career when she marries Hector and has a family. What are your thoughts about that sacrifice?

10. Annie had a troubled childhood in Australia with an abusive father, and she has largely put her past behind her. Returning home for her mother's funeral has stirred many old emotions. How do you think this affected her choice to leave her family?

11. *Wifehouse* unfolds over the course of one year—it starts with a Christmas gathering and ends with one as well. Annie's life is in very different at the beginning and at the end. How does the passage of time mirror her transformation and her changed world, and what route do you envision her future life taking?